THE WEISER CLASSICS SERIES represents the full range of subjects and genres that have been part of Weiser's publishing program for over sixty years, from tarot, divination, and magick to alchemy and esoteric philosophy. Drawing on Weiser's extensive backlist, the series offers works by renowned authors and spiritual teachers, foundational texts, as well as introductory guides on an array of topics.

The HERBAL ALCHEMIST'S HANDBOOK

The **HERBAL ALCHEMIST'S HANDBOOK**

A Complete Guide to Magickal Herbs
and How to Use Them

Karen Harrison

Foreword by Arin Murphy-Hiscock

WEISER
BOOKS

This edition first published in 2020 by Weiser Books, an imprint of
Red Wheel/Weiser, LLC
With offices at:
65 Parker Street, Suite 7
Newburyport, MA 01950
www.redwheelweiser.com

ISBN: 978-1-57863-705-8
Library of Congress Cataloging-in-Publication Data available upon request.

Cover by Kathryn Sky-Peck and Kasandra Cook
Interior by Debby Dutton
Typeset in Brioso Pro

Printed in Canada
MAR
10 9 8 7 6 5 4 3 2 1

Series Editors
Mike Conlon, Production Director, Red Wheel/Weiser Books
Judika Illes, Editor-at-Large, Weiser Books
Peter Turner, Associate Publisher, Weiser Books

Series Design
Kathryn Sky-Peck, Creative Director, Red Wheel/Weiser

Contents

Foreword

Lately, I've been doing a lot of thinking about what a modern practitioner's personal grimoire should include. Everyone's is different, of course, because our needs are unique, and it will include what is specific to your interests. Something we all include, however, is lore.

Lore is an aggregate of knowledge associated with something that we can use to interpret how people felt about that thing. It also allows us to transmit wisdom and information, providing a way of educating others. Lore finds its expression in superstition, old wives' tales, folklore, anecdotes, and mythology. Historical documents that tell us how practitioners used plants can also inform our modern approach in magical practice.

Immersing yourself in lore situates you within your field, giving you a sense of a larger community, a history that informs your modern practice. How people have previously approached a plant, how they interpreted its physical form, how they associated that with what it might be used for—all this can support your personal interpretations of that plant's uses. It is a foundation upon which you can base your own experimentation.

Part of occult history is the study of alchemy, a field of natural philosophy with the goal of transforming matter. In that respect, it is concerned with purification and perfecting, stripping away the dross to refine the remaining matter into something as pure as possible. In the physical field of science, alchemy was a forerunner of chemistry. In esoteric fields, alchemy became the pursuit of personal spiritual perfection, the transformation of the dross of mundane self into a higher self. In this sense, the transmutation of lead into gold is symbolic, an allegory for the journey from ignorance to enlightenment.

With this understanding of alchemy we see how it is well suited to the study of magical herbalism. The life cycle of plants—from seed growing to plant with the application of light, water, and earth; then to harvest; then to magical ingredient—can be understood as an alchemical development from basic seed to spiritual application. The use of plants in magic is a means to create change, to transform a situation into something else, to draw specific energy toward a goal with the objective of altering it. More than that, magical herbalism is one of the ways through which we can work for self-transformation, the magical alchemy of using materials from the world around us to help us refine our spirits and achieve our highest possible spiritual state.

Karen Harrison's *Herbal Alchemist's Handbook* is a book you can grow with, as you develop your personal practice. It has several layers of depth, allowing beginners to access it while still useful to more advanced practitioners. It is a reference as well as a guide, a history lesson as well as a recipe book.

Karen's book is also an excellent way to dip your toes into incorporating astrological correspondences into your magical work. Not only does she offer ways to do it and the information to use as a foundation, but she also explains *why* you might want to do it and lists the benefits and bonuses of working with planetary energies in your practice of magical herbalism.

Planetary correspondences add a layer of complexity to working with herbs and plants. An examination of planetary energies allows you to learn about the sphere of influence of each planet and luminary, with an accompanying list of the plants classified under that planet's rule. Rituals associated with the planet's sphere of influence are provided to help you explore the energies connected to it. Likewise, if you are primarily an astrologer, this book offers you extrapolated information to incorporate herbal correspondences into your astrology practice.

The formulas section offers a variety of methods by which to explore the applications of magical herbalism. Recipes for oils, bath salts, philtres, elixirs, amulets, and incense allow you to experiment with different techniques to draw upon the properties of plants. The different methods are explored and explained, allowing you to learn new techniques as you expand your knowledge of magical herbalism. One of my favorite parts is Karen's lists suggesting combinations of herbs and other components such as stones to provide ideas for enhancing or focusing certain energies in magical work.

In short, if you are seeking self-transformation and refinement of the mundane self to achieve your highest spiritual potential through working with plants, this is an excellent book to have at hand.

—Arin Murphy-Hiscock, author of *The Green Witch*

Preface

Since the age of four I have been fascinated with nature, herbs, and scents. As a child my initial interest was in communing with plant and nature spirits while picking herbs and flowers to dry to create simple potpourris. By the age of seven, I decided I would make the most amazing perfume in the world. So I gathered up all my mother's colognes and perfumes and mixed them into one big creation. As you can imagine my creation was an olfactory disaster and my mother was less than pleased. It was at that time that my grandmother, Ysleta, took me under her wing to show me how to really use herbs and scents, and I've never looked back.

Over the decades one of my greatest joys has been researching the composition of sacred incense and ritual oil recipes from every corner of the earth as well as composing my own trademark custom recipes. To me, the practice of blending the scents and energies of the sacred plant materials to aid in the manifestation of magick is an amazing gift, and I have been blessed to make this practice a big part of my life's work.

In writing *The Herbal Alchemist's Handbook*, my goal is to share the ways of herbal magick in a straightforward and accessible fashion. I designed the book so that my readers would be able to open my book to any chapter and have the information they need immediately at hand to make the changes in their life that they are seeking. I offer information in a way that hopefully piques creativity and curiosity while teaching new skills and adding to a person's magickal "toolbox."

My work is based on traditional Western herbal practices with a strong foundation created by the ancient greats—Paracelsus, John Gerard, and Nicholas Culpeper. My work has also been inspired by writings by modern herbalists such as Paul Beyerl, Scott Cunningham, Judith Hawkins-Tillirson, Richard Alan Miller, Ann Moura, and Arin Murphy-Hiscock.

Introduction

The use of herbs for Magick and medicine has fascinated people for millennia—and for good reason. Herbs have been used effectively in Magick and religious ceremony for tens of thousands of years. The Healing Arts and the Magickal Arts developed together as our ancestors sought ways to control and sustain their survival in the days well before a pharmacy was located on every corner. Indeed, what our forebears discovered and experimented with was the fact that a pharmacopeia existed in every meadow, forest, and river bend—if you knew what to look for and what to do with the herbs once you found them.

As the compiled knowledge of our ancestors evolved, they developed complex, integrated systems of information in order to understand and affect the world around them. Based on their keen observations of the natural world's flows of energy, the movement of the stars and Planets, the cycles of the Earth's seasons, and the Waxing and Waning Phases of the Moon, the ancients could begin to predict the course of the weather and what its effects would be on their lives, as well as the paths that the herds would follow and therefore when to go on the hunt. They could foretell where the herbs that healed would grow and when they would be ready to harvest.

The components of herbs (roots, leaves, flowers, resins, and essential oils) were certainly used for their physical healing properties in the creation of salves, poultices, tinctures, fomentations, and much more, but they were also extensively used Magickally in conjunction with their medicinal properties. Our ancestors knew that the value of the herb was not just in the physical ailments it could alleviate or heal, but also in the energy, the *spirit* of the plant. This energy/spirit could be harnessed to heal an individual or influence events and so could be used for Magickal purposes as well. This wisdom and understanding of the cycles of the natural world combined with knowledge of the effects of herbs, Magickal and medicinal, forms the foundation of Herbal Alchemy and Herbal Magick.

Alchemy (*al-kimia* in Arabic; or *al-khimia* in Hebrew) is a philosophy and practice that has as its goal the attainment of ultimate wisdom and connection with the Divine. Alchemy became known in the 16th century as the *spagyric* art with the Latin motto *solve et coagula,* meaning "to separate and to rejoin," as one of its practices is the infusing of natural materials such as herbs or metals with spiritual and/or Magickal intention and then using the result to transform one's life. Steeped in mysticism and mystery, Alchemy is also an ancient path of spiritual purification and the transformation of the spirit: the expansion of consciousness and the development of insight and intuition with the goal of uniting the Alchemist with her True Self and higher consciousness. Alchemy is the investigation of and joining with nature via a philosophical and spiritual discipline, combining elements of chemistry, metallurgy, Astrology, medicine, mysticism, and art—all components that when combined create a greater whole.

Alchemy is a science and philosophy that focuses on the innate character of the four Elements—Fire, Water, Earth, and Air—in conjunction with the energies of the Planetary bodies and the Planetary correspondences of organic materials abundant in nature such as metals, herbs, and stones.

Although it has been practiced worldwide—we find treatises on Alchemy in Mesopotamia, ancient Egypt and Persia, India, China, Japan, and Korea, classical Greece and Rome, and Europe and the Americas through the modern day—the roots of Alchemy are in Khem, the ancient name for Egypt (from which we get the Arabic word *al-kimia*), and inTaoist Chinese practice of creating medicines from combinations of herbs, stones, and metals along with energy (*chi*) practices. Taoist Alchemy focuses mainlyon the purification of one's spirit and body in the hopes of gaining immortality through the practice of Qigong and/or consumption and use of various concoctions—alchemical medicines or Elixirs, each of which serves different focused purposes.

In this book, we explore Herbal Alchemy as practiced in the West, through the uses of the plants and their Planetary signatures as developed by the 14th-century philosopher and Alchemist Paracelsus. Paracelsus said, "As Nature is extremely subtle and penetrating in her manifestations, she cannot be used without the Art."

A fascinating figure, Philippus Aureolus Theophrastus Bombastus von Hohenheim was a philosopher, physician, Astrologer, mathematician, Alchemist, and more. This eminent gentleman took the title Paracelsus, meaning "equal to or greater than Celsus," who was an earlier botanist and a 1st-century Roman encyclopedist. Aulus Cornelius Celsus was famous for his writings on medicine and compilations of notes on plant life and its medicinal uses. Inspired by Celsus's work, Paracelsus traveled extensively in the Old World visiting the healers of villages, talking with the wise men and wise women in hundreds of hamlets about their uses of local herbs, their observations of the herbs' effects, and the best growing conditions for those herbs as well as their best gathering times. As he traveled, he kept a diary of what he was learning and gathered it into a large body of work. Up to this point, the lore, use, and history of each plant had been given to an apprentice only orally. Through the use of writing and the printing press, this information would make its way into the wider world.

Paracelsus's work with herbs utilized his experience as an Astrologer, aligning each known herb with the energy of a Planet. As an Astrologer, he organized his Doctrine using the system of the Planetary energies to designate the effects and disposition of each herb. The Doctrine of Signatures recorded each plant and its medicinal and Magickal uses. The way that Paracelsus used the term *signature* was to signify and organize eachherb according to its specific appearance, geographical location, and the physical effects of the herb on the human system. The Doctrine of Signatures organized each herb in terms of its unique properties: what type of climate in which it grew, what time of day it bloomed, the form and color of its flowers and leaves, what type of physical ailments it addressed, what type of Magickal uses for which it was customarily employed, whether it had a heating or cooling effect on the body, whether it was bitter or sweet tasting, sweet smelling or acrid, and more. For example, he placed herbs that affected the heart; were primarily golden in color; thrived in sunny areas; and promoted a sense of well-being, success, and confidence in an individual under the dominion or rulership of the Sun.

Paracelsus was also revolutionary in his work with plant life, as he combined spiritual alchemical practices with the herb's use in addition to traditional basic medicinal herbal concoctions. In subsequent centuries, Paracelsus's Doctrine was expanded and built upon by medieval herbalists like Nicholas Culpeper and John Gerard, and his Doctrine of Signatures continues to be the cornerstone of Western Magickal herbal practice today.

The aim of this book is to give you the knowledge and tools for your own personal transformation using readily available tools and herbal ingredients. Partnered with each chapter on Planetary/herbal energies you will find tried and effective rituals, meditations, and workings that highlight the use of Magickal herbs designed to improve your life in all its myriad aspects. Each working has been used in a real-life situation, and each one has manifested its purpose. These rituals and meditations include practical and Magickal techniques to solve and improve both physical-world issues and workings devoted to understanding and actualizing your spiritual goals.

A famous Hermetic axiom states, "As above, so below." Your spiritual life is reflected in your physical life, and your physical life mirrors your spiritual condition. If the problems you face in your mundane existence can be resolved and transmuted in ways that will change your challenges into opportunities, you will have much more time and energy to devote to your true work—your spiritual transformation.

The Herbal Alchemist's Handbook is eminently practical. The use of it will teach you the energies and Magickal properties for each herb and how to use each singly or in combination. In most herbal Magickal applications, combinations of Planetary/herbal energies are utilized. In part 1 of this book, we explore each Planet and consider very specific applications for each Planetary energy and its corresponding herbs. In each chapter, we apply the Planet's energy in a ritual, energy working, or meditation as an example of its practical use.

Part 2 explains in detail how to compose your blend or formula in any form you deem the most efficacious for it, such as Incense, Fluid Condenser, or blended essential oil. Part 3 discusses creating custom formulas based on Numerology and Astrology. Also included are appendixes of herbal materials, Planetary energies, and suggested formulas making use of their natural affinities.

The blending of Incense, ceremonial oils, Bath Salts, Herbal Amulets, Fluid Condensers, and Herbal Philtres, along with a multitude of recipes, are here at your fingertips. I hope you will enjoy the recipes and find them useful, but my main goal is to show you how to create your own Alchemical combinations using natural substances so that you claim this work and make it your own.

This book is a culmination of the decades of medicinal and Magickal experience I have with herbs. I was raised in a family that was considered strange at the time, which I have realized over the years was quite fortunate for me, as I am certainly their product . . . they prayed to the Moon, talked to trees, communed with spirits, called to the lightning, and used natural things like herbs, rocks, and bird feathers to contain power and make Magickal changes in their lives. Just as I live today.

PART 1

THE HERBS

and

THEIR PLANETARY SIGNATURES

CHAPTER 1

The Herbs of the Sun

Personal Power, Health, and Success

Energies: self-confidence, success, vitality, courage, authority, dignity, fame, self-knowledge

Colors: gold, orange

Number: 1

Metal: gold

Stones/materials: diamond, citrine, yellow jasper, topaz

Deities: Ra, Apollo, Helios, Lugh, Isis, Diana, Brigit

Herbs: angelica, ash, bay, calendula, chamomile, celandine, eyebright, frankincense, juniper, mistletoe, rosemary, saffron, safflower, Saint-John's-wort, sunflower, tormentilla, walnuts

In Astrology, the Sun and Moon are called "Planets" for ease of interpretation, but they are obviously not Planets in the scientific sense. In medicinal terms, the Sun could be considered the great restorative. Even as the returning Sun allows plant life to flourish on the Earth, the herbs attributed to the Sun act to restore health and vitality. They stimulate and balance the human health system that suffers from either excess or deficiency. Many of the plants attributed to the Sun may be considered Solar simply on the basis of their appearance, of course. For example, chamomile, celandine, Saint-John's-wort, and calendula all produce bright yellow flowers, many of which blossom around the summer solstice. The sunflower follows the path of the Sun during the day, facing the East as the Sun rises and bending its head to the West as the Sun sets. Saffron produces a dye that may be considered Solar because of its bright yellow-gold appearance.

It is in healing, however, that the Solar herbs really "shine" in their diverse healing efficacy. Solar herbs restore equilibrium to the entire physical system, often serving as tonics to the heart and promoting the free flow of vital energy. The heart is commonly considered the Solar center of the body (the organ ruled by Leo, the Astrological Sign associated with the Sun), and many effects of Solar herbs center around this organ. Angelica relieves circulatory conditions, such as gout, when used as a compress. It works well to alleviate fever, inflammations, and headache (all conceivable symptoms of excess heat or high blood pressure). Saint-John's-wort relieves headaches, and chamomile and celandine reduce fever. The restorative Solar heat of chamomile, celandine, juniper, and Saint-John's-wort relieves swellings, inflammations, and rheumatic conditions; eyebright and Saint-John's-wort alleviate symptoms due to colds, such as rheumatic joints and congested lungs. Angelica and Saint-John's-wort also have restorative properties that recommend them for use in cases of weakness and anemia. In addition, Saint-John's-wort is known to balance the effects of mental depression, leading to more confidence and the ability to take action toward personal and professional goals and responsibilities.

Another herb of the Sun, mistletoe is a parasite/symbiote to the oak, a tree attributed in a wide variety of cultures to Solar Deities. Mistletoe produces a drastic and often fatal effect on the heart and circulatory system. The berries are never used, but the leaves and twigs can be made in a weak Infusion to reduce bleeding by lowering blood pressure, and the leaves can be used to reduce uterine bleeding after parturition. As one of the few spots of green in the forest in the dead of winter, the mistletoe is often viewed as a symbol of the Sun and returning life.

Because the Sun is seen in Astrology and Magick as the Planet of the ego or personality, the Magickal/energy effects of Solar herbs are to promote self-confidence and personal success. The energies of Sun herbs are represented and expressed by people in the public eye: rulers and authority figures, as well as people in successful, self-expressive endeavors that bring them pleasure. Sun herbs impart a sense of purpose and a strong will. Just as the Sun Sign in one's Natal (birth) Astrological Chart indicates the ways that a person presents himself to the world and tends to apply his energies, Sun herbs help to draw power toward self-expression and personal success in whatever endeavor toward which a person is directed. Utilized in Solar

Incenses, oil blends, Philtres, and other herbal formulas used in ritual, Sun herbs give vitality, health, creativity, dignity, success, and authority.

When used in ritual and Magick, Solar herbs help us to define and understand our true purpose and Will in any specific endeavor. They inform our thought processes and how we wish to harness our motivation and energy toward the success of any given goal. Sun herbs strengthen our self-expression (the expression of our True Will), impart the confidence to embark on actualizing our goals, and give us the power to manifest our visions into the physical, emotional, mental, or spiritual realm toward which we are aiming this energy. With the self-expression of our Astrological Sun Sign, we each have our own gauge of what success means to us. The various areas of interest and aspiration a person has at a given time, how success will express itself in the final outcome of the manifestation of a goal, and what life is presenting to an individual at the diverse stages of her life will all have a bearing on the ways that a person defines success at that particular juncture. We all have personal definitions of success that can never be defined solely by the outside world.

Because of their extensive benefits to physical health, as well as the emotional, mental, and spiritual levels of being, Solar herbs are excellent for use in ritual to balance and maintain your system for optimal energy and enthusiasm leading to success in any area you choose. In this exploration of the energies of the Sun, we create a Health Philtre (a Magickally charged Herbal Infusion), which you can use now for any health issues or save for later use when the need arises.

Health Philtre

A Philtre is an Herbal Infusion that has been charged with your intention and sometimes, depending on the type of ritual, by the energies of the Sun or the Moon. An Infusion is created by adding dried or fresh herbs to room-temperature water and allowing them to steep for a time, releasing their properties into the liquid.

For the creation of this Health Philtre we utilize the herbs of the Sun as well as the energy and heat of the Sun. Gather calendula, Saint-John's-wort, chamomile, and juniper berries. At sunrise, place approximately one tablespoon of each of these herbs into a chalice, bowl, or cauldron that can hold at least sixteen ounces of liquid. As you place each herb in your container, focus on the healing properties that each one brings to your Philtre:

Calendula for the intake of vital force and energy;

Saint-John's-wort for confidence and mental/emotional equilibrium;

Chamomile for calmness and serenity;

Juniper for expelling any negativity or imbalance.

If you wish to include the dynamic, natural qualities of a gemstone of the Sun, now add one sunstone, one diamond, or one gold topaz to your herb mixture.

Sit for a few minutes, meditating on health, energy, and vitality as you consciously direct your slow, quiet breathing over the mixture. Next, pour spring or distilled water over your ingredients until your container is three-quarters full, focusing on the blending of these energies into a synergistic, balanced whole. Begin to stir clockwise (the direction of growth and activation) as you charge or vitalize the Philtre with your focused intention. You may visualize your aura radiating and pulsing with life and energy or recite a mantra or incantation as you stir and activate your mixture to add additional focus and energy to the brew.

Now place the Philtre mixture in an area where it will absorb the rays of the Sun all day, and let the ingredients steep together until sunset. Cover your container and allow your blend to continue steeping overnight. The next day at sunrise, strain the herbs out of the water (bury the spent herbs in your yard or in the woods) and pour the Philtre into a sterilized bottle that has a cap. You can sterilize your bottle beforehand by running it through the dishwasher with the drying element on high or by microwaving it for thirty seconds. Store the Philtre in the refrigerator and add one tablespoon of it to a cup of herbal tea at any time you feel fatigued or suspect you are getting sick. You may also wish to use some as a wash for a burn, cut, insect bite, or sprain to hasten the healing process.

CHAPTER 2

The Herbs of the Moon
Dreamwork and the Inner Self

Energies: psychic knowledge, dreamworking, childbirth, fertility, past life recall, imagination, the subconscious mind

Colors: lilac, silver

Number: 2

Metal: silver

Stones/materials: pearl, abalone, moonstone, selenite

Deities: Selene, Nuit, Luna, Artemis, Sin, Inannur, and Khonsu

Herbs: almond, anise seed, cabbage, camphor, cucumber, fennel, iris, jasmin, lettuce, lily, lotus, moonwort, mugwort, pumpkin, violet, watercress, white sandalwood

The energies of the Moon affect the activities of the subconscious mind, the intuition and psychic centers, reproductive system, dreamwork, and the emotions. The plants attributed to the Moon act principally on the major fluids of the body and on the stomach (attributed to Cancer, ruled by the Moon). Their fluidic action is primarily regulatory and eliminative. Much of digestive activity seems also to influence an individual's moods— the effect of one's emotions on digestion and the actions of the stomach are well-known and universally experienced, so this dual action of many of the Lunar herbs makes a great deal of sense.

Several Lunar herbs bear marked resemblances to the Moon in her various phases, both in color and shape of plant, fruit, and flower. The white fruits of fennel grow in pairs of curved, oblong shapes that resemble the waxing and waning Lunar crescents. The lily, long associated with Lunar Goddesses, has round, bell-shaped flowers that are frequently bright white, and its leaves are oblong or crescent shaped. The fruit of the almond generally is also pure white and ovoid or crescentic.

Those Lunar herbs that deal with fluidity generally act upon water and blood most specifically just as the Moon herself controls the tides and the flow of blood. We are all aware of how the Moon cycles affect the rhythms of the female system and the menses. It is also known by healers involved with surgery that treatments involving the cutting of the body are best scheduled around the New Moon period, when blood flow during operations has been documented to be decreased.

Cucumber helps eliminate excess water from the body and is both laxative and diuretic, particularly effective in dissolving uric acid accumulations such as kidney stones. Fennel and lily are eliminators, laxatives, and diuretics. The lily acts as a digestive antispasmodic, and fennel is commonly used to stimulate the flow of milk in nursing mothers. Mugwort is particularly apt in its Lunar attribution (note the presence of the Moon Goddess Artemis in mugwort's scientific name, *Artemisia vulgaris*). In addition to its digestive and purgative qualities, a decoction (herbal tea created by steeping the herbs in cold water for twenty-four hours) of mugwort can be used quite effectively to regulate the flow of menstrual blood.

Moon herbs and plants can also aid the female reproductive system, which depends on the Moon for the pituitary gland's signals in releasing estrogen and progesterone, the female hormones. Anise, fennel, flaxseed, and cucumber all contain phytoestrogen, a natural estrogen. So does brown rice (ever wonder why the bride and groom are pelted with rice? For fertility, of course!).

Several Lunar herbs act on other fluids of the body (generally to eliminate excess) and serve as digestives. Camphor, by reducing fluid accumulation in the lungs and pleural sac, is an excellent remedy for whooping cough and pleurisy. Bitter almond is used as a cough remedy, while sweet almond is used internally as a soothing syrup and externally as an emollient. White sandalwood is used to reduce inflammation of mucosal tissue and is also a diuretic—a decoction of the wood can be used for indigestion.

Myrrh and sandalwood share both astringent and stomachic properties, but along with jasmin and bitter almond, they share qualities attributed to the Moon that surpass the simply medicinal. Bitter almond and jasmin both have sedative effects, calming the nerves and allowing a more intuitive, psychic Lunar mode of brain function to manifest. Almond, jasmin, sandalwood, and myrrh, when used in Incense, also can trigger the subtle, Lunar mode of perception that is so effective in meditative work involving intuition, psychic awakening, and meditative pathworking through the sense of smell.

Magickally speaking, herbs of the Moon affect the subconscious mind. They aid in the development of intuition and psychic gifts. Since they are so useful in accessing the subconscious, they are excellent for dreamwork, recalling past lives, and breaking old ingrained habits. Moon herbs are often white or pale in color, night-flowering, and soothing to the senses.

Moon Incense and Meditation for a Dreamworking

Gather your mortar and pestle, a dropper bottle half filled with alcohol, a small scoop, and the following herbs and essential oils:

jasmin flowers

white sandalwood powder

jasmin oil

cucumber oil

white sandalwood oil

myrrh gum

Place one small scoop of jasmin flowers and two small scoops of white sandalwood powder in your mortar. Gently crush the flowers into the white sandalwood powder with the pestle. Squeeze any alcohol out of your dropper and shake it well to expel any droplets. Draw up into your dropper the jasmin oil and disperse twenty drops of it into the flower-sandalwood mixture. Clean out your dropper with the alcohol and shake it out again, then draw up the cucumber oil. Disperse thirty drops of the cucumber oil into your mixture. Repeat again with the white sandalwood oil, dispersing forty drops into the blend. Combine well with the jasmin flower–sandalwood powder mixture. Last, stir in a half scoop of your myrrh gum.

In your bedroom, prepare a simple altar. Cover a nightstand or other small table with a cloth. Center an Incense burner on the altar and surround it with a circle of jasmin flowers. Fill your Incense burner halfway with sand to insulate the burner from the heat of the Incense charcoal that you now nestle on top of the sand. Place a lighter or matches by the Incense burner along with a journal and pen. Turn on a soft night-light.

Go draw yourself a comfortable bath. If you like, add a few drops of your jasmin, cucumber, or sandalwood oil to the water (or all three, if you prefer). Relax into the water, slowing your breath. With each exhalation, imagine that you are dispelling any negativity or stress, letting your body melt into the water. With each inhalation, imagine that you are awakening your mind, expanding it, and encouraging your subconscious to emerge. Bathe as long as you like, doing your mindful breathwork throughout.

After your bath, dry off and don comfortable sleeping attire. Go back to your bedroom and light your Incense charcoal. Hold it between your thumb and forefinger and light the end farthest from your fingers. When its sparks are almost to your fingers, place it back on the sand in your burner. Let the coal ignite completely across, then place a small bit of your Incense in the center of the coal. Waft some of the smoke up toward your face and breathe deeply as you greet your subconscious. Tell your inner mind that you will be listening closely tonight. You may ask a specific question or just let your subconscious show you something you need to know.

Leave the Incense burning (if you have an active cat or dog, you may wish to put it in another room for the night so that your burning coal doesn't get knocked onto the floor). Pick up your journal and place it in a convenient spot by your bed along with a writing utensil. Retire into your soft bed and let yourself drift into sleep. During the night you may be half awakened by active dreams—write down any images, impressions, themes, or characters in your journal any time you wake. Go back to sleep for more dreams. You may be awakened by some of your dreams, but it is not uncommon to sleep the night through.

Before you get up in the morning, while you are still in that half-sleep state, write down any dreams and their major symbols, people, emotional qualities (joy, fear, freedom, amusement . . .). Over the next few days and nights, you may find that additional dream memories rise to the surface of your conscious mind or that you get psychic impressions that *feel* important. Keep your journal handy wherever you go so that you can jot down these memories as well.

Later the next day, you can dispose of the charcoal and Incense ashes by simply stirring them into the sand in your Incense burner. As you use your burner in several different sessions over time, you can bury the sand or sprinkle it into your yard, but you don't have to use new sand each time. Just dispose of the sand when it gets too much Incense debris in it and reuse it until then.

CHAPTER 3

The Herbs of Mars

Courage and Motivation

Energies: victory, aggression, achievement, energy, action, assertiveness, strength, sexual desire

Colors: scarlet, red, vermillion, orange

Number: 5

Metal: iron

Stones/materials: garnet, ruby, carnelian, bloodstone

Deities: Ares, Hercules, Tiw, Minerva, Maeve, Pallas Athena

Herbs: aloeswood, asafoetida, basil, broom tops, briony, cactus, cayenne, cumin, dragon's blood resin, galangal, garlic, gentian, ginger, hawthorn, horseradish, honeysuckle, mustard, nettle, peppercorn, red sandalwood, rue, safflower, sanicle, tobacco, wormwood

The Planet Mars has a bad reputation, as it is often associated with destruction, impetuous action, strife, and aggression, but these are qualities that Mars expresses when its energies are not in balance. These energies are also those that protect and vitalize. Their catabolic effects destroy and transform—breaking down and clearing away waste or dead tissue. The balanced, positive energies of Mars can be represented in the activities of firemen, police officers, and the military—all professions that can be dangerous yet protect life and, in the case of the police and military, preserve law and justice. The energies of Mars can be intense and uncomfortable at times, yet they are necessary in the protection of life and health.

Red is the color of Mars, which makes the Martian attributions of dragon's blood resin and cayenne obvious. In ritual, dragon's blood resin has its uses in binding, protection, and purgation, all of which fall under the dominion of the powers of Mars. Mars's herbs in general are irritants, purges, and stimulants, and they act to build up body heat, increase energy, and promote an assertive vitality. Rue, for example, is an aromatic stimulant whose energizing qualities have been known to relieve nervous heart problems such as arrhythmia and palpitation. Rue also alleviates colic, eliminates worms, and can provoke menstruation. One quickly learns upon handling fresh rue that its juice is a highly effective, though fortunately local, irritant.

Nettle, another herb of Mars, possesses thorns that act as hypodermics, injecting subcutaneous doses of stinging fluid. It is this same irritating juice, however, that when properly prepared becomes a powerful internal astringent, eliminating infections and blood in the urine, regulating blood pressure and flow, cleansing and relieving hemorrhoids, reducing susceptibility to colds, and by virtue of its heating action, soothing rheumatic conditions.

The mineral sulphur is also attributed to Mars and is an extreme irritant, being hot (in fact, flammable) and explosive—all properties that exemplify that Planet's energy. Peppercorns and cayenne share this quality of producing extreme heat (peppers are classified by the amount of BTUs—British Thermal Units—that they produce), and the efficacy of their use depends largely on the resilience of the individual's constitution. Peppercorn and cayenne are noteworthy digestive catabolics, aiding immeasurably in the aggressive breakdown of food and waste products. Cayenne, in building up body heat, is excellent for maintaining resistance to colds and will increase blood flow to any area that it is applied to when used in a plaster (although watch out for the danger of blistering).

The internal effects of these irritants as well as the olfactory stimulus of sulphur used in Incense are highly effective in the induction of a Mars temperament, especially where aggression is called for and in meditative pathworkings pertaining to the Qabbalistic sphere of Geburah, which is also associated with Mars.

Magically speaking, herbs of Mars give vast amounts of energy to projects and health. They bring protection, independence, assertiveness, and motivation and stimulate the passions. When mixed into an Incense or formula with herbs of other Planets, Martian herbs lend their immense energies to the effects of the other herbs, thereby strengthening and vitalizing the whole. Like Mars, Saturn is another Planet of protection, but there is a difference in how Saturnian and Martian energies protect. You might think of Saturnian protection as the shield, Martian protection as the sword. You might choose to use Mars's energy for protection in instances of real danger to you or those you love. Saturn's energy would be more appropriate in situations where you are shielding from negativity, such as in a Home Blessing.

Since so many of the herbs and oils of Mars are hot in nature, be careful when you choose the ingredients for any of your herbal Magick. Cayenne, chili peppers, nettles, aloeswood, mustard, and peppercorns should never be added to a Mars Incense, because when burned, the smoke from these herbs severely irritates the mucous membranes, throat, and eyes. Adding cayenne, chili peppers, nettles, or aloeswood to an Herbal Philtre or Fluid Condenser is also not recommended, as these mixtures are often ingested, and the above herbs would be very unpleasant and possibly irritating when drunk.

Composing a Magickal Potpourri

Let's explore the effectiveness of Mars energy by making an Herbal Potpourri to use in your workplace. Oftentimes, people feel uncomfortable having to stand up for themselves with co-workers or the boss. Or perhaps you might feel that you are often passed over for promotions or new tasks. Maybe you could use this energy to give you motivation to start or complete an important project. This Potpourri can sit on your desk, lending its strength to your immediate environment and giving you courage and motivation to achieve your goals and stand your ground gracefully yet firmly.

In a Potpourri, the herbal ingredients do not need to be powdered or cut up into very small pieces. In fact, the more whole your ingredients are, the more attractive the end result will be.

Gather together your choice of the following Mars herbs and oils:

safflower

red sandalwood

dragon's blood resin (small chunks will look better than the powdered form, or you can use the oil)

ginger (root and/or essential oil)

honeysuckle (flowers and/or essential oil)

Combine one scoop each of the chosen herb, stirring them together gently so that you don't crush the materials. Distribute each herb thoroughly throughout the mixture. Now add twenty drops of each of the essential oils you've chosen. Toss the herbs together with the oils as you focus on being strong, motivated, courageous, and energetic. This focus will charge your Potpourri with your intention.

Now place your Potpourri in a red or orange bowl—the colors of Mars—and set it on your desk. Whenever you feel the need to add a little "oomph" to your work or your confidence, just fluff the herbs lightly with your fingers. This will release the scent, and you will feel energized and effective. After a month or so, if you feel that you need to reactivate the bowl or that the scent is not as strong as you prefer, just freshen it with a few drops of some of the oils that you originally added to your Potpourri.

Martian herbs are often used for protection or to rid yourself of troublesome people. Traditionally, pieces of chili pepper are strewn across the front doorstep to keep people you don't want away from you and from entering your home. Small pieces of chili pepper can also be placed in the shoes of a person you are trying to remove from your life.

Martian energy is intense, and most of the time Mars's herbs and oils are used in conjunction with the energies of other Planets to intensify their effects, rather than in a "simple"—a formula that uses only one Planet's herbs. Here are some examples of how a touch of a Mars herb can act with and upon other Planetary energies to enhance their effectiveness:

Sun with Mars

Sun is confidence, personal power, health, and self-expression. Add a little Mars and increase your control over your life, enhance your ability to express your interests and goals with even greater success, or enable yourself to stroll through life with energy, health, and personal charisma.

Moon with Mars

Lunar energies keep you in touch with your emotions, your psyche, and your subconscious. Add some Mars to quicken the development of your psychic abilities, motivate yourself to transform bad habits into good ones, or add vitality to your system if you are working on fertility issues.

Mercury with Mars

Eloquence, intelligence, and business endeavors are some of the energies of Mercury. Combining Mercurial herbs and oils with an herb or oil belonging to the dominion of Mars will help you to be more persuasive, have an even quicker mind, and be charmingly assertive enough to get the job you deserve.

Jupiter with Mars

Expansion, honor, authority, and growth all belong to Jupiter. Add a Mars energy to grow and expand faster in an area of your ambition, garner recognition of your accomplishments, intensify your authority in any area of your life, or expand your understanding of the best ways to accomplish your goals.

Venus with Mars

Romance, beauty and the arts—what's not to love? Combining Venusian energy with a touch of Mars will add passion to the romance, help you to express yourself confidently as an artist, and make people look twice when you pass.

Saturn with Mars

Protection, understanding of karma, endurance, self-discipline, and control are the areas where Saturnian herbs are used. Add strength and energy with a Saturn-Mars combination to protect your home if you live in a particularly dangerous area, to work through karmic debt, to vitalize yourself in a situation which requires hard work and endurance, or to accomplish a difficult task requiring much self-control.

Neptune with Mars

Neptune is the Planet of out-of-body experiences, creative genius, and the mystical. Bringing a little Martian energy into the equation will help you to harness and express the creativity residing in your subconscious, master astral projection more quickly, and experience more intensely any meditation, trancework, or altered state.

Uranus with Mars

Intellectual genius, innovative thought, and transformation of thought patterns fall under the dominion of Uranus. Mars will increase the workings of your mind to higher levels, bring action to your original thoughts, and hasten your ability to change the way your brain works, taking you out of any thought doldrums.

Pluto with Mars

Karma, unconscious behavior patterns, letting go, facing fear, and your Shadow Self are all Plutonian in nature. Partnering Pluto's herbs and oils with an herb or oil of Mars will help you open those scary "memory boxes" in the back of your mind that make you so uncomfortable, break through barriers when you are working in psychotherapy, recognize karmic debt, and enable you to actively work to release it. This is not a fun combination, be warned. It is very intense, and if you choose to work with this combination, expect dramatic changes that will rock your life.

CHAPTER 4

The Herbs of Mercury
Communication, Knowledge, and Business

Energies: communication, divination, business success, intellectualization, learning

Color: yellow

Number: 7

Metal: quicksilver

Stones/materials: quartz, opal, Herkimer diamond, yellow calcite, optical calcite, yellow jasper

Deities: Janus, Hermes, Thoth, Ogma, Maat, Shesat, Calliope

Herbs: bergamot, caraway, cinnamon, dill, ephedra, gum arabic, gum mastic, horehound, lavender, licorice, marjoram, mouse-ear, mullein, papyrus, peppermint, star anise, savory, thyme, woodruff

The activity of herbs attributed to Mercury is quite multifaceted and diverse, mirroring the ways that the energies of Mercury tend to perform in Magick, but a common thread runs through them. Mercury is the connector, the communicator, and the messenger, representing the bright intelligence and the free flow of nervous energy. Mercury governs both the nervous and respiratory systems and is intrinsically involved in matters of conscious perception and mental focus. Like the Martian herbs, stimulation is a principal element among Mercurial herbs, though it is somewhat gentler and more precise than that of the Martian herbs.

Mercury energy is about communication and comprehension—communication by electrical impulse in the brain as well as with the verbal and written word. Mercury energies are those of the orator, writer, computer programmer, and actor. The herbs associated with this Planet are often spices that act to excite the nervous system and the brain through the sense of taste. Cinnamon, licorice, and star anise are noted examples of this function. Gum mastic exemplifies the interconnecting messenger function of Mercury. Though it is a fixative and binder, it provides the medium in which a multiplicity of elements may blend, or communicate.

Mercurial herbs relieve respiratory difficulty, hoarseness, and headaches caused by stress. Mullein taken as a tea relieves respiratory ailments, as well as coughs, hoarseness, and bronchitis, while inhalation of the steam serves to break up congestion in the chest. Application of a mullein fomentation or poultice, on the other hand, soothes skin inflammation, itching, and warts. Licorice also relieves sore throat, hoarseness, and bronchial conditions and calms nervous ulcers.

Lavender essential oil or an Infusion of lavender flowers provides excellent relief for insect bites when applied directly, and aids in relieving headache when massaged into the temples. It is also a beneficial herb to use in a sleep pillow to help focus and quiet the rambling thoughts of the mind in preparation for rest. Drinking a tea of equal parts cinnamon and lavender flowers is also very helpful before studying to help focus the mind in order to retain the information.

Mercurial herbs facilitate clear thinking, eloquence, and conscious understanding. They aid in business success and excite and vitalize the nervous receptors throughout the body. They help to facilitate quick recovery from illness. The herbs of Mercury enable the conscious mind to communicate more easily with the subconscious mind, thus aiding psychic work with the Tarot or any other divination method that visually incorporates symbols and requires memorization.

Among Mercury's areas of expertise are business acumen and positive self-presentation. Let me illustrate how to use the energy of Mercury and Mercurial herbs and essential oils in a ritual to gain a new professional position.

New Career Ritual

Choose a time when you will not be interrupted—unplug the phone, put the pets away if they tend to disturb you when you are doing energywork, and gather your tools for your ritual. You will need the following materials:

three yellow candles

Employment Oil (see Formulas for Manifestation of Goals in appendix E, Formulas and Recipes)

Incense charcoal (see Note)

Employment Incense (see Planetary Formulas in appendix E, Formulas and Recipes, for an Incense made from Mercurial herbs)

parchment

yellow feather quill (see Note)

yellow calligraphy ink

small yellow or gold plate placed in the center of your altar

stone of Mercury (clear quartz, yellow jasper, yellow calcite, optical calcite, or opal, or Herkimer diamond are some choices)

yellow pouch or bag

whatever you will be leaving at your interviews (your resume, job application, or business card)

Now it is time to begin. If it is traditional with the way you work when focusing your energy for a ritual, cast a Circle in your usual manner. If you prefer not to create a sacred space in which to do your work, focus your

---

* Incense charcoal: It is always a good idea to use an insulating material in your burner because the charcoals get very hot! Fill the burner halfway with an insulating material like sand, garden soil, or kitty litter and flatten the surface so the charcoal will lay flat. Holding the charcoal between two fingers, light one end and let it spark completely across. When the sparks are almost at your fingers, place the charcoal, divot-side up, on the sand. Do not smother the charcoal with Incense—put a pinch on at a time. A charcoal can burn for several hours, so once you have finished your ritual, just leave the charcoal safely in the Incense burner and dispose of the ashes the next day. Be sure that you close off the room so that small children or animals don't knock it over and start a fire.

* Feather quill: Be sure that you have prepared your quill beforehand by cutting the end into a point so that you can gather the ink into it. You may want to practice writing with your quill before your ritual so that you know how much ink to gather in it and to be sure that the point is the right shape (there's nothing more frustrating than finding in the middle of a ritual that something is not working the way you expected!).

thoughts and energy on the work at hand. Breathing slowly and deeply, imagine that you are connected to the Earth and that you are radiating a pale, clear light from every pore in your body, surrounding yourself with this light.

Now anoint your candles with your Employment Ritual Oil, from the wick down to the bottom of the candle, while visualizing (seeing in your mind's eye) the result you want. You will anoint in this direction because you are drawing a new job to yourself; as the candle burns down, it will attract energies of opportunity like a magnet. Focusing on the idea of "the perfect job," see yourself receiving a paycheck or walking down a hallway being greeted by friendly co-workers. Light the candles and then, from the flame of the middle candle, light the Incense charcoal. Let it spark almost to your fingers and then place it in your Incense burner on some insulating sand. Place a small amount of Incense on the charcoal and imagine that you see your new job in the smoke of the Incense. Now, on a piece of parchment, draw a simple image of your business card or the word *career* with your feather quill and calligraphy ink.

Place the parchment onto the yellow or gold plate in the center of your altar, image-side up where you can see it. Pick up your Mercury stone and, holding it in your hands, fingers cupped over it, again visualize your desire. With each breath, see your desire more clearly and blow this energy image into the stone in your cupped hands. After you have filled the stone with energy, hold the stone briefly in the flame of each candle and over the Incense smoke. Place the charged stone in the center of your parchment on which you have drawn your image and pour a small amount of Ritual Oil over it. Breathe quietly for a few moments, keeping your concentration on your goal in a gentle but intense fashion. Now place the stone in the yellow pouch or bag and sprinkle some of your Incense over it in the bag. Set the bag down and, from the center candle flame, light one end of your parchment. Let the flame get going and then set the parchment down on the small plate on your altar. Once it has burned into ash, let it cool, then add the ashes to your yellow pouch or bag.

Now it is time to cense, anoint, and activate your resume, job application or business cards. Hold whichever you are charging with energy (or all three!) a few inches above the flame of the candles as you focus on "the perfect job." Allow the heat of the candle flames to be felt on the paper, but be careful not to mar your materials with soot from the candles or by catching them afire. Imagine the power of fire activating and enlivening the materials. Next, bathe them in the smoke of your employment Incense and focus your energy. Last, put a small amount of your employment oil in the palm of one hand and rub both palms together, distributing the oil over your palms. Lightly place your palms on the back of the resume, job application, and/or business cards, making sure not to leave oily splotches behind for your prospective employer to wonder about.

Place the charged materials in the center of your altar and put the power bag on top. Leave everything there overnight to blend their charged energy.

Extinguish your candles, and you are done! You can use the candles again later if you wish to recharge your bag or charge up more copies of your resume to take on your job search. Bring your power bag with you for each job interview to lend energy to you as you speak eloquently and with confidence about your abilities. When you are looking in the paper for prospective jobs, keep the bag right by you, or when you are making phone calls to set up interviews, hold the bag as you talk on the phone. Happy hunting!

CHAPTER 5

The Herbs of Jupiter

Prosperity and Honor

Energies: expansion, career, ambition, luck, material success, spiritual growth, humor

Color: royal blue

Number: 6

Metal: tin

Stones/materials: sapphire, turquoise, blue topaz, lapis lazuli

Deities: Zeus, Llyr, Thor, Hera, Gaea, Rhiannon

Herbs: agrimony, borage, carnation, cedar, cinquefoil, dandelion, figs, fir, hyssop, linden, magnolia, maple, meadowsweet, oak, oak moss, pine, poplar, saffron, sage, sassafras, sumac, rosin, wood betony

The energies of our largest Planet, Jupiter, are represented and expressed in the vocations of ruler, magistrate, philosopher, village elder, or priest and priestess. Jupiter is the Planet of the All-father in many pantheons, and the corresponding properties of generation, mercy, expansion, and beneficence are consistently fulfilled by the herbs attributed to Jupiter. While sage and wood betony wave the Jovian banner of royal purple in their crowns of leaves and flowers, it is in the healing, soothing, and vitalizing functions that the Jupiter herbs as a whole medicinally typify the beneficial influence of their patron Planet. Many of the herbs act to soothe and gently heal several conditions that are well-known for causing extreme discomfort.

Wood betony is particularly useful for digestive difficulties that are commonly attributed to overly enthusiastic and unrestrained gastronomical expressions of appetite—overindulgence, overeating, a regular diet of very rich and fatty food—that are represented by the energies of Jupiter.

As a stomachic, wood betony is effective in relieving cramps, vomiting, constipation, diarrhea, and dysentery. While it acts to relieve the effects of Jovian excess, many of the other attributed herbs reflect the expansive, philanthropical aspects of Jupiter by acting as soothing salves, balms, tonics, and emollients. Used internally, aloeswood is generally a purgative, but when used in an external wash it is one of the most effective of known emollients. It draws out infections and is useful as a wound wash, soothing and healing minor burns, cuts, insect bites, and wrinkles. Dandelion (expansive and prolific, as a proper Jupiter plant should be—just check out your lawn!) and linden, when used as teas, act as external astringents for skin irritations and mouth and throat sores.

Oak bark is another Jovian astringent effective on skin irritations and sores when used as a wash. As an internal astringent and digestive, it helps control rectal problems, hemorrhoids, bloody urine, varicose veins, and internal hemorrhage. Just as the oak tree represented the All-father, the king of trees as it were, to the Druids, the strength of the oak radiates its majesty, and its dramatic presence and the towering, beneficent shelter it provides to the forest have earned it its attribution to Jupiter. Pine and poplar are plants of Jupiter that also produce healing balms. Poplar in particular produces a soothing salve for internal use and an exterior application for skin rashes, burns, and scrapes that is without comparison. The ascorbic acid content of pine makes it effective as a balm and liniment where a revitalization of systemic activity is needed. Pine-resin vapors, when inhaled, are excellent in soothing respiratory ailments. Burdock root serves as an incredible tonic for the liver (the organ attributed to Jupiter) and clears the blood of hepatitis.

On the Magickal front, Jovian herbs are expansive herbs. They bring growth, both spiritual and material. On the spiritual level they allow us to expand our consciousness and highlight spiritual/religious values; on the mental level they bring insight, clear judgment, and a delight in philosophical thought; on the emotional level they encourage mercy and beneficence toward others; and on the physical plane they draw abundance, prosperity, and recognition. Herbs of Jupiter expand the mind and the heart, allowing for an intellectual understanding of the workings of the Universe and the laws of nature and of humankind while lending a sense of the connection we all share.

Utilizing the expansive effects of some of the herbs of Jupiter, we'll create and use an oil blend for attracting prosperity and abundance to our lives.

🌸 Prosperity Oil

Gather together your supplies:

one-ounce bottle of alcohol with dropper cap

glass dram-size vial with cap (cork or screw-top cap work equally well)

carnation essential oil

cedar essential oil

oak moss essential oil

pine essential oil

small bottle of carrier oil such as sweet almond oil

Jupiter stone such as lapis lazuli, amethyst, or turquoise (optional)

Focusing your intention of expanding and attracting prosperity into your life, breathe slowly and deeply. Imagine glittering green and gold confetti softly raining down upon you, and being absorbed into the auric energy field surrounding your body. Taking up the dropper bottle of alcohol, draw the alcohol up into the dropper, then squeeze it back into the bottle to cleanse the dropper. Taking the dropper from the bottle, shake the dropper vigorously to release any droplets of alcohol that might remain in it. The dropper provides the convenience of being able to count the number of drops of essential oil you will be dispersing, and the alcohol ensures the dropper is clean and will not cross-contaminate any of your essential oils. You want to be sure to get all the alcohol out of the dropper between applications so that you don't accidentally mix alcohol into your essential oils, which would make them cloudy.

Now, carefully draw carnation oil a quarter of the way into the dropper and drop three drops of the essential oil into your empty glass vial. Squeeze out any excess carnation oil back into its bottle. Fill the dropper again with alcohol, squeeze it out, shake out any excess alcohol from the dropper, and draw your cedar oil a quarter of the way into the dropper. Drop three drops of the cedar oil into your vial. Squeeze any excess cedar oil back into its bottle and repeat the process again with your oak moss and pine oils, cleaning out the dropper with alcohol between each oil. Remember to keep your focus and intention and add it energetically as you add each oil.

If you wish to add more energy to your prosperity oil, you may include a small Jupiter stone of abundance to your oil. If you are adding a stone, place it in the bottle with intention before you fill the bottle up the rest of the way with carrier oil.

Now fill the vial of blended oils the rest of the way with your carrier oil. Essential oils are very concentrated so there is no need to have an undiluted solution. Shake the oil blend well and let the oils mix and react with each other overnight. If you smell the oil blend right after you mix it and then again the next day, you will see how the oils create their own synergistic aroma after being given some time to link their properties of both odor and energy.

You have blended your oils using numerical alchemical values. The number attributed to Jupiter is 6. You have used twelve total drops of essential oils in your blend. By using twelve drops, you have doubled the number 6 of Jupiter's expansion and created the number 3 (12 = 1 + 2 = 3), the number of harmony. Let's look at it another way and add the number differently: by using the number 12, you have also utilized the numbers 3 and 4 in your formula—three drops of four different essential oils, or 3 (drops) x 4 (herbs) = 12. The number 4 is the number of manifestation and form, and 3 the number of harmony and balance, which is the way in which you want your prosperity to manifest—on the material plane.

Now that you have your blend, note how very versatile Magickal oils are in their use. You can use them to anoint candles to burn during a Prosperity Ritual or meditation, or anoint a silver dollar that you keep in your wallet or purse to draw money to it. You can pour a few drops in your bath as you prepare for an Abundance Ritual. A little oil can be placed on a lottery ticket before the drawing or you can rub some of the oil into your hands before you purchase a ticket or go play at a casino. You may also decide to wear the oil as a Magickal perfume to attract opportunities to yourself throughout the day. Just remember to focus on your attention as you apply the oil in any of these ways to *set* and *charge* the energies for your specific purpose.

CHAPTER 6

The Herbs of Venus
Love and the Arts

Energies: love, friendship, artistry, attraction, music, pleasure, sensual delights, beauty, balance, compassion

Color: green

Number: 3

Metal: copper

Stones/materials: emerald, malachite, apatite, green fluorite

Deities: Aphrodite, Aradia, Persephone, Eros, Cupid, Faunus

Herbs: catnip, cherry, coltsfoot, damiana, feverfew, lemon verbena, lilac, maidenhair, mandrake, myrtle, orchid, passionflower, peach, periwinkle, plumeria, rhubarb, raspberry, rose, spikenard, tansy, tonka bean, vanilla, vervain, violet

As Venus rules the arts, using Her herbs can help to influence and enhance creativity and self-expression in painting, writing, music, dance, and all acts of artistic expression. Love, however, is the arena where these herbs tend to be used the most often—romantic love, to be sure, but also love of family, friends, community, the Planet, and all other beings, as well as love and acceptance of oneself. It is this *love*, this coming together in empathy, that creates the harmony of Venus. Venus is the Planet of relationships and your capacity for giving and receiving love and emotion in any type of relationship. It is also the Planet that works to bring together opposites in a union of balance. Venusian herbs can be useful in physical beauty, as well, when they are applied to the skin to bring smoothness, moisture, and youthfulness to the face.

Venus rules over the metamorphosis of the cells, the reproduction and enrichment and transformation of cells, the preservation of the body, the complexion, the reproductive system, and the harmony between all the systems of the body. To access these energies through the use of herbs, you may wish to consider the following rose water or rose oil, when applied to the skin, stabilizes, helps clear blemishes, and generally nourishes the skin. Eating strawberries or drinking strawberry juice also heals the skin, and strawberry slices laid on the skin provides a healing facial. For balancing health and enhancing the function of your metabolism and cells, tansy, vervain, and raspberry leaves and berries can be drunk in a tea or taken in capsule form. Reproduction and sexuality are also under the dominion of Venus. Raspberry, cherry, banana, and periwinkle can help to nourish and balance the reproductive system, thus influencing the male and female hormones that are key to sexual interest.

The key concept of Venusian symbology and attributes is *harmony*. The balancing force represented by one of Venus's rulerships, Libra, the scales, is a good metaphor for harmony on every level. Using the energy of Venus allows the sense of the aesthetic to blend with empathy and love. This sense is thus manifest on all levels and emphasized with the energies of this Planet. Venus is attributed to the Qabbalistic sphere of Netzach—the ecstatic consciousness that is a wellspring of creativity. Venus is the Planet of the arts: dance, music, drawing, and sculpture all express the Venusian energies and can be aided by the use of Venusian herbs in Incense, oil blends, and teas. It is true that "beauty is in the eye of the beholder," and so it is with the Venusian appreciation of form in harmony. Beauty is found in perfect function, proportion, and balance—not necessarily only in fashion magazines. Utilizing the energies of this Planet doesn't just make you or your artistic creation more physically beautiful. Venus has the power to unite all aspects of a person or a project into a balanced, harmonious whole, which others then respond to with appreciation and affection.

A Ritual Herbal Condenser that attracts the perfect person into your life is the perfect use for Venusian herbs. Use this ritual carefully—it works very well. Before embarking on this work, clear out of your life any extraneous activities that you no longer enjoy in order to free up time for your relationship. I would also suggest that you do some soul-searching to be sure that you are no longer engaging in behavior patterns from the past that have made your love life go sour—no need to bring the perfect person into your life when you're not yet ready.

Soul Mate Ritual

First, we need to talk about some ethics. This ritual is designed to help bring a great love to your life. It directly asks the Divine to determine who is best suited to you (and vice versa) and to bring that person into your life—not to break up someone else's relationship so that you can have your whim, or to bind to you a specific individual whom you have in mind. Those types of actions are unethical because they thwart the free will of other people for your personal gain. Besides, you don't really know as clearly as the Divine who will be best suited for you—you are judging on looks, money, sexiness, or whatever mundane quality that has entranced you, and that quality is not the one that necessarily helps to create a relationship that will last for life (or many lifetimes). For this ritual, you must be ready to accept what the Divine brings you, and you must be ready for *real* love in your life.

To make your Soul Mate Herbal Condenser, you will need the following supplies:

three edible Venusian herbs (banana, catnip, cherry, damiana, lemon verbena, lilac, maidenhair, myrtle, passionflower, peach, plumeria, rhubarb, raspberry, rose, strawberry, tansy, vanilla, vervain, and violet) (see Note)

glass or enamel cooking pot with lid

spring or distilled water

measuring cup

---

* *Venusian herbs:* Research your herbs for their physical effects on the body—remember, not all herbs should be ingested. Mandrake, for example, is an herb of Venus but medicinally speaking can cause seizures, coma, and liver failure, none of which are conducive to love Magick. Mandrake would, therefore, be better used in an Herbal Amulet where you can draw upon its properties, but it would not be affecting your physical self. Tonka beans can be poisonous, so their use should be limited to Amulets as well.

vodka or grain alcohol

gold flake (see Note)

amber- or cobalt-colored glass bottle

Place a handful of each of the three herbs you have chosen into an enamel or glass pot (glass or enamel will not react and seep into your mixture—aluminum or iron pots will react). Cover the herbs with spring or distilled water and bring to a simmer. Cover, turn down the heat, and let them simmer softly together for twenty minutes with the lid on. Allow your mixture to cool to room temperature and strain out the herbs. Now boil again at a medium heat until the liquid has been reduced by half. Cool the extraction again, and when it is room temperature, pour it into a measuring cup so that you can see how much liquid you have. Add an equal amount of vodka or grain alcohol as the amount of liquid extract in your measuring cup. Add a pinch of gold flake. Pour your Condenser into an amber- or cobalt-colored glass bottle (this keeps light from ageing your mixture) and store in a cool, dark place. Be sure to shake it before each use. Now that you have your Condenser, you are ready to perform your Soul Mate Ritual.

Here are the supplies you will need for your rite:

deep green cloth for the altar

three pink candles

vase of beautiful flowers

lovely chalice half full of fruit juice, wine, or spring water

piece of rose quartz

Incense burner

Aphrodite Incense and Oil (see Formulas for Manifestation of Goals in appendix E, Formulas and Recipes)

---

* *Gold flake:* This you can obtain at an art supplies store that carries materials for gold leafing. Gold leaf is a thin sheet of gold on glassine paper. You can scrape the gold from the paper to create flakes.

parchment paper

writing pen

"flame" candle with which to light your pink candles

rose petals

Soul Mate Condenser

On a Friday during the Waxing Moon, at a time when you will not be disturbed or interrupted, gather together your supplies and set them on your altar, which should be covered with a deep green altar cloth. Place the three pink candles in the center of your altar in a triangular pattern, with base of the triangle nearest you. Put the vase of flowers just to the left of the top candle, and your chalice just to the right of the top candle. Now place the rose quartz in the middle of the candle triangle. Place your Incense burner and Incense to your right near the edge closest to you. Your parchment and pen lie directly in front of you on the altar. Place your flame candle to the left top side of your altar and light it. Sprinkle your rose petals randomly all over the altar.

Anoint the candles from the wick down to the bottom with the Aphrodite Oil, then anoint your Third Eye (the spot just above and between your eyebrows) and over your heart with the Aphrodite Oil. Light the pink candles with your flame candle, and then using the top pink candle, light your Incense charcoal and place it in your Incense burner atop some insulating sand. While your charcoal is igniting completely across, draw a heart on your parchment paper and, inside of the heart, a spiral. Place some Incense on the charcoal and bathe the parchment in the Incense smoke, imagining the parchment absorbing the love energy.

Now, charge the parchment by placing it above each candle flame (but not so close you ignite it!) while saying three times:

> *Aphrodite, Queen of Night,*
> *Bring to me the one who's right*
> *Aphrodite, Morning Star*
> *Whether near or whether far*

Bringer of Love, O Aphrodite
Draw my soul mate now to me
Most lovely of Goddesses, O Aphrodite,
And as I will, So Mote It Be.

Then place a drop of your Soul Mate Condenser on your finger and seal the energy you have placed in the parchment by firmly anointing the spiral in the center of the heart with the liquid. Drop three drops of the Condenser into the libation your have prepared in your chalice. Drink the liquid slowly as you concentrate on your heart chakra, opening and strengthening it. Feel it opening like a beautiful red rose. Let the candles burn all the way down, then fold your rose quartz stone inside the parchment and place it inside your pillowcase.

Each Friday evening as you relax, pour some fruit juice, wine, or spring water into your chalice and add three drops of your Condenser. Relax and daydream and continue working on opening your heart chakra.

It can take up to a full twelve months for the Divine to locate your love and bring him or her into your life, although this ritual has also been known to work within a month's time. Drink the Soul Mate Condenser each Friday evening, and keep the parchment-wrapped rose quartz in your pillowcase as you dream of your love!

CHAPTER 7

The Herbs of Saturn
Grounding, Protection, and Stability

Energies: form, stability, karma, discipline, occult knowledge, protection, patience, endurance

Color: indigo

Number: 4

Metal: lead

Stones/materials: jet, onyx, hematite, smoky quartz

Deities: Kronos, Dionysus, Anubis, the Cailleach, Danu, Ceres

Herbs: asafoetida, balm of Gilead, bistort, boneset, comfrey, cypress, dill, fumitory, garlic, hawthorn, hemlock, hyssop, patchouli, petitgrain, rosemary, Solomon's seal, Saint-John's-wort, valerian, vetivert, wolfsbane, yew

The energies of the Planet Saturn are central to spiritual creatures who live in the physical world, such as humans. Saturn's dominion encompasses those powers that rule the knowledge of karma acquired during one's lifetimes. Saturn's force slows down and calms chaotic events and gives endurance. This force restricts and binds but also assists with self-control, self-responsibility, and the wisdom learned through overcoming challenges. In addition, Saturn is important in rites of protection and shielding. This Planet's energy serves as a passive form of protection rather than the assertive form of protection, which is that of Mars.

Saturn is sometimes known as a malefic Planet because Saturn's flavor of energy can bring what, at the time, we may interpret as events of hardship and difficulty. But challenges requiring self-control, time, and endurance teach us our karmic lessons, and it is in the overcoming of these challenges that we begin to comprehend and apply our karmic heritage, thus enabling us to be more spiritually focused individuals.

There are many symbols that encapsulate the power and expression of Saturnian energy as it applies to the concept of karma. Kronos, the god of time, is the Greek form of the Roman god Saturn. Adherents to the Gregorian calendar symbolize the passing of the year's months by the image of Kronos, or Saturn, as the old man with a scythe giving way to the new year on January 1, symbolized by a baby. By harnessing the scythe power of Saturn, we can cut away that which binds us karmically when we become responsible for the path we choose to follow. The Hermit and the High Priestess cards in the Major Arcana of the Tarot exemplify the way that Saturn expresses energy. In their own ways, they both symbolize time, wisdom, inner secrets, and slow contemplation.

Saturn's various energies can be found in those herbs that are the foundation of plants—the roots binding the plant to the Earth, such as comfrey root or Solomon's seal root. They are also those herbs that grow in dark, dank places, like the cypress tree, or are dark themselves, such as patchouli leaves. Herbs that clear or cleanse, such as garlic, or that are used as a fumitory also fall under the dominion of Saturn. Garlic is a natural antibiotic, restricting and binding the growth of bacteria. Garlic is also found to be medicinally beneficial in controlling and stopping the growth of plaque in the blood vessels that can lead to heart failure or stroke.

Saturn energy represents the force of limitations and restrictions both in time and space. This energy provides the structure and foundation, without which existence would dissolve into chaos. It is interesting that two of the most foul-smelling herbs, asafoetida and valerian, have been used for millennia in rites of banishment and exorcism and, medicinally speaking, are powerful antispasmodics, acting to limit and sedate potentially damaging overflows of energy. Other herbs of Saturn such as rosemary, dill, and Saint-John's-wort are also antispasmodics, working principally on the nervous and digestive systems. Rosemary also reduces scrofulous sores and acts as a mild astringent, restricting and eliminating infection. Other Saturnian astringents include Solomon's seal, hyssop, Saint-John's-wort, and garlic. Solomon's seal and hyssop bear indigo fruit—the color associated with Saturn—and the flowers of the garlic plant are sterile, corresponding with the limiting, binding, and ending energies associated with Saturn.

Garlic is a great limiter in terms of internal infection and is an eliminative for worms. Admirably suiting the Saturnian aspect of protection, Garlic is widely credited as a preventative against a broad variety of diseases (including bubonic plague). It regularizes the liver and gall bladder (while rosemary stimulates bile production) and has a limiting effect on the circulatory system, lowering blood pressure and combating arteriosclerosis. Sharing the pungent, aromatic qualities of valerian and asafoetida, it exemplifies the Saturnian medical principal of essential healing agents that are at times difficult to swallow.

The energy of Saturn is very helpful to our lives in many ways. Creating a Protection Amulet allows you to apply the power and lessons of this valuable Planet and aids in shielding you from the unbalanced, negative energies that you often encounter as you work toward your goals.

Protection Amulet

The words *amulet* and *talisman* have come to be used interchangeably for an object or charm that repels negativity. I generally used the word *talisman* to indicate something that has symbols or words written or inscribed upon it, while I view an Amulet as an object that is composed of natural materials. Both can be worn on the body or placed in a location of significance. Amulets are quite versatile in their use. You may use this Protection Amulet to shield and protect. Really, your imagination is the limit as far as the myriad places and uses you will find to take advantage of this Magickal tool.

For the manufacture and charging of your Amulet, you will need the following materials:

six-inch-square black cotton or silk cloth

one yard white cotton cord or ribbon

four protective herbs (hyssop, Solomon's seal, rue, garlic, coriander, agrimony, rowan, patchouli, or chaparral), each in a separate small dish container

one protective stone (onyx, smoky quartz, hematite, jet, or obsidian)

Incense burner

Protection Incense (see Formulas for Manifestation of Goals in appendix E, Formulas and Recipes)

Incense charcoal

white candle and holder

Protection Oil (see Formulas for Manifestation of Goals in appendix E, Formulas and Recipes)

matches or lighter

Arrange your materials on your altar or a flat surface as such: the cloth and ribbon in the center; your herbs (each in a separate small dish or container) and your protective stone to your right; an Incense burner half filled with sand, Protection Incense, and a ready piece of Incense charcoal at the top right of your table; your candle, candleholder, Protection Oil, and some matches or a lighter at the top left of your table.

Now it's time to do the work.

If you typically cast a Circle when you do any energywork, do so in your usual manner. If you prefer not to create a sacred space in which to do your work, focus your thoughts and energy on the work at hand. Breathing slowly and deeply, imagine that you are connected to the Earth and that you are radiating a pale light from every pore in your body, surrounding yourself with light.

Now anoint the white candle with Protection Oil from the top of the wick to the bottom of the candle. You will anoint in this direction because you are drawing protection to yourself; as the candle burns down, it will attract protective, shielding energies like a magnet. Place the candle in the candleholder and light it. Now, light your Incense charcoal from the candle's flame, let the charcoal begin to ignite across its entire surface, then place it on top of some sand or other insulating material that you have placed in your Incense burner. Once the ignited charcoal ignites all the way across, apply a small spoonful of Protection Incense.

Lay your black cloth out flat in the center of your altar and place about a tablespoon of each of your four chosen herbs in the center of this cloth. As you place each herb in the center of the cloth, concentrate on the protective qualities of the herb and activate the energies of the herb with your thoughts. Hold the chosen stone in your hands and, focusing and activating the protective qualities of the stone, warm it in your hands, then place it on top of the herbs. Taking two opposing corners of the cloth, bring them together and hold the edges with the fingers of one hand as you then take the other opposing corners and bring them together, creating a bag or pouch. Let the corners lie flat while you gather your cord or ribbon, then pinch all the cloth corners together and twist them one or two times to secure it. Tie your cord tightly around the twisted portion of your bag and knot it four times. With each knot you tie, focus your mind entirely on protection. Now hold your Protection Amulet in the smoke of the Incense, then briefly over the candle flame to set the Magick. You can now put the Amulet by your front door to safeguard your home, keep it in your car's glove box for protection while traveling or to ward off thieves, carry it in your purse or in your pocket to protect you wherever you go, tie it to your pet's collar to keep your pet safe, or store it in a cash drawer to shield money from theft—anywhere that you have determined protection is needed.

You will notice that for this Amulet, in addition to herbs and stones of protection, you have been using the colors white and black. White is a color of purification, while black is a color of shielding and absorption. Using both for protection helps to bring purity, shielding, and the quality of absorbing any negative energy. You have used four herbs and tied your cord with four knots. This is the number of Saturn and of binding. By using the number 4, you are binding and sealing the power of your Amulet. In addition, 4 herbs + 4 knots = 8, the number of power.

CHAPTER 8

The Herbs of Neptune
Creative Inspiration, Mysticism, and Imagination

Energies: illusion and imagination; useful in hypnosis, trance, dreamwork

Color: green-blue

Number: 11.

Stone/material: seashell, amber, labradorite, cat's-eye, lemurian crystal

Deities: Poseidon, Apa, Dylan, Tiamat, Ceridwen, Nimue

Herbs: cannabis, datura, lobelia, lotus, orange blossom (also known as neroli), peach, poppy, skullcap, wild lettuce, willow, wisteria

Up to this point, we have been working with the original seven "ancient" Planets—the orbs of energy that the ancients could identify by eye. These seven Planets form the basis of the Doctrine of Signatures developed by Paracelsus. The next three Planets we will explore—Neptune, Uranus, and Pluto—are often known as the "Outer Planets." They must be viewed through a telescope, and their discovery coincided with the explosion in technology and science over the last 250 years. Astrologers and people who work with Magickal energies have identified the Outer Planets' energies as reflecting in a more subtle yet intense fashion the energies of some of the traditional seven "ancients." Neptune is paired with Venus, Uranus is paired with Mercury, and Pluto is paired with both Mars and Saturn.

The energies of Neptune are those of the mystic and the artist, the same ecstatic energy represented by Venus, transmuted to a higher level of psychic and imaginative power that nurtures the sources of creativity, perception, and inspiration through the experience of illusion, fantasy, imagination, and occult intuition. Neptune is the dreamer—an aspect perhaps represented by the image of the sleeping Vishnu dreaming the dream of infinite creation.

The herbs attributed to Neptune are the mind-altering plants of dream weavers. Their principal effects are psychotropic, opening up recesses of higher and lower levels of consciousness not normally accessible to the waking mind, revealing or at least indicating that most occult of all entities: the Hidden Self. A study of Neptunian herbs sheds light on their hidden aspects, revealing their connection. For example, an Infusion of dried orange blossoms produces a stimulating effect on the nervous system. The oil distilled from the blossoms, however, upon inhalation of its alluring scent, enables the inhaler to achieve a state described in the texts as hypnotic, thus rendering orange blossom oil an excellent medium for trancework, which falls under the dominion of Neptune.

Neptune is considered to be the higher octave of Venus, thus those properties of Venus—the arts, music, beauty, and love—are brought to an even higher, more intense and pure level. As such, all the Venusian herbs apply to Neptune as well. The Neptune energies inspire the artist in finding his Muse and enable one to connect with the collective unconscious to explore the depths of art, music, beauty, and dance in a deeply emotional way, which in turn ignites the subconscious, ideally leading to a clearer and more intense expression of creative talent.

Opium is distilled from poppy, a Neptunian herb, and while its use is not recommended to achieve trance states or astral travel due to problems with addiction and overdose, poppy seeds used in a tea or burnt in an Incense will result in a less intense opiate state while still aiding the user in obtaining the desired effects. If you use poppy seeds this way, be aware that your use of it will show up in drug tests. Cannabis is another Neptune herb and is still illegal in the United States, but those flower children of the '60s could attest to its hypnotic effects and the heightened sense of creativity it provokes (although I'm not sure how much creativity was actually expressed!). Passionflower is used medicinally as a calmative, sedative, and soother. If you have ever viewed the live plant, you have seen its amazing otherworldly appearance. Wisteria, like orange blossom, has an intoxicating scent that leads to a calm, inward contemplation ideal for meditation and calming the mind prior to creative activity.

The use of Neptune herbs to enhance the creative process is the perfect way to experience the intoxicating energies of this Planet of the Mystic. A Bath Salt using Neptune herbs and essential oils is a lovely Neptunian experience before applying yourself to self-expression, whether painting, music, dance, poetry—your imagination is the only limiting factor. With the activation of your Muse through the mystical opening that Neptune provides, your imagination will delight in the unfolding of talents of which you may not have even been aware. The use of the herbs and oils in a Neptune bath will allow you to relax into an altered state of consciousness and open your creative mind while you soak in a warm, mini-sea of intoxicatingly scented water.

Creativity Bath

For a bath, you have two choices of how you wish to combine your herbs and oils. One way, Bath Salts, is the literal and simple application of essential oils mixed into sea salt. The second way is to create a Bath Tea, which contains herbs and essential oils, but is applied to the bath in a teabag, tea ball, or cloth pouch to prevent the herbs from floating freely in and on the water. You will want to contain them—otherwise you will have a bathtub of herb debris to clean up later, and when you emerge from your bath, you will look as if you stepped out of a swamp, covered with bits of soggy herbs!

Bath Salt

To create a Bath Salt, the supplies you will need are as follows:

mortar or small bowl

four ounces sea salt

orange blossom essential oil (or other Neptune-associated essential oil) lotus essential oil (or other Neptune-associated essential oil)

two ounces bicarbonate of soda (baking soda; optional)

blue and green food coloring (optional)

Breathing slowly and deeply, ground yourself and focus on your purpose and intention in creating your Bath Salt. In your mortar or small bowl, pour the sea salt. Add eleven drops of orange blossom oil, and then eleven drops of lotus oil, blending lightly after each addition. If you wish your bath to have a slight bubbly effect, now is the time to stir in the bicarbonate of soda. At this point, if you wish to tint your bath with the color of Neptune, add three drops of blue food coloring and four drops of green food coloring. This will cause your bathwater to be the lovely green-blue of Neptune.

Bath Tea

To create a Bath Tea (also known as a Tussie) you will need the following materials:

mortar and pestle

Neptunian herbs (willow, orange blossom flowers, skullcap, or whatever you like)

one Neptune essential oil

ironable teabag (available at many health food stores), six-inch-square cloth (cheesecloth works very well as it is a loose weave) and string, muslin pouch with a drawstring, or a tea ball

In your mortar, place a healthy pinch of the herbs you have selected and crush them lightly together with your pestle. This will begin to release their oils. When you have combined your herbs to your satisfaction, add eleven drops of your essential oil and then fluff lightly with your fingers—you don't need to crush the oils in with your pestle.

Now stuff your teabag, tea ball, pouch, or cloth with the herb mixture. If you are using a flat piece of cloth, place the herbs in the center of the cloth while it is flat, bring two opposite corners up over the center of the cloth, tie them snugly, and then repeat with the remaining two corners.

Drawing the Bath

Once you've created your Bath Salt or Bath Tea, prepare whatever medium you plan to use in your creative exploration. Get your journal and pen ready, or boot up the computer if that's where you write; clear space in your studio so that you can dance freely; set up your easel and get out your paints, brushes, charcoals, or pastels; lift the keyboard cover from the piano keys; take your guitar from its case—prepare the instrument of your expression for its work with you.

Turn off the phone, lock the doors, contain any rambunctious pets so that you will not have any interruptions.

Now it's time to draw your bath and use your Bath Salt or Bath Tea. Bring a CD player or other music player into the bathroom and put on some music that inspires and relaxes you. Turn on the bathtub water spigot, adjust the water to a temperature you find pleasurable, and let the tub begin to fill. Light a green-blue candle and disrobe. Turn off the electric light in the room and stand at the side of the tub, breathing slowly and deeply, holding your bath creation and drinking in its intoxicating scent. When the tub is full, drop the Bath Salts or Bath Tea into the warm water. Step into the bath and relax your body down into the water. Continue to breathe deeply and slowly, with intention. Stretch out your body in the water and, as you breathe, feel each breath lightening your body and filling your mind with relaxation. With each breath, exhale any extraneous thoughts and stress; with each inhalation, open and relax your mind.

Now breathe deeply of the Neptune aroma and begin to expand your consciousness. Imagine that with each breath your mind is reaching out into space, farther and farther, caressing the stars and skipping around amazing, whirling nebulas. There is a star out there in the black vastness that is waiting to connect with your mind and share with you the mysteries that reside within you, and your connection to the Universe. Let your mind and imagination wander, seeking that star in a relaxed and playful state of mind. You are drawn to it; there is no way that you can miss it. Breathe.

Allow yourself to play in space and completely melt into the experience. You will know when you have reached the center, the star. Absorb the feeling, the nudge, the image that you receive and give thanks. Stand up, get out of the bath, put out the candle, and dry off. Put on whatever attire that you plan to create in, and get to work!

CHAPTER 9

The Herbs of Uranus

Innovation, Originality, and New Thought Patterns

Energies: enlightenment, objectivity, technology, genius, eccentricity, breaking free from old patterns and electrical impulses of the brain

Color: electric blue

Number: 22

Metal: white gold

Stones/materials: quartz, rutilated quartz, kunzite, amazonite

Deities: Merlin, Shu, Ur-annu, Prometheus, Urania, Varuna

Herbs: allspice, betel nut, chicory, clove, coffee, elemi, guarana, mahuang

As Neptune is the Planet for the dreamer and the mystic, so Uranus is for the eccentric and the Magickian as she strives to transform herself and her environment in accordance with the Magickal Will. Neptune governs the irrational, nonlinear, intuitive functions of the mind, while Uranus governs the same functions of conscious perception as Mercury but on another, higher level. You might look at the energies of Mercury as the college math professor and those of Uranus as Einstein, with his intuitive thinking patterns that, once they become a part of the conscious, linear mindset, make sense of the workings of the Universe. The Uranian sphere of endeavor may be considered to be the conscious exercise of lucid Magickal perception.

Each somewhat eccentric herb attributed to this unique Planet does something to facilitate the achievement of a highly energized mental state. While Mercury may rule the nervous system, Uranus governs the electrical flow of nervous energy itself. While most Planets seem to rule a system or set of organs, Uranus rules the ongoing, kinetic processes. Each Uranian herb acts as a nervous stimulant, producing an abundance of circulated energy flow that can cause the mind and the perceptions to act and react in a decidedly eccentric manner.

Coffee was originally brewed as a sacramental drink among the Aztec, Maya, and Inca. A powerful nervous stimulant, due principally to its heavy caffeine content, coffee produces a state of temporary alertness that may be useful in Magickal operations and perceptions. The danger arises with prolonged use or overindulgence, which can produce both a physical addiction and a state of mental and emotional burnout—where what was once only charmingly eccentric becomes dangerously erratic. It is a sort of a Sorcerer's Apprentice effect wherein what was once useful becomes out of control.

Kava kava is also a sacramental drink among Pacific Islanders, though in effect it seems to be the polar opposite of coffee. It was used in ritual to induce a tranquil sleep filled with visions and is thought to be a principal agent in the astral endeavors of the Hunas. It was also thought to act— once again in contrast to the effects of coffee—as an aphrodisiac. Both coffee and kava kava act upon the electrical impulses that allow the brain to signal behavior to the body.

Nutmeg is an aromatic stimulant and mild hallucinogen that serves to kick the brain into overdrive. Neural synapses seem to fire all at once, and associational thought processes have a momentum all their own. A clear symptom of overindulgence is doubled or blurred vision. If used in excess, nutmeg can cause symptoms that express themselves as severe stomach pain, hemorrhaging, and even death.

Change, innovation, objectivity, and the repatterning of thought processes are all hallmarks of Uranian energy. You can make fundamental changes in your life and its future opportunities by harnessing the power of Uranus.

Innovation Ritual

When we want to make changes and new beginnings in our lives, we often must first make room for them by releasing old habits, people, or ways in which we currently use our energies that are no longer working for us. This can be in any area of your life, so before doing this ritual, first begin by looking at the person, thought pattern, job, or lifestyle that you feel is hampering your efforts. Decide what you need to release in favor of new thoughts or perceptions that will allow you to alter your attitude and ingrained reactions. This will give you the mental space to plant new roots of behavior and to have them to grow in your life. Next, determine how you want to grow or change: spiritually, monetarily, emotionally, physically, or intellectually. Once you know where you need to let go and what you wish to change about your life, you will be ready to do the ritual.

The supplies you will need for this spell are the following:

electric blue candle and candle holder

Incense burner

calligraphy ink

green quill

piece of parchment

an object that represents the new you (see Note)

three- or four-inch-long black silk or cotton cord (*not* polyester)

small box (such as a matchbox)

Uranus Oil (see Planetary Formulas in appendix E, Formulas and Recipes)

matches

Uranus Incense (see Planetary Formulas in appendix E, Formulas and Recipes)

On an evening when you will not be disturbed, arrange your altar with your candle at the left top edge; your Incense burner at the right top edge; your ink, quill and parchment at the right bottom edge; and your

---

* *An object that represents the new you:* This object can be a piece of jewelry with a clear quartz, rutilated quartz, amazonite, or kunzite stone set in it, or a small, lovely art object that you feel sums up the changes that you will make. If you use an art object, you will later set this piece in a prominent place in your home after the ritual so that you can see it every day to reinforce your changes. If you have chosen a piece of jewelry, you will wear it every day after you have charged it in your ritual to keep drawing that innovative energy to you.

"new you" object at the left bottom edge, leaving the center for the black cord and small box. For the moment, just lay the cord coiled in the center of your altar. Cast your circle or center your energy. Anoint your candle with your Uranus oil, from the bottom of the candle to the wick, and light it. Light your Incense charcoal from the candle flame. Let it ignite almost completely across, then set it down on a bed of insulating sand in your Incense burner. Place a small spoonful of your Uranus Incense in the center of the charcoal.

In the center of the piece of parchment, draw with your ink and quill a symbol that represents the thing that you are releasing from your life that has been holding it back. If this is a person, you can draw his Astrological Sign or initials, for example. If it is your employment, draw the logo of the company or its initials; if it is a bad habit, draw a simple image that represents this lifestyle choice. Next, around this symbol, draw a square, which represents the limitations that this has set on you. Set this parchment sigil in the center of your altar. Pick up the black cord and knot the two cut ends together, concentrating on the problems or limitations that you have encountered with this person, job, or lifestyle, placing the energy of the problem in the knot. Lay the cord in a circle around the parchment sigil in the center of your altar. For a few moments, continue to focus on the problem while you also become aware of your breathing. Each time you exhale, imagine yourself exhaling the hold that this problem has on you. Feel yourself becoming lighter and more relaxed. After each exhalation, say, "I release you." Work on this release for about three minutes, or until you feel very relaxed and light.

Next, pick up your cord and carefully hold the knot in the flame of the candle, igniting the knot and burning away the problem. Set the remainder of the cord in the box. Next, holding the parchment by the very edge, ignite it with the candle flame. Let it burn toward your fingers and go out. If it burns dramatically, you can blow on it lightly to control the flame and blow it out while concentrating on release. Place any unburned parchment in the box with the burned cord and put the box to the side. When you have finished with this part of the ritual, relax for a few moments, enjoying the release and lightness.

Now take in your hands the "new you" object, concentrating again on your breathing and what you are bringing into your life. With each inhalation, breathe in energy, motivation, and optimism. As you exhale, breathe on the object, filling and charging it with this new, exciting change. After you have filled it, set the energies by anointing it with your Uranus oil, then hold it in the smoke of your Uranus Incense and place the object next to the candle. Leave the candle to burn down all the way and go outside to dig a hole to bury the box with the parchment ashes and cord. Bury the box, firmly tamp down the dirt, and walk away, never looking back. Feel the freedom and lightness.

The next morning, take the jewelry from the altar and go to a mirror. Watch yourself adorn yourself with the jewelry, focusing on the changes it represents. If you have chosen an art object, take it up from the altar and place it in a location in your home where it will be prominent, being mindful of the changes it represents.

---

* *Note:* In this ritual, you are literally "playing with fire," so *be careful.* You may wish to also have a plate on your altar on which to set the burning parchment in case you get nervous. That way you can let it continue to burn without scorching your fingers. Also, since you are letting the candle burn all the way down, which will take several hours, your altar needs to be set up in a room that is closed off to all children and pets. You do not want to set your altar up near curtains or other flammable things. Your jewelry or object is going to be on the altar next to the candle, and you don't want it covered with melted wax in the morning. Be sure that the candleholder you choose has a bottom that can contain melted wax. You may wish to place your jewelry or object in a small container set next to the candle just to be safe.

CHAPTER 10

The Herbs of Pluto
Karma and the Unconscious Mind

Energies: death, alchemical transformation, regeneration, decay, sexual instinct, the deep unconscious, catharsis

Color: smoky black

Number: 33

Stones/materials: ash, lava stone, obsidian, black opal, apache tear, black tourmaline

Deities: Arawn, Pwyll, Osiris, Demeter, Rhea, Astarte

Herbs: barley, black cohosh, corn, damiana, fly agaric, galangal root, mushrooms, myrrh, oats, patchouli, pomegranate, psilocybin, rye, saw palmetto, wheat, wormwood, yohimbe

Pluto has been somewhat of an occult enigma since its discovery. Its attributions and rulerships have been debated, often bitterly, for the past fifty-some years. In fact, astronomers differ on whether Pluto is a Planet at all. Those of us who work with the energies of Pluto concur that Pluto should, indeed, be classified as a Planet, as its effects and energies are intense and discernable to the average person. The current (and most intuitively workable) hypothesis defines Pluto as the Planet of sex, death, and regeneration; of things hidden and subterranean—those primordial forces of evolution and inner compulsion that can represent and express themselves through the "Shadow" aspects of the personality. Pluto is considered officially to be the higher aspect of the energies of Mars and, in my experiences and studies, also partakes of the higher karmic and subconscious energies of Saturn. The attribution of grains such as rye, barley, wheat, and all cereal grains (plants sacred to Ceres/Demeter) associated with the planetary energies of Pluto tend to bear out the previously ascribed qualities, particularly if grain parasite-symbiotes such as ergot are added to the Plutonian catalogue.

This attribution of the cereal grains to Plutonian energies is shown in our myths of Pluto's abduction of Persephone into the Underworld, a well-known story in Western culture. In a nutshell, Pluto spies the young Persephone, daughter of Demeter, exploring the forests and meadows. Stunned by her beauty and desiring a companion, he abducts Persephone and takes her into the Underworld with him. Demeter, the Goddess of all grains and animal husbandry, grieves as she cannot find her beloved daughter and withdraws her energies from the propagation of life. The plants begin to die, the animals will not mate, and the Earth goes into a wintry sleep. Persephone becomes aware of the demise of life on the Earth's surface and begs Pluto to allow her to live part of the year in the underworld (the unconscious) with him and part of the year on the Earth's surface with her mother and living things. He agrees, noting that while she has resided with him in his kingdom, she has eaten six pomegranate seeds and thus must stay with him six months out of the year but can live the other six on the surface of Earth. The myth securely connects Pluto as an essential component of the continuing cycle of the death and regeneration of the plant life and ultimately (and metaphorically) all life.

There are, however, other levels of meaning and perspectives regarding this primal legend and Pluto's herbal attributes. When one considers the effects that ergot, a naturally occurring fungus that infects rye and other grains, has on the human system, it becomes very interesting and clear. The Eleusinian Mysteries were held around the Demeter-Pluto-Persephone legends and became, over the centuries, a profound initiatory experience. Central to the rites was the consumption of a potion made of barley water containing a decoction of ergot, the progenitor, of course, of our own LSD, the discovery of which virtually accompanied the astronomical discovery of the Planet Pluto. This powerful hallucinogenic was first synthesized from ergot alkaloids by the Swiss chemist Albert Hofmann in 1938. In small amounts the ingestion of ergot can lead to hallucinations and bodily sensations sometimes termed *rushes*.

One of the few common threads amid the bewildering variety of experiences catalyzed by ergot and its derivatives is the feeling of death and dissolution of the ego (which from an egocentric viewpoint amounts to total annihilation) and its subsequent reconstitution and regeneration. Those who partake of ergot are taken on a voyage through their own psychic Underworld that closely parallels the experience of Persephone as the Underworld bride of Pluto. There is also a great deal of evidence to indicate that the experience involves a triggering of genetic memory and so opens the floodgates of evolutionary force.

Ergot also serves as a vasoconstrictor, narrowing the large arteries, small arterioles, and veins. Ingesting fungus-infected grains subjects the body to ergot poisoning, which constricts the blood's flow to the extremities. The resultant feeling of the hands and feet being on fire, full-body convulsions, and even hallucinations as blood flow to the brain was impeded was called St. Anthony's Fire in the Middle Ages. Vasoconstriction can also have positive effects, such as in the natural retention of blood in the phallus during sexual arousal. With Mars's association with sexuality, blood, and our circulatory system, ergot's vasoconstriction may be considered an appropriate effect for an attribute of the higher octave of Mars.

Pluto may indeed be the dread dark lord whose experience is, to say the least, cathartic. Pluto rules our deep unconscious, our animal instincts, and past-life memories. When we first open the Pandora's box that the experience of Pluto offers us, we must be prepared to acknowledge that some of what resides in our deep memory has been repressed because it stirs fear within us. When we bring these fears into conscious light, it may first feel overwhelming, but as we face our dread and work to transform our Shadow Selves, we release the negative energy and emotions attached to these memories and purify ourselves. Through the use of ergot, it is possible to put oneself on the pathway to the experience of death or radical transformation while providing for the possibility of human frailty by eliminating (just as in real life and death) the possibility of turning back. In this way we initiate reconnection with our Deep Selves and our past lives, enabling us to meet any unresolved or traumatic challenges again and overcome them.

Pluto is correlated to other fungi as well. Fly agaric and psilocybin subsist and multiply on decaying organic materials and were once commonly associated with dark, deadly subterranean origins. Pluto herbs bring about dramatic, sometimes traumatic change, particularly within the psyche. They promote dramatic growth and insights normally through cataclysmic circumstances. Pluto herbs, such as yohimbe, saw palmetto, and damiana, aid the sexually impotent and help to balance the physical with the spiritual.

While Pluto's effects and energies can be dramatic and difficult to integrate into one's life, gaining wisdom through the knowledge of one's karma and karmic debts can be very useful and, in most cases, not usually upsetting. The actions and events of previous lifetimes tend to be experienced in the present lifetime with a sense of distance and objectivity. Knowing what you came into this lifetime to accomplish and recognizing the challenges you will need to overcome can be invaluable gifts. With this in mind, we use the herbs of Pluto to draw back that veil between the worlds and time and take a look at a past life.

Recalling a Past Life

To discover the primary karmic lessons with which we came into this lifetime, we utilize the occult principles of Scorpio, which rules Pluto, with the karmic comprehension of those energies in a Past Life Ritual.

Spend the day lightly fasting on a Saturday, a day whose energy is very useful for understanding karma. When evening falls, gather your ritual materials:

Incense burner

Incense charcoal

Past Lives Incense (see Formulas for Manifestation of Goals in appendix E, Formulas and Recipes)

matches

two purple candles and candleholders

journal

pen

divisionary tool such as a crystal ball or scrying mirror (optional)

Past Lives Oil (see Formulas for Manifestation of Goals in appendix E, Formulas and Recipes)

Arrange your altar with an Incense burner, charcoal, Incense, and matches close together to one side on the surface of your altar. Place one of your candles in a holder *behind* you so that when you light it, it does not reflect in your crystal ball or scrying mirror (if using); place the other on your altar in the center behind the crystal ball or scrying mirror (if using). Place the journal and pen within easy reach of the altar so that you can jot down information as it comes to you.

Cast your circle in your usual way or, using your breathing, surround yourself with light and peace. Anoint your candles (one on the altar, the other behind you) with your Ritual Oil, then light them. Light your Incense charcoal from the altar candle, let it ignite most of the way across, and then place it on insulating sand in your Incense burner. Place some of your Incense onto an Incense charcoal and allow the smoke to waft into the air. Ground yourself with your breathing and connect your energy field with that of the Earth. Anoint your Third Eye (the spot just above and between your eyes on your forehead). Breathe in the scent of your Incense and Ritual Oil. Allow yourself to relax into a light trance state while gazing at the candle flame on your altar. When your body is completely relaxed and your mind is clear, blow out the candle on your altar and shift your focus to the crystal ball or scrying mirror. If you are not using a scrying device, you can let the altar candle continue to burn and return your eyes to the flame periodically to refocus yourself.

Visualize an ancient leather-bound, parchment-paged book on the surface of your scrying tool or visualize it in front of you. As you gaze at the book, it slowly begins to open and the pages begin to turn by themselves as if by an invisible hand. Ask yourself what lesson you are here to learn, what karmic balance you are here to redress or enforce. Keep concentrating on this question until the pages stop turning and a dim light illuminates the parchment page.

At this point, you may see the words and be able to read them, you may see static images or view a montage or "movie," you might hear the answer directly inside your head, or you may simply gaze at a page that has no words or words in a written language that you currently do not understand.

Write down the information you acquire; emotions you are feeling; names you receive; and any impressions of geography, clothing style, architecture, foliage, or timeframe that you have during this experience. Be very observant of any dreams you have during the next three nights, as they will contain additional information and even the key to the information that you witnessed on the page.

During the same working or at another time when you wish to get more information, you may use some of the imagery, names, time sense, or clues to obtain more details. It is important after doing a working of this type that you do two things: (1) eat a light snack to re-center and securely anchor yourself into your present-day body, and (2) act on any insights you receive that will help you to balance, resolve, and initiate the karmic lesson(s) you came into this lifetime to carry out.

PART 2

PRACTICUM

THE CREATION, COMPOSITION,

and

BLENDING OF ALCHEMICAL

HERBAL FORMULAS

CHAPTER 11

Magickal Incense

The use of Incense is as old as mankind. It has
been used in religious and Magickal practices in
every culture around the world. Incense has always
been associated with Magick, and for good reason.
Although Magickal practitioners have known for
centuries that herbs, flowers, resins, and oils carry
with them their own vibrations that attract sympathetic events and/or people, science has finally con-
firmed through studies over the last thirty years that
this "folklore" is true. It has been established that the
scents of specific herbs and oils stimulate a predictable
response in the brain receptors—whether it be sexual,
meditative, aggressive, or relaxing.

The smell of Ritual Incense as it burns works directly on the subconscious mind, helping the Magickian to focus on the work at hand
and direct the energies. In addition, as it is inhaled, the scented smoke is
directly, physically connected to the brain through the nose, immediately
stimulating the brain synapses. Burning Incense represents the Elements
Fire and Air. The smoke can be used to send the Magickal energy forth via
visualization and focus, or write the desire on a small piece of parchment
and then burn it in the thurible (Incense burner) along with the Incense.

A good Ritual Incense should be composed of natural, nonsynthetic
ingredients—herbs, flowers, resins, and essential oils. These natural ingredients' energies should be sympathetic (attracting) to those you wish to
raise during a ritual. For example, if a ritual for psychic development is to
be performed, then an Incense composed of a combination of Lunar herbs,
oils, and resins should be used—such as white sandalwood, cucumber, and

water lily—because the Moon rules the psychic realms and the subconscious mind. A success Incense would be made from Sun herbs, the Planet of success and personal power, or perhaps a combination of Sun and Jupiter ingredients since Jupiter is the Planet of authority and expansion.

The ability to compose an Incense that will stimulate the desired response is both an art and a science. You must be familiar with the Planetary symbology and meaning of each herb or oil, the Planetary affinities of the ingredients you plan to use, and the phases of the Moon so that you can take advantage of the Lunar tides as part of the energy or power of your Incense. Learning all these correspondences and then being able to apply them confidently takes many years of study and practice. But your study is very satisfying when you can apply it to make a special Ritual Incense that fits every aspect of your rite perfectly.

Natural, loose Incense, which is burnt on Incense charcoal, is a combination of dried herbs, flowers, gum resins, and essential oils. The essential oils and gum resins are the ingredients that give the Incense most of its scent; the dried herbs and flowers provide an attractive base and additional energy/Planetary vitality. You can use root parts in your Incense, but remember: root parts are quite dense and often have a very acrid smell when burnt. They must be kibbled into very small pieces, or they will just sit there on your charcoal, smoldering unpleasantly. These natural ingredients may be obtained at your local health food store, at your favorite local occult shop, or through a mail order supplier.

The composition of Incense is not difficult and can be done with a minimum of equipment and space. All that is required is a mortar and pestle to crush and mix the ingredients and, of course, the herbs, flowers, gums, and oils. A mortar and pestle can be found at your pharmacy, health food store, or local occult supply. Some modern-day Incense makers use food processors or blenders to cut up and mix the ingredients for their Incense, but I don't think this is a good idea. Part of the creation of your Incense is the energy and focus you put into it as you mix it in your mortar. Simply pressing a button doesn't have the same psychological and focused energy effect. If a food processor is used, the resins will still need to be mixed in by hand, as the heat raised by the whirring blades of the machine can heat and melt the resins sufficiently to gum up the blades and potentially burn out the motor—and it can't be much fun to try to clean up those blades afterward.

Since you will be burning the Incense, it is also necessary to understand the physiological effects of the ingredients you are using. You want to be sure that you won't be breathing in something that you are allergic to or an herb that has some toxic qualities. Always be sure to consult a medicinal herbal as you create your formulas so that you know all your ingredients can be safely ingested. Even if an herb is ingestible, you will still also want to consider the possible physical effects—cayenne, for example, should not be burned because it will sting your eyes and irritate your throat and nose.

When you make your Incense, be aware of the Moon Phase, the Planetary affinities of your ingredients, the Planetary Day, and, if you want to be very precise, the Planetary Hour so that all the components of your mixture will enhance your Magickal operation.

When blending your herbs, resins, flowers, and oils, always begin with the herbs and flowers. They don't need to be powdered but should be in small pieces so that your Incense will burn smoothly on your Incense charcoal. Blend the dried herbs and flowers together thoroughly and then begin to add your oils. You will want to have on hand a one-ounce dropper bottle half filled with alcohol for this part of the blending. Using a dropper bottle will allow you to disperse combinations of your oils easily and be precise with the number of drops of oil you use. Before you first begin to distribute the oils into your herbal mixture, draw some of the alcohol into the dropper. Squeeze it back into the bottle and then shake the dropper to rid it of any alcohol that may be clinging to it. Then draw about a half dropper full of your oil and distribute however many drops of the oil you deem appropriate. Follow this procedure between each different oil you use so that you don't contaminate the next oil with the previous one. You don't want your essential oils to end up smelling like each other, especially the stronger-smelling oils such as cinnamon and lavender.

Begin by adding only ten or so drops of each oil and blending each into the mixture thoroughly so that you can slowly develop the scent you like the most. Remember, you can always add more of an oil, but it's impossible to take it out! I would suggest that after adding what you think smells like what you are trying to create, you let the mixture sit for an hour or so. This will allow the materials to interact with each other and let your olfactory sense rest. You can then come back to the blend for one last sniff and add a bit more of anything to finish it up. After you have blended your desired combination of oils into the dry mixture of herbs and flowers, add your resins—frankincense, myrrh, arabic, or whatever. Adding the resins last will keep them from getting sticky. If the resins become sticky, the rest of your herbal ingredients will adhere to them, making your Incense less visually beautiful.

Developing your own formulas is part of the fun of Incense composition. To give you an idea of the possible combinations and to illustrate the process of making Incense, we will use a recipe for Mercury Incense.

Gather together your materials:

mortar and pestle

one part powdered cinnamon

one part lavender flowers

one part finely cut licorice root

cinnamon oil

lavender oil (optional)

one part gum arabic

Incense charcoal

Pour the powdered cinnamon, lavender flowers, and licorice root into your mortar and begin crushing and blending the herbs thoroughly with your pestle. When they are as fine a consistency as possible, add ten drops of the cinnamon oil and mix again. If you like the smell of lavender, you can add ten drops of lavender oil as well. Smell your Incense and see what you think about the strength of the scent. If you would like it to smell stronger, add your essential oil(s) five drops at a time until you are satisfied. After you have the amount of oil you like blended into the mixture, add your gum arabic. Set the mixture aside for at least twelve hours to allow the oils to completely permeate the herbs and to let the scents combine.

You will need Incense charcoal upon which to burn your Incense. Be careful not to completely cover the charcoal with the Incense, or you will smother it and put it out. Once it is smothered, it is no longer usable, and you'll have to start over with a new charcoal. A scant teaspoonful is the perfect amount for one application. You may be doing a ceremony where you will want to apply Incense several times, and this is fine. Your charcoal will smolder for forty-five minutes to an hour, giving you plenty of time. If you plan to use many applications of Incense, you should turn off your smoke alarm, or you will have a very unpleasant interruption to your meditation or ritual. Just remember to turn it back on before you retire for the night or leave the house.

If you prefer a self-igniting Incense that burns without a charcoal, first crush your herbs, oils, and resins into as fine a mixture as possible. Then add two teaspoons of potassium nitrate (also known as salt peter) and distribute it evenly through your Incense. Potassium nitrate will cause your Incense to burn unevenly if not distributed thoroughly throughout the Incense and may spit sparks. For this type of burning, you will need to mix the herbs, flowers, oils, and resins into a very powdered or finely minced form, or it may stop burning. If your Incense is too chunky, it will burn unevenly.

Store your Incense in small glass jars out of the sunlight and away from a heat source (a closet or inside a drawer is perfect) so that it will last for several years. Happy mixing!

CHAPTER 12

Ritual Oils

The composition of Ritual Oils is relatively simple once you know your Planetary and energy correspondences. Just as each herb, plant and resin is associated with a specific Planetary energy, the essential oil from the plant from which the oil is gathered shares the same association.

What are essential oils? They are the oils collected from freshly harvested herbs, flowers, resins, and roots. There are varying methods to extract the essential oils depending on the nature of the herb material and the amount of oil that is naturally contained within the plant. Maceration is the method of crushing the freshly picked plant material and submerging it in alcohol. The crushed fresh plant is placed into a jar and then alcohol is poured into the jar to fill it about three-quarters full to allow for expansion of the materials. The bottle is then sealed and stored near a low heat source such as a radiator. It should not be placed directly on the radiator, as the heat should not exceed 100 degrees Fahrenheit (38 degrees Celsius), or the resulting oil will be destroyed. This mixture is then shaken several times daily to disperse the oil into the alcohol. After approximately two weeks, the plant material is strained from the alcohol, and the remaining alcohol-oil mixture is left open for the alcohol to evaporate, leaving the essential oil behind. Maceration is typically used for less delicate plant material such as orange peel or thick, aromatic herb leaves like bay.

Another method is enfleurage. This technique is used most often with delicate fresh flowers such as jasmin. To extract the essential oil in this way, you would apply a thin layer of a neutral oil like sweet almond oil or nonscented fat to a flat glass plate (something like the glass for a picture frame works well). Place your flowers evenly over the glass plate on the oil or fat. Now apply another thin layer of oil or fat onto the surface of another flat glass plate and place the coated surface face down on the plant material. Press lightly to seal the glass plates together. Let them sit in indirect sunlight for a day, then remove and discard the plant material but leave the oil or fat, and repeat the process, applying fresh plants to the oil. Depending on how much oil you intend to extract, repeat this method for several weeks, leaving the same oil or fat so that you are building up a concentration of essential oil. When the oil layer on the glass has a strong scent, you scrape the scented oil or fat into a jar for future use.

Water and steam distillation is another method and may be the one most often used in commercial essential oil extraction. With this technique, fresh plant material is placed in a colander set over a pot filled with a few inches of water and then covered. The water is heated to a slow simmer, and the steam passes through the plant material, collecting the essential oils. The oil rises on the steam to the lid. When you see that a layer of steam has collected on the interior of the lid, pour it off into a wide-mouthed bottle. You now have a mixture of water and oil. Repeat the process until you have obtained as much volume as you need for your work. At this point you can let the liquid cool and then pour off the oil on the surface of the water, or simply let the water evaporate, leaving the extracted essential oil.

Essential oils are extremely concentrated. They are sixty to one hundred times stronger than the plant material from which they are extracted because the oil distillation process intensely concentrates the herbal properties.

You may find the extraction of essential oils to be too much trouble or the obtaining of fresh plant material to be problematic. Fortunately, in this day and age there are many companies that specialize in extracting essential oils, making the oils readily available. You can find a nice selection of essential oils through mail order and online companies or at your local health food store.

A Ritual Oil is blended from selected natural essential oils and then diluted by at least half with a neutral-smelling carrier oil such as sweet almond oil. You want it to be neutral smelling so that the scent of the blended essential oils is not compromised by the scent of the carrier oil. Peanut oil is much too strong smelling, as are most olive oils, even the most virgin. There are specific traditional blends such as Abramelin that call for olive oil, but the scent of olive oil is intentionally part of those formulas' smell.

Ritual Oil blends are very versatile. After blending and diluting your oil formula, your oil can be added to bathwater or used in an aromatherapy oil diffuser as a smokeless Incense. Or you may use your oil to charge Amulets and Talismans, to dress and dedicate candles for specific purposes, and to anoint the different Chakras for activation and balance. Oils also can be worn on the body to influence events in the immediate vicinity (a Love Oil worn on a date for example, or an Employment Oil on a job interview). If you want to create a specific feeling or effect in an area such as your bedroom or office, you can add some of your blended oil to a Magickal Potpourri.

If you do plan to wear your oil on the skin or put it in your bathwater, do some research first to make sure that the oils you plan to blend won't harm the skin. Cinnamon oil, for example, burns the majority of people who place it on their skin. You'll want to use it very sparingly, if at all, in an oil blend, and be sure to dilute the blend by at least 75 percent to prevent blistering. Clove oil can make some individuals' skin sensitive to sunrays, making the potential for sunburn more likely. Many people are sensitive to eucalyptus oil as well—so do your homework before you put essential oils on your skin. It is a good idea to test a small amount of your blend on the inside crook of your elbow a few hours before you plan to use it in a ceremony. This way you can ensure that you won't have an unpleasant surprise during your rite. After you have worked with essential oils for a few months, you'll know if you have a sensitivity to any of them.

If you wish to combine all the energies most effectively when making a Ritual Oil, be aware of the Moon Phase, the Magickal Day, and the Planetary affinities of the oils (they will be the same as the herb's affinities). This way you are combining all the aspects of influence and energy in your oil. The general rule is to combine the essential oils three drops of each at a time, then smell the combination with each addition to make sure it still smells pleasant. As you begin to build your scent, you may find that you have the perfect amount of one particular oil and just need to add a few more drops of one other to balance it for your nose. The spicy oils (nutmeg, ginger, clove) should be added just one drop at a time, for they quickly overpower any other scent. Lavender, jasmin, patchouli, and rose can also overtake the smell of a blend, so go easy at first with those as you learn how much you like in a mixture.

When diluting the oil, be aware of the Element to which your final product is attributed. Water energy and Earth energy oils should be diluted with sweet almond oil. Fire energy and Air energy oils should be diluted with safflower oil. For example, a Love Oil falls under the Element of Water because it deals with emotions and would be diluted with sweet almond oil. A Mercury Oil falls under the Element of Air because the Planet Mercury is ruled by Air and thus would be diluted with safflower oil.

I like to use a dropper bottle to disperse the different essential oils into a blend as I work. It makes it much easier to keep your essential oils untainted by the scent of the other oils. Essential oils can be pricey as well, so you may not want to depend on a steady hand when you are pouring several different oils into another bottle. As you blend, keep track of how many drops of each scent you are using so that you have a record of each formula you create. I have found that using a one-ounce dropper bottle full of rubbing alcohol makes the process very easy. Using the dropper, you can count exactly how many drops of oil you are adding at any given time. Cleaning out the dropper between applications of different oils by drawing some alcohol into the dropper and shaking out the excess ensures that you don't inadvertently get any oils into other oil bottles, keeping the scents pure. You just want to be sure that before drawing up a new essential oil into the dropper all the alcohol is out of the dropper. If you drip alcohol into your essential oil, it can make it cloudy.

The general supplies you will need handy to create your blends are the following:

selection of small, pharmaceutical-grade glass vials to contain each formulated oil (one dram-size vial is perfect—it contains one-eighth ounce of oil)

bottles in varying sizes from one-half ounce to four ounces to store alcohol

carrier oils

labels for marking which formula is in which bottle

Keep all your oils in a cool, dry place out of sunlight and away from heat. Essential oils are very volatile, meaning that UV rays and heat cause them to evaporate. If you store them correctly, they can last for years. In some of the excavations of Egyptian tombs, researchers have found vials of essential oils and essential oil blends buried with the owner of the tomb. When the vials were opened for testing, it was found that many of the contents are just as useable today as they were when they were first stored.

CHAPTER 13

Bath Salts and Purifying Bath Herbs

Ritual Baths are used to purify your body and thoughts prior to a ritual working. You may wish to use a standard Purification Bath Salt for all your rites, or you may choose to create a specific Bath Salt that you have composed specifically for the work at hand. The Ritual Bath will help you to focus on the Magick you are about to begin and cause your auric (energy) field to begin vibrating at the same frequency as the type of Magick in which you will be engaging.

Each time you use a Bath Salt or mixture of purifying bath herbs, you will immerse yourself in the water, visualizing all negative vibrations washing away from your body and your energy field. You will allow your muscles to relax and your mind to empty of all thoughts except those that pertain to your ritual.

There are several ways to use Bath Salts or their herbal derivatives as you purify yourself in preparation for your work:

Bath Salt: Make a Bath Salt composed of sea salt and essential oils.

Bath Tea: Compose a mixture of herbs and oils and place it in a tea ball or ironable tea bag (these bags are open on one end to stuff with herbs; after you have put your herbal mixture inside, you then iron it shut with a clothing iron).

Bath Tussie: Place your herbs, essential oils, and a tablespoon of sea salt in a cloth bag with a drawstring or on a flat piece of tightly woven cheesecloth that is then knotted closed. With a Tussie, draw your bath, step in without sitting down, dip the Tussie in the hot water, and scrub your body with it. Then place the Tussie in the bathwater and proceed to soak.

Bath Elixir: Create an Elixir by simmering two cups of your herbal mixture in a quart of water for twenty minutes. Strain the herbs from the water, squeezing out the excess water from the herbs and into the liquid you are collecting. This liquid Elixir is then added to your bathwater.

Certainly not everyone has a bathtub. If all you have available is a shower, don't despair. Bath Salts can be used as a scrub directly on the body as you shower. You may also use a Tussie in this same manner, scrubbing your body and then hanging the Tussie directly under the showerhead so that you are completely doused with the essences of the herbs as you bathe.

As the herbs and essential oils composing your Bath Salt or purifying bath herb combination will be coming in contact with your skin (and in the case of a bath in which you soak, coming in contact with very sensitive and intimate parts of your body), you do not want to use any oils or herbs that will sting, blister, or otherwise harm your body or make you uncomfortable. If you know you have an allergy to any particular herb recommended for use with a specific Planetary energy, don't use it. It is very hard to concentrate during a meditation or ritual when you are sneezing or have raised hives on your body!

Herbs you should never use in the bath include nettles, cayenne (it shouldn't hurt your skin but will wreak havoc if you get some of the bathwater in your eyes), valerian (unless you want to emerge from the water smelling like an old sock), cinnamon, cloves, dragon's blood resin (this won't hurt you but will be hard to remove from the bath tub and can also permanently stain enamel), and asafoetida (whose aromatic effects are similar to valerian's). Ragweed is an herb that often grows among chamomile. Many people are allergic to ragweed, and if you have pollen- or plant-based allergies, I recommend that you not use chamomile in the event that ragweed was inadvertently harvested with it. You will always want to use fine sea salt in your mixtures rather than a larger rock salt type. Sit down in the bathtub on the rock salt and you'll immediately know why.

If you store your Bath Salts in airtight glass containers, you should be able to use them in their full strength for approximately one year. Do not store your Bath Salts in a metal container. The metal can react with the salts, leaving bits of corroded metal debris in your salts. Most people will use about three tablespoons of Bath Salts per bath. You can certainly use more or less depending on your personal tastes.

Pour one cup of fine sea salt into a glass bowl or mortar. Add your essential oils one by one, thoroughly mixing in each one before adding the next and smelling the salts before adding the next oil. Start with five drops of each oil—you can always add more of a scent that you particularly like, but it is impossible to take the oil out. For one cup of sea salt, you will usually end up using around one hundred drops of oil. You want your Bath Salts to look slightly damp but not oily. After combining the essential oils to your liking, add one-quarter cup of bicarbonate of soda (baking soda) if you would like your bath to be slightly bubbly and fizzy. You may also want to add color to the salts in accordance with the Planetary or energy color of the Magick you plan to do: green for a prosperity bath, blue for a tranquility bath, and so on. You may use regular food coloring that you can find in the baking section of the grocery store or go to a store that has food coloring for cake frosting. These colors come in small jars and are in a paste form. You need to add only a tiny bit to get intense color. You will find the purple cake frosting coloring to be very helpful, since when you mix blue and red liquid food coloring, no matter what you do, it will come out gray. For a full listing of the energy properties of color, see the list under "Colors for Your Herbal Amulet" in chapter 14. For a Bath Salt, you will be combining only essential oils, not herbs. This is purely for an aesthetic reason. If you put a Bath Salt containing herbs directly into the bath, you will have herbal debris floating on the top of the bathwater. This debris will stick to your skin when you emerge from the bath, and you'll have to thoroughly wipe down the tub when you are done.

When making an herbal bath mixture to be placed in a bag or tea ball and then infused in the hot bathwater, you will determine the herbs and oils you wish to use. Keep in mind that myrrh resin granules will dissolve and be sticky and mastic; arabic and pine resins will become soft and sticky. I would advise using myrrh or pine oil in place of the resins in a bath herbal mixture, and the oil of elemi in the place of mastic or arabic resin if you desire to include Mercurial or Uranian energy. In your mortar or a glass bowl, place one teaspoon of each of your herbs. Crush and mix them together with the pestle and then add a few drops of your chosen essential oils. Mix thoroughly, then fill your tea bag half full and iron shut, or fill your tea ball halfway. The herbs will expand as they absorb water from the bath. When you use the tea bag, immerse it in the hot water for a few minutes, then squeeze it in your hand to release the liquid that has absorbed into the herbs. If using a tea ball, let it steep in the bath for five minutes or so and then hang it under the water spigot if you are still running water into the bath. If you are not running water, you can just let it bob along in the water as you soak and meditate.

In making a Tussie, combine one or two teaspoons of your herbs in your mortar or glass bowl and add your essential oils and, last, about a quarter cup of sea salt. Since you won't be putting this mixture loose into the bathwater, you can use either a finely ground sea salt or a larger rock sea salt. Place the mixture into a cloth pouch with a drawstring or onto the center of a flat cloth that you will tie shut. Immerse the Tussie in the bathwater after you have entered the tub or shower and scrub your body with it. Then let it float in the bathwater or hang it from the showerhead.

If you choose to make an Herbal Bath Elixir, combine your herbs into a mixture that is two cups in volume. Crush and mix the herb mixture in your mortar or glass bowl, then simmer the mixture in a quart of water for twenty minutes. Let cool until the herbs are comfortable to handle. Strain out the herbs, squeeze any additional water from the herbs into the resulting Elixir liquid, and add any essential oils you desire at this time. After you have drawn your bath, add as much of the Elixir as you like to the water. If you are showering, dip your washcloth into the Elixir and wipe down your body at the end of the shower, leaving an herbal wash on your skin.

Of course, with any of these methods, create your bath mixture with intention. As you add each herb, meditate on the qualities of that herb and focus your intention as you mix and crush the herbs together. As you disperse each drop of essential oil into the bath mixture, focus on the energy qualities of that oil. The composition and making of anything you intend to use for meditation, Magick, and ceremony is the beginning of the rite. By infusing it with the correct focus and intention, half your work is done.

Here are some suggestions for the herbs and oils most easily and effectively incorporated into a Ritual Bath:

Sun Baths

Herbs: calendula, chamomile (if you know you do not have allergies), eyebright, juniper berries, Saint-John's-wort, angelica, bay laurel

Oils: frankincense, calendula, juniper, bay laurel, heliotrope

Moon Baths

Herbs: white sandalwood, camphor, fennel, lotus seeds, watercress, jasmin

Oils: white sandalwood, jasmin, fennel, lotus, myrrh, cucumber, hyacinth

Mars Baths

Herbs: ginger, safflower, basil, gentian, patchouli

Oils: ginger, basil, geranium, patchouli, wormwood

Mercury Baths

Herbs: lavender, white sandalwood, horehound, marjoram, thyme

Oils: lavender, white sandalwood, marjoram, anise

Jupiter Baths

Herbs: pine, cinquefoil, cedar, poplar

Oils: pine, cedar, sage, oak moss

Venus Baths

Herbs: rose, vervain, catnip, raspberry leaves, myrtle

Oils: rose, catnip, verbena, violet, coriander

Saturn Baths

Herbs: patchouli, rosemary, dill, agrimony, comfrey

Oils: patchouli, cypress, myrrh

Neptune Baths

Herbs: willow, lobelia, skullcap, poppy seed, orange blossom

Oils: orange blossom (neroli), lotus, tarragon

Uranus Baths

Herbs: nutmeg, anise, coffee, ginseng

Oils: nutmeg, anise, elemi

Pluto Baths

Herbs: galangal, saw palmetto, yohimbe, wormwood

Oils: opoponax, myrrh, patchouli, wormwood

CHAPTER 14

Herbal Amulets and Magickal Potpourri

Herbal Amulets are combinations of herbs, resins, and essential oils along with special stones, written wishes, and any other natural power object you like (such as a shell, acorn, or feather) gathered into an appropriately colored pouch for a ritual purpose. Herbal Amulets are also called medicine bags, power bags, mojo bags, and sachet bags in different folk cultures.

If you choose to include a written wish, try to consolidate that wish into a short phrase or word that encompasses the goal. It should not be a paragraph or article. Let's say that your goal is a better job with more pay, more creativity, and lots of perks. You don't need to write all that—just write "perfect job" and you can meditate on and infuse the paper with all the things that you believe would go into a perfect job as you are writing your wish, I have found that if you state your goals concisely but leave a bit of the goal unstated, the Universe has an uncanny way of bringing you exactly what you need and usually in a much better way than what you would have originally imagined.

It is important that as you place each herb in the pouch you focus on the Magickal properties of that herb. As you anoint your stone, concentrate on the Magickal powers of the stone and the energies of the oils with which you are anointing it. If you are using a natural power object, concentrate on what the object represents in relationship to the spell you are working. This charges each item with the specific intention that you have for it. While the "tools of Magick"—like the herbs, oils, and stones you have chosen—have energies that are sympathetic to your Magickal goal, it is *your* energy, *your* focus that ignites them to draw to you that which you desire.

Gather together your materials: herbs, resins, oils, stones, natural power object, and pouch. If you know how to crochet or sew, you may wish to make your pouch by hand out of the appropriately colored material. This way you can also incorporate Magickal intention as you stitch, which is a very traditional and effective practice. If you don't sew, you can make a type of Herbal Amulet in what is called a "sachet" with a six-inch-square flat piece of natural material such as cotton or silk in an appropriate color. You can also purchase a premade pouch in the correct color for your working. Pouches in various colors are available at your local occult store.

If you are using a bag or pouch, place a healthy pinch of each herb and resin that you have chosen in the bottom of the bag, being mindful of the Magickal energies of each herb as you place it there. Anoint your stone(s) with the oil(s) you have chosen, again focusing on the Magickal properties of each. Place the anointed stone(s) in the pouch with intention, visualizing your goal. Last, place your natural power object or written wish. Tighten the strings of your bag and leave it overnight to soak up the energies and blend them.

If you are making a sachet-style Herbal Amulet, place your six-inch-square material flat in the center of your altar. Concentrating on the Magickal properties of each herb, place a healthy pinch of each herb, one by one, in the center of the material. Focusing on the powers of the stone(s) and oil(s) you are using, anoint your stone(s) and place on top of the herbs. You can also drop a little oil onto the herbs, but you need to have a steady hand here or you will add more than you intend to and end up with an oil-stained Amulet. Hold the natural power object or written wish in your hands and concentrate on its meaning for your ritual, then place it on top of the herbs. Gently draw up and together two opposite corners of the material, then do the same with the other two corners. Twist gently but tightly and then tie the bag with a natural ribbon or string of the proper color.

You can wear your Herbal Amulet or keep it in an area where it is meant to influence. For example, keep a Prosperity Herbal Amulet in your purse or wallet. You could wear a Love Herbal Amulet round your neck, near your heart, or keep it in the drawer with your lingerie. You might wear a Protection Herbal Amulet or keep it in your pocket or purse. You could also keep it in your car's glove box or bury or hang it near your front door. Put a Dream Herbal Amulet in your pillow or on your nightstand—you get the idea!

Stones for Your Herbal Amulet

Every crystal and gemstone has its own Magickal and energy property that corresponds to its color and aligns it with the energies of a Planet. Here are some basic, low-cost gemstones that will help you in your workings:

Sunstone is ruled by the Sun and the Element of Fire and is good for abundance, personal success, and personal power. You can make a power bag with Sun herbs and a sunstone to draw success to your endeavors.

Moonstone is ruled by the Moon and the Element of Water. It helps develop psychic awareness, dreamwork, and fertility. Wear it when reading Tarot cards or using a crystal ball. Moonstones are also useful as you lie down to sleep to help you remember and understand your dreams. You can charge a moonstone with the task of helping you to be fertile if you are trying to get pregnant. Then wear it or keep it in your pocket each day and particularly while making love.

Carnelian is ruled by Mars and the Element of Fire. It helps to dispel depression and anger and brings courage and energy. You can use it in protection spells, or carry it with you for protection as well as vitality and health.

Quartz crystal is ruled by Mercury and the Element of Air. Wear it to focus and sharpen the mind as well as to help you communicate more clearly. Set a quartz cluster on your desk as you work to aid your creative thinking and writing. You can also rub a quartz crystal on an afflicted part of the body to remove energy blockages and promote healing.

Amethyst is ruled by Jupiter and the Element of Water. If you have insomnia, place one under your pillow to help you relax and sleep. Hold one in your hand or wear one during meditation to go deeper. You can also harness the prosperity energies of Jupiter by placing an amethyst in the center of your altar and burning green candles around it.

Jade is ruled by Venus and the Element of Earth. It draws luck, health, long life, love, and prosperity. Surround jade on your altar with pink candles to bring love or orange candles for health. Wear jade while gardening to help your garden grow.

Onyx is ruled by Saturn and the Element of Earth. It stabilizes and protects. Bury one by your front door to repel negativity or wear onyx to protect your aura. If you tend to be flighty or indecisive, wear one to help you to ground your energies.

Fluorite is ruled by Neptune and the Element of Water. Inspiring creativity and calm, this stone of Neptune can bring dreams, enhance trancework, and help you to connect with the deep mysteries.

Herkimer diamond is ruled by Uranus and the Element of Air. Innovation, originality, and unexpected events are attracted by this stone. Carry a Herkimer in a pouch or add it to the energy of a Philtre to change the ways that energy is flowing and break up stagnation.

Lava stone is ruled by Pluto and the Element Fire. For intense inner transformation, the ending of karmic patterns, lava stone draws forth the vibrations of death and rebirth of the soul.

Stone Combinations

To combine the energies of gemstones and crystals for special projects, first charge them with the focus of your intention, then place them in a bag of the proper color and carry or wear them to draw the results to yourself. What follows are some possible desired results and the combinations to achieve them.

Protection: garnet, onyx, obsidian, and quartz crystal in a white bag

Prosperity: jade, peridot, tiger's-eye, and sunstone in a green bag

Love: rose quartz, jade, malachite, and red jasper in a pink bag

Intuition: spectrolite, lapis lazuli, moonstone, and tanzanite in a purple bag

Serenity: amethyst, blue lace agate, quartz crystal, and jade in a blue bag

Colors for Your Herbal Amulet

Red is vital and active. It is the color of life energy and sexuality. It is sensual and of the material plane. Red is energizing, heating, and exciting when it is used in a positive manner. Red is used to bring vitality and movement to projects, in spells of love, and seduction.

Pink is used in love and friendship rituals. It helps to create and sustain emotional connections. It is really better to use pink than red in love spells because red can bring more lust than love into a relationship. A healthy love relationship is composed of both sexuality and friendship.

Blue is spiritual and intuitive. It is the color of the subconscious mind and creative artistry. Blue is soothing and can be used for meditation, peace, and astral projection. Light or bright blue are the tones best used for positive results.

Yellow is the color of the workings of the conscious, intellectual mind. It aids in logical, linear, analytical thinking processes such as enhancing memory, writing, speaking eloquently, and studying.

Purple is a combination of the energies of blue and red. It helps to integrate the subconscious and conscious minds and can be used to enhance your psychic powers and spirituality here on the physical plane. It is also the color of royalty and gives dignity and authority.

Green is a combination of blue and yellow. It is the balancing of the subjective with the objective, our dreams with reality. Green denotes growth and creativity and is an excellent color for healings.

Orange is a combination of red and yellow. It is the vital life force of red with the mental activity of yellow. It is the most creative, energizing color and is good in healings when regeneration is needed. It is also helpful when there is a mental block that is leading to inaction or confusion.

White is the combination of all colors and denotes purity, perfection, and completeness. It is a good color to use for protection, meditation, and exorcism.

Black is the absence of color and light and has been used many times for negative purposes. However, it can also be used to protect in case of psychic attack by burning a candle of this color to represent the power and intentions of your enemy. It can also be used to represent a disease such as cancer or a bad habit. In this case, the burning of the black candle burns away the power of the disease or of the bad habit. Black can transform and absorb negative energy.

Brown in warm tones such as russet is used to stabilize and unify the home. Darker browns can help ground (bring down to Earth) intentions and actions but can also stagnate and slow.

CHAPTER 15

Philtres, Elixirs, and Fluid Condensers

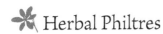 Herbal Philtres

An Herbal Philtre is a combination of herb materials and liquid that is intended to be ingested. Therefore, you must do some investigation into the physical effects of the herbs you are considering and choose herbs that react well in the human physical system and to which you have no known allergic reactions.

You can make a tincture-style Philtre that incorporates the plant substances in alcohol or wine, or you can create an Infusion-style Philtre in which you incorporate the plant materials into distilled water. The tincture style is self-preserving due to the alcohol's property of keeping the resulting Philtre liquid fresh, but the Infusion style will need to either be consumed within a few hours or kept refrigerated.

For a tincture-style Philtre, the herb material is crushed with mortar and pestle and then steeped in an alcohol that is at least 70 proof. You can use a grain alcohol or vodka if you prefer to taste the herbal content, or a brandy or liqueur if you prefer a smoother taste. In a glass or enamel pot, heat one cup of your preferred liquid to almost a simmer, then turn off the heat. Stir in one-half cup of your dried herb mixture or one full cup of fresh herb materials. Let this combination of alcohol and herbs steep for three days and then strain out your plant materials. Pour the resulting tincture into a bottle and seal it. This type of Philtre will last indefinitely if stored in a cool, dark, dry space.

When making an Infusion-style Philtre, crushed herbs are added to simmering distilled water. Place one cup of distilled water into a glass or enamel pot and bring it to a slow simmer. Meanwhile, crush and mix one-half cup of dried herbs or one cup of fresh herbs in your mortar and pestle. Turn off the heat under the distilled water and stir in the crushed herbs.

Let this mixture steep in the water for approximately eight hours. Strain out the plant material and pour the Philtre into your chalice for immediate use.

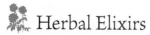

Herbal Elixirs

An Herbal Elixir is an alchemically prepared liquid that contains properties of the Planetary energies, thanks to the inclusion of herbs possessing the chosen Planet's equivalent vibrations.

In an Elixir, the herbs are blended with the physical, astral, and spiritual aspect in mind so that the energy vibration of the final result is one in which all three levels are balanced. Thus, the physical, astral, and spiritual being of an individual is affected when the Elixir is used.

An Herbal Elixir can be used in the same ways that a Philtre is used but is most often utilized in conjunction with internal (self-transforming) rituals such as pathworking rites.

You will begin by preparing what is known as the Menstruum. This is an alcohol-based substance such as brandy in which you will place the herbs to extract the "sulphur" (astral qualities of the herb). Place one pint of brandy in a small enamel or glass saucepan and bring to a simmer. Simmer with the pan covered until you have reduced the liquid alcohol by half. Turn off the heat.

Pour the reduced alcohol into a dark, wide-mouthed jar. Now, add one-half cup of your chosen dried herbs or one cup of fresh herbs to the reduced alcohol in the jar and seal it. The alcohol is considered to be the "mercury" (the spiritual qualities of the herbs used). Keep the herbs and alcohol in your sealed jar in a slightly warm place for about two weeks. At this point, strain the mixture until it is clear and has no particles of herb left in it. Take the herbs that you have strained out of the liquid (reserving the liquid for the last step of this process—store it in your dark, wide-mouthed jar) and allow the herbs to completely dry. This may take a few days. When they are dry, place them in a fire-resistant dish and ignite them. Allow the herbs to burn to ash. Next, place the ashes in their fire-resistant dish over the low flame of a Bunsen burner and heat the ashes to a red glow while grinding them occasionally. This produces the alchemical "salt" (physical qualities of the herb).

Mix the alchemical salt back into the liquid in your dark jar and store the mixture again in its warm place. Let it sit for another two weeks. After that time, pour the liquid off, leaving the solid matter in the jar, and seal it. Allow it to sit another two weeks and then open the jar to allow any moisture remaining to completely evaporate. After the Elixir is completely dry, scrape it out of the jar and place it into a small, airtight container.

You can certainly save the liquid that you removed from the solid matter in the jar and use it in the bath, or, if you prefer to discard it, you may pour it in a running stream to disperse your desires into the Universe.

When you wish to use the Elixir, mix one-fourth teaspoon of dry Elixir with two cups of distilled water and take it internally over a week's period just prior to your Magickal working.

By using this alchemical process, you have worked with the physical (salt), astral (sulphur), and the spiritual (mercury) properties of the herbs. This will then affect those levels within yourself when used in ritual.

Herbal Condensers

An Herbal Condenser is more simple to prepare than the Elixir but can be used in similar ways. For your Condenser, take a large handful of an herb or herbal combination and place it in a small glass or enamel pot. Cover the herbs with distilled water. Let the mixture simmer for twenty minutes with the pot covered. Turn off the heat and allow your mixture to cool, leaving the pot covered. When it is cool, strain out the herbs and return the liquid to the pot again. Simmer with the lid on until the liquid has boiled down to half. Cool the liquid again and mix it with grain alcohol equal to the volume of the liquid. Now, add ten flakes of gold and stir. Bottle it in a dark amber or blue bottle to keep any light from touching the liquid and store in a cool, dark place.

When you wish to use the Condenser, shake well first, then drink a liqueur glass full each day for a week prior to your rite.

Suggested Gemstones and Metals

With any of these Magickal liquids, you may add a gemstone of the appropriate Planet or the metal/material of the Planet to the jar or bottle in which you are storing them for added energy.

Sun

Gemstones: sunstone, gold topaz

Metal: gold

Moon

Gemstones: moonstone, pearl

Metal: silver

Mars

Gemstones: garnet, ruby

Metal: iron

Mercury

Gemstones: clear quartz, opal

Metal: Mercury's metal is poisonous to the human body. *Never* add quicksilver to an Elixir, Philtre, or Condenser.

Jupiter

Gemstones: sapphire, turquoise

Metal: tin

Venus

Gemstones: rose quartz, emerald

Metal: copper

Saturn

Gemstones: onyx, smoky quartz

Metal: Saturn's metal is poisonous to the human body. *Never* add lead to an Elixir, Philtre, or Condenser.

Neptune

Gemstones: amber, fluorite

Material: abalone shell

Uranus

Gemstones: rutilated quartz, Herkimer diamond

Metal: white gold

Pluto

Metal: hematite, obsidian

Material: lava stone

PART 3

COMBINING

THE PLANETARY

and

ELEMENTAL INFLUENCES

CHAPTER 16

Custom Formulas to Balance, Transform, Empower, and Manifest

Thus far we have been exploring the energies of the Planets and their associated herbs as "simples"—formulas with only one Planet's herbs—in order to fully acquaint you with each Planet's energy signature in a concentrated fashion. However, for many if not most of the goals that you are working toward or the challenges that you face, you will find that what will be the most effective is when you combine the energies of several Planets and their herbs to attain the desired end result.

The way to determine which Planets to combine and in what amounts is first to analyze and break down the individual components of your final goal. In other words, when you fully examine how you wish your goal to manifest, you will often find that the energies of several different Planets will be employed in a synergistic union.

To begin, let's review the energy signatures of the Planets:

Sun

Herbs of the Sun promote self-confidence and personal success. They impart a sense of purpose and help to develop a strong sense of identity and willpower. Sun herbs bring vitality, health, creativity, dignity, and a sense of well-being and abundance. Look for the color yellow in your Sun herbs: sunflower, calendula, frankincense, celandine, and safflower are some examples.

Sun herb keywords: personal success, health, prosperity, fame, confidence, authority, vitality

Moon

Herbs of the Moon affect the subconscious mind. They aid in the development of intuition and psychic gifts. As they help to access the subconscious, Moon herbs are excellent for dreams, recalling past lives, and bridging communication between the conscious and unconscious mind to access and interpret psychic impressions. The Moon rules the subconscious mind, where habits and attitudes reside: if you wish to break the old, ingrained habits that may be stuck in your subconscious mind, Moon herbs would be the energy you would utilize. Moon herbs are often white or pale in color, night blooming, and hypnotic in effect. Some that I use often are white sandalwood, jasmin flowers, mugwort, cucumber, and lily.

Moon herb keywords: psychic awareness, emotions, childbirth and fertility, subconscious mind, dreamwork, reflection

Mars

Herbs of Mars give vast amounts of energy to projects and health. Mars herbs promote independence and assertiveness and tend to stimulate the passions. Mars herbs can be used very successfully to protect one's person and one's home and are excellent in developing or maintaining motivation. When mixed with herbs of other Planets, they lend their immense energies to make the whole stronger and more vital. Herbs that are red and can irritate the skin or mucus membranes are often those with Martian tendencies, such as red sandalwood, nettles, ginger, mustard, and galangal.

Mars herbs keywords: courage, strength, protection, victory, overcoming obstacles through determination, motivation, sexual force

Mercury

Herbs of Mercury facilitate clear thinking and eloquent communication. They aid in business, where a clear head and clear communication is needed for success. Mercury herbs help the body recover more quickly from illness and enable the conscious mind to communicate more easily with the subconscious, thus facilitating memory and study. Using Mercurial herbs while studying the Tarot or other divination system, which visually incorporates the use of symbols, can often be quite helpful to memorization. The word *mercurial* is a derivative of *Mercury* and means to change quickly. The energy of Mercury brings fast change, and the herbs of this Planet can be added to formulas where speed or change is desired. Many Mercury herbs are those with a multitude of small stems or flowers, such as lavender. Mercury herbs tend to stimulate the central nervous system and brain. Some herbs are cinnamon, lavender, cardamom, licorice, and gum mastic.

Mercury herb keywords: communication, eloquence, intellect, persuasion, job opportunities, luck, divination, quickness, focus, humor, health

Jupiter

Herbs of Jupiter expand consciousness and opportunity. They bring growth on all levels and can be very helpful in health matters, as they enhance the body's ability to heal itself. Herbs of Jupiter also expand the mind, allowing for a greater understanding of the workings of the Universe. In this way, they also work to expand a person spiritually, as the mind's ability to comprehend the workings of the Divine leads to spiritual unfoldment. Herbs and plants of Jupiter tend to be large themselves, such as oak, pine, magnolia, but also include the smaller flowering herbs agrimony and meadowsweet.

Jupiter herb keywords: ambition, fame, honor, law, expansion, recognition, leadership, spiritual awareness

Venus

Herbs of Venus bring joy, beauty, artistry, sensitivity, compassion, and appreciation of the bounty and beauty of the Earth and all her creatures. Venus herbs activate love—romantic, familial, and platonic—as well as a *joie de vivre* and can be used quite successfully by those engaged in the creative arts. Venusian herbs tend to have prominent, sweet-smelling flowers or sweet fruit. Some herbs of Venus are rose, vervain, raspberry, columbine, and cherry.

Venus herb keywords: romance, friendship, beauty, the arts, artistic expression, pleasure, attractiveness, sensuality

Saturn

Herbs of Saturn give structure, foundation, grounding, stability, and an understanding of how the physical plane of existence works. They are great teachers of self-knowledge and one's karmic debts and tend to slow down and calm situations. They teach that success comes through perseverance and patience. Saturn herbs are binding herbs and protect in a nonaggressive, shielding manner. Saturnian herbs are dark and woodsy smelling, like myrrh, wormwood, patchouli, cypress, and Solomon's seal.

Saturn herb keywords: endurance, shielding, grounding, past lives, slowing, patience, practicality, structure

Neptune

Herbs of Neptune are those of the mystic and are useful in dreamworking, trance, and hypnosis. They intensify the imagination and lead to concepts, visions, and ideas far beyond the physical plane. Neptune herbs can be used to good effect for those who are developing telepathy and astral projection as well as those artists who seek the Muse directly. Many Neptunian herbs are mind-altering and intoxicating. Some Neptune herbs are orange blossoms, poppies, lobelia, peach, and lotus.

Neptune herb keywords: creativity, artistic inspiration, imagination, fantasy, mystery

Uranus

Herbs of Uranus excite, energize, and stimulate the human energy system and the thought processes. They lend themselves to inspiration, practical idealism, genius, and the development of telekinesis. Like the Mercury herbs, these plants stimulate the nervous system and, in particular, the brain wave patterns. They stimulate change on all levels and sometimes lead to unforeseen results. Some herbs of Uranus are allspice, calamus, betel, guarana, and ephedra.

Uranus herb keywords: genius, innovation, idealism, objectivity, independence, originality

Pluto

Herbs of Pluto transform and illuminate the shadow side of ourselves. They can bring about dramatic, sometimes traumatic, growth and promote insight into cataclysmic circumstances. Pluto herbs act on the unconscious levels of the brain and upon the thalamus portion of the brain, which dictates instinctual response. Pluto herbs aid the sexually impotent and help to balance the physical self with the spiritual Self. Some Pluto herbs are yohimbe, saw palmetto, damiana, rye, and amaranth.

Pluto herb keywords: endings, regeneration, deep unconscious, karma, renewal

Typically, when you formulate a blend of herbs, you consider the situation in its entirety and a combine various Planetary energies in your mixture for a holistic effect. When investigating the energy effects of a single, specific Planet, you could certainly compose a blend using only the herbs of that Planet, but in most cases the result you are working toward would encompass a blending of several Planetary influences and energies.

For example, say that you want to make an Herbal Amulet for the perfect job. You need to analyze the components of the perfect job for you: the right amount of money, the chance to learn new skills, people with whom you will be compatible, and the potential for advancement could all be parts of what you see as the "perfect job." Therefore, you would combine Sun herbs for abundance, success, and personal satisfaction; Mercury herbs to be eloquent and clear-sighted as you interview for various positions; Jupiter herbs for expanded opportunities; and, perhaps, Venus herbs for compatible associates.

To reach the desired manifestation for your ritual, you will often emphasize one specific Planetary energy while enhancing its effects with smaller quantities of the herbs and oils of other Planetary energies. By combining your energy effects in this way, you fine-tune and heighten the entire formula.

Generally speaking, in workings involving success and attainment, always include an herb or oil of the Sun. If you want to be able to access your intuition or in areas of fertility, have Lunar herbs and oils as part of your formula. For workings involving motivation or protection, always incorporate Mars. When you are seeking to gain the ability to touch and influence the thoughts or responses of other people, utilize Mercury. If expansion in any area is sought, Jupiter is the primary energy source to tap. Love, artistry, or added harmony to your life require that Venus herbs be employed. Bindings and karmic work use the energy of Saturn. Mystical inspiration utilizes Neptune; innovation and repatterning take Uranus herbs and oils. If you see the need for transformation on deep levels leading to renewal, Pluto as a primary energy source is where you begin as you choose your ingredients.

Here are some ways that you may choose to combine the herbs, resins, and essential oils of a grouping of Planetary energies to capture all the components that will result in the manifestation of specific goals.

For example, you wish to awaken and attract *abundance* in your life. How do you define its components? For me, abundance is the manifestation of opportunities for growth in desired parts of one's life—both the physical acquisition of the results of that growth as well as the ability to recognize and take advantage of opportunities as they are presented. Abundance is the manifestation of growth in all areas and the recognition of opportunities that have the potential to manifest their results in a flowing, successful way.

Planets that partake of the idea of abundance would be the Sun (personal success) and Jupiter (opportunity and growth); manifestation in a physical fashion would be ruled by Saturn (structure and form in the physical world); the ability to recognize opportunities as they arise falls under the dominion of Mercury (quick mind), Jupiter (awareness of the ways that spirit is expressed in the physical world), and Mars (motivation). In looking at that detailing of the components of abundance, you will see that you have determined that the Sun is delineated once; Jupiter twice; and Saturn, Mercury, and Mars are determined to be factors once each. So your formula will be composed of two Jupiter components and one each of Sun, Mercury, Saturn, and Mars. You will then choose among the various herbs, resins, and oils of each of those Planets to create your blend. For an Incense or Magickal Potpourri, you can choose which form of herb (plant, resin, or oil) you wish to employ in your mixture for each of the Planets. For a bath formula such as a Tussie or Bath Elixir, you have the choice of both herbs and oils, or solely oils if you are creating a Bath Salt. For a Ritual Oil, you use only the oils of each Planets; for an Elixir, Condenser, or Philtre, simply the dried or fresh herbs. When blending an Herbal Amulet, you can use herbs, resins, essential oils, and the Planetary stone that corresponds the most to the desired manifested effect.

A formula for an Abundance Incense could include cedar chips and pine oil (two parts Jupiter), frankincense resin (one part Sun), cinnamon chips or cinnamon oil (one part Mercury), myrrh resin or cypress oil (one part Saturn), and red sandalwood or honeysuckle oil (one part Mars).

A blend for an Abundance Oil could take cedar and pine oils for Jupiter, frankincense or calendula oil for the Sun, lavender oil for Mercury (remember, you don't want to use cinnamon oil in a formula that might be used on the skin), cypress or patchouli oil for Saturn, and honeysuckle or ginger oil for Mars.

A combination that could be used for a Magickal Abundance Potpourri could be pine needles and cedar oil for Jupiter; calendula petals or juniper berries to incorporate the Sun; lavender flowers or oil for Mercury; myrrh resin, patchouli leaves, or either of those oils for Saturn; and red sandalwood or honeysuckle flowers or honeysuckle oil for Mars.

An Abundance Bath Salt could incorporate cedar and pine oils for Jupiter, frankincense oil for the Sun, lavender or Anise oil for Mercury, cypress or patchouli oil for Saturn, and honeysuckle or basil oil for Mars. If you plan to make a Bath Tussie, you could use any of the above herbs and oils.

When creating an Herbal Amulet to bring abundance, you could use cinquefoil herb and pine oil for Jupiter, eyebright herb for the Solar energy, licorice root to bring in Mercury, comfrey root for Saturn, and dragon's blood resin to activate Mars. Or you could replace one of the herbs with the stone of one of the Planets: turquoise for Jupiter, sunstone for the Sun, clear quartz for Mercury, onyx for Saturn, or carnelian for Mars. In addition, you would want to incorporate a color appropriate for Abundance in the bag or pouch that contains your herbal/stone mixture: green for growth or orange for activation.

As another example, what if you wanted to create a formula that would allow you to access your psychic abilities, be more intuitive, and remember your dreams? You would combine Moon, Neptune, and Mercury herbs, oils, and resins to accomplish this goal. Moon is dominant, as She rules the psychic life, intuition, and dreamworking. You would choose two Moon herbs to represent this dominance. Neptune is the mystical Planet having dominion over soul connection, trancework, and imagination; Mercury rules the conscious mind and memory, helping you to remember the information you receive in your psychic work. Your main goal is enhancing your psychic abilities and giving your subconscious mind a voice, therefore you use two Lunar herbs. Neptune and Mercury each contribute one herb to bring their energies, thus rounding out your experience of the intuitive side of your life.

To create an Incense that will open your psychic senses and intuition, draw upon the wisdom of your dreams, and delve into past life information, you could use myrrh resin and jasmin oil for the Moon energies, neroli oil for Neptune, and white sandalwood chips or powder to bring in Mercury.

When creating a Ritual Intuition Oil, you might select any of the oils in the above Incense example, or you could blend lily and fennel oils for the Moon, neroli or lotus oil to bring in the Neptune connection, and white sandalwood or lavender oil to activate Mercury. These would be the same oils that you could mix into salt to create a Ritual Bath Salt, and the same herbs—in herb or essential oil form—could be combined to create a Ritual Bath Tussie.

To blend a Magickal Intuition Potpourri, you would choose two Moon herbs or essential oils and one Neptune and one Mercury herb or essential oil. This might comprise mugwort and jasmin flowers for the Moon, lotus oil for Neptune, and cinnamon chips to incorporate Mercury. The same formula could be the base for your Herbal Amulet with the addition of a stone in place of one of the Planetary herbs: moonstone for one of the Moon herbs, amber instead of the Neptune herb, or opal in place of the Mercury herb. You would place your Herbal Amulet ingredients in a bag or pouch in the color appropriate for psychic work: light blue, lilac, or purple.

There are lists and lists of herbs, stones, colors, and metals available in a plethora of books that correspond to the Planetary energies. You are free to select the ones that you like the best, the ones that have the most meaning for you, or the ones that you simply have on hand when you want to begin composing your blend. What you want to keep in mind is, what physical form is your alchemical herbal creation going to take? Incense? Then you know you have the whole selection of herbs, flowers, roots, resins, and essential oils at your disposal. When making an Herbal Amulet or Potpourri, you again have the entire gamut of herbs to choose from, but you also might want to consider adding a Planetary stone. If you decide to create a Ritual Oil or Bath Salt, you know that you have only the essential oils to work with for best results, which might make your selection process a little trickier. And with all Ritual Oils or Ritual Bath formulas, you must be aware of which oils may not react well with skin.

If what you want to create is an offertory to a Deity to whom you have a connection now or with whom you wish to create a relationship, research the herbs, plants, and oils mentioned in conjunction with that Deity as you read the myths and lore. Find out what type of plant life grows in the geographical area favored by that Deity. Look into the herbs that share an affinity with the powers, strengths, and duties of that particular Divine figure. At any time as you are creating your formula, you might get a psychic "hit" to include a particular herb or oil in your combination. Always go with the nudge of intuition—your subconscious mind is giving you useful information.

CHAPTER 17

Creating Custom Formulas Using Numerology

One of the most creative, challenging, and satisfying ways to blend herbs, oils, and resins for a beautiful alchemical and transformative result is by determining a formula based on an individual's numerological or astrological chart. You may create a custom formula that represents, through scent, the strengths and aspirations of an individual or a formula to help her to find the tools she needs to achieve her goals and overcome her natal challenges.

You, the Alchemist, can rectify imbalances or negatives in a chart by including Planetary and Elemental energies that may be missing or causing difficulty. Balancing the energy with the addition of an herb or oil of a missing Element will enable the person who is using the formula to have an outlet of expression for the missing or misaligned energy. Or perhaps you decide that you want to enhance or highlight a natural strength or talent inherent in a person's chart for a specific goal that she is working toward—in effect, creating her unique herbal scent signature. That, too, is possible when you create a custom blend.

Numerology is a science that is easily mastered by anyone who can do basic math. The two main areas looked at in Numerology are the number vibration of a person's name and the number vibrations of a person's birth date. To divine the energies of a person's name, one simply adds together the Numerological value of the name's letters to discover the number vibration that influences the individual's conscious and unconscious perceptions and actions. When examining the influences of a birth date on an individual's vibratory numbers, the birth date is dissected into the vibration of the birth month, the birth day, and the birth year. These numbers are first interpreted individually and then added together to discover the individual's Destiny Number—the number that reveals what that person came into this lifetime to accomplish and the best way for him to express his energies. When creating a formula using Numerology, you may work with the Numerological values of a person's name or birth date or use both to completely express that person's Self.

In Numerology, each number is associated with a Planet, and the herbs and oils of that Planet would be the herbs and oils corresponding to that number:

Number	Corresponding Planet	Energies
1	Sun*	personality, self-expression
2	Moon	union, partnership
3	Venus	artistic expression, harmony
4	Saturn	organization, responsibility
5	Mars	driving force, motivation
6	Jupiter	social consciousness, teaching
7	Mercury	intellectual development, linear views
8	Sun, exalted*	recognition, material accomplishment
9	All Planets	universal awareness, completion
11	Neptune	mysticism, union with spirit
22	Uranus	genius, innovative accomplishment
33	Pluto	transmutation

* You will have noted that there are two numbers associated with Sun energies. The number 1 corresponds with the energy of the *personal* ego Self: personal expression, success as it applies to specific personal goals, and such. The number 8 corresponds to the Sun, exalted: works and goals that effect more than just one's individual Self, those accomplishments with goals that can impact the world at large.

In Numerology, double numbers (11, 22, 33) are known as Master Numbers and correspond to the Outer Planets Neptune, Uranus, and Pluto, respectively. Master Numbers occur when you add together a string of numbers and they naturally equal 11, 22, or 33. Master Numbers can be reduced to a single digit by adding the two digits together (11 is 1 + 1 = 2; 22 is 2 + 2 = 4; and 33 is 3 + 3 = 6). You may choose to work with the more intense energy of the Planet associated with the Master Number or the Planet associated with the single digit from the reduced Master Number. Your choice will be determined by the way in which you want the energy of the formula to express itself.

To determine the number associated with each letter, use this traditional chart:

1	2	3	4	5	6	7	8	9
A	B	C	D	E	F	G	H	I
J	K	L	M	N	O	P	Q	R
S	T	U	V	W	X	Y	Z	

Some Numerologists believe that the name parents give to a child is the name most important to the identity of that individual and how he will tend to react to opportunities and challenges during his lifetime. This works in the same way that one's Natal Birth Chart shows the energies working upon a person at the exact time of his birth. In Astrology, the Natal Chart (Birth Chart) shows the talents and challenges that a person came into this lifetime to work with. A person's Progressed Chart (how the energies and Planetary placements have "progressed," or moved forward during the lifetime) shows what energies are most active whenever the chart is consulted. It works the same way with Numerology.

While we usually begin life with one surname, when we marry, we have the option to change our last names by adopting our spouses' surnames or hyphenating our birth surnames. Sometimes over the course of a lifetime, a person may elect to change the spelling of parts of his name to make it different from his original birth name; he may never use his middle name; or he may have decided to rename himself entirely. The name and spelling that a person elects to use is what you will use to create the formula to represent the energies here and now for that person.

Here's an example from a name I have chosen at random:

KEVIN ABERLE
Using the Numerological Chart, we find these values for the letters:

K	E	V	I	N	A	B	E	R	L	E
2	5	4	9	5	1	2	5	9	3	5

Add the numbers for the first name together: 2 + 5 + 4 + 9 + 5 =25
Reduce the sum to a single digit: 2 + 5 = 7
KEVIN = 7

Add the numbers for the surname together: 1 + 2 + 5 + 9 + 3 + 5 = 25
Reduce the sum to a single digit: 2 + 5 = 7
ABERLE = 7

Add the numbers for the first and last names together: 7 + 7 = 14
Reduce the sum to a single digit: 1 + 4 = 5

Kevin's basic vibratory number is 7 because both his first and last name equate numerically to 7, the number of Mercury. This will be the base herb or oil for his formula. We note that Kevin is missing the numbers 6 and 8 in his name/number value. Therefore to balance his energies, he needs Jupiter/6 and exalted Sun/8 in his formula. He has a predominance of 5's in his name. The number 5 expresses the energy of the Planet Mars, indicating that Kevin tends to be impatient, impulsive, and perhaps overly energetic. He has only one 1, 3, and 4 in his name/number. He could use the calming and balancing influences from each in his formula to better express his talents and dilute all that fiery Mars/5 energy. We'll add one herb or oil of Sun/1, Venus/3, and Saturn/4, which should balance it out nicely, allowing him to recognize his goals and enjoy the process of achieving those goals as they manifest.

In this example, we then choose an herb or oil of Mercury/7, Jupiter/6, exalted Sun/8, Sun/1, Venus/3, and Saturn/4 to create his formula. In Planetary/number order, this formula could then be composed of lavender, cedar, frankincense, calendula, rose, and cypress.

You may elect to create a formula from the birth date Numerological values of an individual. The birth *month* number represents the First Cycle of your life, approximately the first thirty years. The birth *day* number represents the Second Cycle of your life, from age thirty-one through age sixty. The birth *year* number represents the Third Cycle of your life, from age sixty-one through the end of your time on the Planet in physical form. Each cycle's number indicates the main strength that a person has to bring to the opportunities and challenges he will face in that cycle.

We'll pretend that Kevin's birth date is May 21, 1946. As his birth month is May, the fifth month, his First Cycle number is 5, the number of Mars, the Planet of motivation, assertiveness, and impulse. His First Cycle will be one of initiating new pathways, and if he uses his immense energies well, he will make great strides. If he succumbs to the impulsiveness of the number 5, he will sometimes spin his wheels with impatience at the slow pace of the rest of the world. If we reduce his birth day (21) to a single digit (2 + 1), we find that his Second Cycle equates to 3, which is the number of Venus. His Second Cycle will be one where he seeks to bring beauty and harmony to those he encounters. By adding together the numbers of his birth year (1 + 9 + 4 + 6 = 20) and reducing this number to a single digit (2 + 0 = 2), we reach his Third Cycle number, 2, the number of the Moon and union. In his Third Cycle, he will find that working in union or partnership with others will benefit him and those he partners with the best. At the last third of his life, he brings people and situations together.

Then we look at his Destiny Number, the number that represents what he came into this lifetime to accomplish overall. His birth month, day, and year, when added together (5 + 2 + 1 + 1 + 9 + 4 + 6) total 28. We want to reduce the 28 to a single number to obtain the Destiny Number, so we add 2 and 8 together, which equals the number 1.

Month	Day	Year	Destiny Number
May	21	1946	
(5) +	(2 + 1) +	(1 + 9 + 4 + 6) =	28; (2 + 8) = **1**

Kevin's Destiny Number is the number 1, associated with the Sun and self-expression. This is also the number of the Self, so he will most likely succeed by his own efforts alone, not with the help of others.

By utilizing the strengths of the Planets related to his cycle numbers he finds the tools to best manifest his destiny. His birth date equals Mars/5 of energy and motivation; Venus/3 of harmony and beauty; Moon/2 union and bringing together in balance. Using herbs or oils of these Planets will help him to be his authentic Self and give him the most satisfaction while fulfilling his destiny of self-expression. For his formula we will choose ginger for Mars/5; myrtle for Venus/3; white sandalwood for Moon/2 and frankincense for Sun/1.

You have a plethora of herbs and oils to choose from as you consult your Tables of Correspondences (appendix F) for Planetary/herbal matches. Take into account any allergies and strong likes and dislikes in terms of scent that the person for whom you are creating a formula may have. For example, most men will not be comfortable wearing a formula smelling strongly of rose, no matter how much Venus is highlighted in their Astrological Charts or Numerology. You have many other Venusian herbs you can pick instead of rose to bring the energy of Venus into a formula.

CHAPTER 18

Creating Custom Formulas Using Astrology

Natal Charts

There are many computer programs that can be purchased that allow you to run a basic Natal Chart for an individual, so don't think "Oh no, now I have to become an Astrologer, too!" You do not have to be an expert Astrologer to use a Birth Chart to help you create a blend. Knowing keywords and concepts associated with the Astrological Signs and the Elements will enable you to create a formula that will help you or a client to live life fully. The following example shows you how you can use Astrology to correct difficult aspects in a chart with Planetary signatures and their corresponding herbs, resins, and oils. The next chapter shows you how to utilize the energies of each of the Astrological Houses.

Briefly, here are the Planets and Astrological Sun Signs and how each can work in an individual's Astrological Chart.

Everyone has all ten Planets working with various Signs in their charts. However, not all Astrological Signs will be aligned with a Planet, therefore there may be a missing Element or energy in an individual's chart. This is something that you will analyze as you decide what energies you will be enhancing or inciting to action in a person's life as he uses your alchemical creation.

Each of the Planets is paired with various Astrological Signs in every person's chart. The way that the energy of a Planet is expressed in a chart is dictated by the Sign paired with the Planet. The following is how the Planets express their energy in an Astrological Chart:

Sun: personality, ego, how the individual presents herself to the outside world

Moon: Inner Self, subconscious, how the individual experiences emotions, the individual's inner motivations and interests

Mars: energy, what drives the individual to accomplish goals and what goals interest her, her strengths

Mercury: conscious mind, intellect, how the individual gathers and collates thoughts and experiences

Jupiter: philosophy of life, social interaction with the world, where the individual may overdo things

Venus: how the individual relates to her senses, where she finds harmony in life and how she applies it, what attracts her

Saturn: where the individual draws her boundaries (or not), where stubbornness can occur, areas of self-discipline and conservation

Neptune: where the individual finds escape from life, imagination and creative impulses, where the individual has a tendency to fantasize and fool herself

Uranus: where the individual can innovate, break out of old patterns, act in an original or bold way

Pluto: intense drives, deep unconscious motivations, where the individual seeks to transform herself, karmic lessons she has come into this lifetime to perfect

A person has the very remote potential to have a pairing between one Planet and one Sign in her Birth Chart, but in most charts, you will see that while all the Planets are present in a chart, they tend to be active in half or less of the Astrological Signs. This is typical and shows that a person came into this lifetime to work on very specific issues.

Each of the Astrological Signs is associated with a specific Element. Fire signs are Aries, Leo, and Sagittarius. Earth signs are Taurus, Virgo, and Capricorn. Air signs are Gemini, Libra, and Aquarius. Water signs are Cancer, Scorpio, and Pisces. A Birth Chart shows imbalance when an Element is missing or when there is one Element working in the majority of Planetary energies. When the Planets congregate in primarily one or two Elemental Signs, it shows that that Element is dominant and can create difficulties or one-sidedness for a person when she attempts to activate other modes of expression in her life.

If you find that one of the Elements (Earth, Air, Fire, Water) is missing from a person's chart, or that she has only one Planet in an Elemental Sign, this will show that she needs an addition of the missing Element to be fully balanced. If she has a preponderance of one Element, she will tend to view the world and take action using only the ways of that Element, to the detriment of expression via the other Elements.

Missing Elements in a Birth Chart can be balanced and rectified by utilizing herbs and oils chosen specifically to bring in and activate that Element, giving the Element expression and energy and thus helping to create a more rounded mode of expression for the individual. Dominant Elements in a Birth Chart can be corrected by adding the herbs and oils to a formula from the other three Elements or the one Element that is its opposite.

If a person has a dominance of Fire Elements in her chart, she may have a tendency to start projects but never finish them, to be impulsive in her behavior, or to be so impatient that it hampers her efforts.

If a person has a dominance of the Element Earth in his chart, he may have a tendency toward inertia, working hard but never taking the risk that is required to succeed. He may be so enamored of physical wealth that he neglects his spiritual side or is stubborn to the extreme, getting in his own way when simply changing the methods he uses to work toward a goal would bring him success.

A person with a dominance of the Element Water in her chart has the tendency to be too emotional, reacting to every experience through her feelings and not using her head. Water dominating a chart can also indicate psychic abilities gone awry, where a person is very intuitive but cannot interpret the information she is getting because she feels so strongly, not being able to differentiate between the psychic impressions she is receiving and the overwrought emotions of the person who is sending out the psychic information.

The Element Air dominating a chart would show a person who views the world only through his intellectual abilities, who is unable to connect emotionally with others, and who tends to superficially solve problems rather than getting to its source and solving it at its foundation.

Water is emotions and psychic impressions. Air is intellect and linear thought processes. Fire is action and what motivates a person to act. Earth is resolve, perseverance, and groundedness. Keep in mind that Water balances Air; Air balances Water. Fire balances Earth; Earth balances Fire.

A person who is missing one of the Elements in his chart will find it difficult to accomplish the types of things that the missing Element represents. If a person is missing Fire in his chart, he will find it hard to get motivated or to gather enough vitality to see a goal through to its successful end. If a person is missing Water in his chart, he won't be able to recognize and interpret his emotions or psychic impressions—he has feelings, but he doesn't know how to express them appropriately. If a person is missing Earth in his chart, he will find it very hard to stay grounded and will often feel confused by events around him. If a person is missing Air in his chart, his thinking processes will be impaired—he will certainly be intelligent enough, but he won't think things through and will act without considering the consequences. By adding the herb or oil of an Element, the missing Element will be given a vehicle of expression and action in his life.

The Astrological Signs show how the Planet in that Sign will tend to express itself via a person's Natal Chart. Not all the Astrological Signs will be active in a person's Birth Chart unless his chart is unusual in the extreme. As long as the other signs that correspond with an Element are present, an individual can function in a balanced fashion in all the areas of his life. Here are the Astrological Signs and the types of energy they bring to a chart:

Aries: driven, impulsive, courageous, active. Ruled by Mars. Fire Sign.

Taurus: patient, appreciative of pleasure and routine, endurant. Ruled by Venus. Earth Sign.

Gemini: spontaneous, humorous, writerly, versatile. Ruled by Mercury. Air Sign.

Cancer: home loving, emotional, psychic, sensitive. Ruled by the Moon. Water Sign.

Leo: self-expressive, generous, fun loving, entertaining. Ruled by the Sun. Fire Sign.

Virgo: natural healer, creates order, analytical, detail oriented. Ruled by Mercury. Earth Sign.

Libra: brings balance, works best in partnerships, social. Ruled by Venus. Air Sign.

Scorpio: intense, mysterious, transformative, secretive. Ruled by Pluto. Water Sign.

Sagittarius: freedom loving, independent, optimistic. Ruled by Jupiter. Fire Sign.

Capricorn: serious, pragmatic, creates structure, career oriented. Ruled by Saturn. Earth Sign.

Aquarius: curious, eccentric, objective, rebellious. Ruled by Uranus. Air Sign.

Pisces: intuitive, emotional, romantic, caregiving. Ruled by Neptune. Water Sign.

The following are the herb/oil associations of the Astrological Signs for you to add to your repertoire.

Aries: cinnamon, dragon's blood resin, frankincense, garlic, ginger, holly, horseradish, marjoram, nettle, pepper, thistle

Taurus: coltsfoot, fern, lady's mantle, linden, myrtle, orris, sage

Gemini: bergamot, clove, elemi, mastic, meadowsweet, mullein, mint, oregano, thyme

Cancer: camphor, caraway, catnip, cucumber, jasmin, lemon balm, mugwort, sandalwood, violet

Leo: angelica, bay laurel, borage, chamomile, dandelion, eyebright, frankincense, heliotrope, marigold, mistletoe, saffron

Virgo: bloodroot, calamus, chicory, fennel, ginseng, lemon verbena, mandrake, patchouli, skullcap

 Libra: carnation, foxglove, galbanum, rose, strawberry, tansy, vervain, violet

 Scorpio: amaranth, basil, black copal, lily, patchouli, pennyroyal, storax, tarragon, valerian, wormwood

 Sagittarius: agrimony, betony, birch, cedar, eucalyptus, hawthorn, oak, pine, poplar, rowan

 Capricorn: benzoin, cassia, comfrey, hemlock, myrrh, plantain, Solomon's seal, witch hazel

 Aquarius: arabic, clove, mastic, nutmeg, Saint-John's-wort, spikenard

 Pisces: fennel, geranium, lobelia, lotus, neroli, poppy, willow

You can capture and express the energies in a chart by simply utilizing the Planetary energies and their associated Astrological Signs as you determine the components of your formula. Once you have become familiar and comfortable with each Planet's keywords and concepts and the way it is expressed in a Sign, you may want to do more advanced analysis of the Astrological Chart to determine the best herbs, resins, and oils for your formula. In the next chapter we discuss how to interpret the Astrological Houses and how to unite the energies or balance any difficulties you see present there.

CHAPTER 19

Advanced Herbal Alchemical Work with an Astrological Chart

The Natal Chart is circular, and all circles are composed of 360 degrees. This 360-degree circle is divided into twelve parts, or "Houses," each composed of 30 degrees. Each House is associated with or "ruled" by a specific Astrological Sign. All twelve Astrological Houses are present in a chart, but not every House will contain a Sign and a Planet. Many times this is not a problem, as a person's chart will indicate the Astrological Houses with which she came into this lifetime to work, and you will see what Houses are active.

The Houses where there are Planets in Signs show a person's primary types of activities for that lifetime and therefore where an individual will be expending her energies and thought processes during that incarnation. For example, if most of the Houses in the upper half of a chart (Seventh through Twelfth Houses) are active, but the bottom half of the chart has no Planets placed there, this indicates that the individual tends to express all her energy and aspirations through the intellectual and spiritual parts of the personality without much emotional understanding or practical grounding. This can lead to frustration and potential failure. Conversely, if a person has all her Planets active in the bottom Houses of her Natal Chart with none or only one active in the top two quadrants, this indicates that she can be shortsighted and unable to view the "big picture" in her life—she needs to balance her overly self-oriented and self-focused tendencies with which she was born by activating the top quadrants with herbs or oils that help her to strive toward a greater understanding of the world around her and her own larger philosophical perspective.

Here is a description of the twelve Astrological Houses for incorporation into your analysis of a Natal Chart:

First House: This house shows your Ascendant, the Planet that was rising over the horizon at the time that you were born. The Ascendant indicates your primary way of expressing your personality and how people tend to view you. The First House is also your physical self—your body style (thin, tall, round), your general health, and how you present yourself to the world. Aries rules this House.

Second House: This is the house of material possessions and how you deal with them. This House expresses how you take care of your possessions and the health of your self-esteem. Taurus rules this House.

Third House: This House is your community and how you interact within it. The Third House is your communication style, your attitude toward change, and how you conduct your mundane life. Gemini rules this House.

Fourth House: This is the House where you are nurtured or feel deprived. It represents your childhood foundation, your family, and the subconscious emotions from which you interpret your world. Cancer rules this House.

Fifth House: This is the House of creativity, romance, and play. The Fifth House is the place of personal interests, how you express yourself in a creative way, your hobbies, the type of partner to whom you are attracted, and where you find joy in life. Leo rules this House.

Sixth House: This is the House of health, work, and your daily routine. It represents how you structure your life and how important routine and responsibility are to you. This House shows where you find it easiest to apply perseverance and where you are willing to spend energy and time. Virgo rules this House.

Seventh House: This is the House of marriage and partnerships. It shows how you relate to other people and how you partner with others for success. Libra rules this House.

Eighth House: This is the House of the hidden side of yourself and how you deal with important issues in your life. The Eighth House holds the key to how you recuperate and survive and the tools you use to do so. Scorpio rules this House.

Ninth House: This House is your area of openness to new experience, higher learning, and your relationship to the world at large via religion, philosophy, and politics. Sagittarius rules this House.

Tenth House: This is the House of reputation, status, and worldly success. It is here that you show your interests in a profession, your overall ambitions, and how you deal with authority—your own or that of others. Capricorn rules this House.

Eleventh House: This House represents the kind of groups you will join or shun, the causes that are important to you, and whether you tend to be social or solitary. This is the House of your hopes, wishes, and dreams. Aquarius rules this House.

Twelfth House: This is the House of solitude, your Inner Self that you show only to those you trust. This House represents areas of your personality that you are not always comfortable expressing in public. It is also known as the House of Karma, and it is here that you find clues about what you are willing to give in the service of the greater good. The Twelfth House is also known as the House of Self-Undoing and can indicate where you tend to get in your own way. Pisces rules this House.

Using my Birth Chart as an example, we now analyze what challenges are present by noting which Elements are missing or out of balance, which Houses need some help in expression, and what strengths can be bolstered to allow full and successful manifestation.

In analyzing this chart, first we note that I have almost all my Planets associated with Signs in the upper two quadrants of the chart. This indicates that I could have trouble grounding my energy and expressing my goals in the physical world. We need to add some Earth to my formula to achieve a grounding/manifestation effect. In looking at the distribution of Elements in my chart, I have six Planets in Water Signs, two Planets in Fire Signs, three Planets in Air Signs, and one Planet in an Earth Sign. This would again indicate that more Earth would benefit my personal formula. In my Twelfth House, I have Mars in Aquarius. Mars is a Planet of Fire and action; Aquarius, ruled by Uranus, is a Planet of the innovator, the humanitarian, and also the eccentric. As this is the House of Self-Undoing, I could have the tendency to rebel for the sake of rebellion,

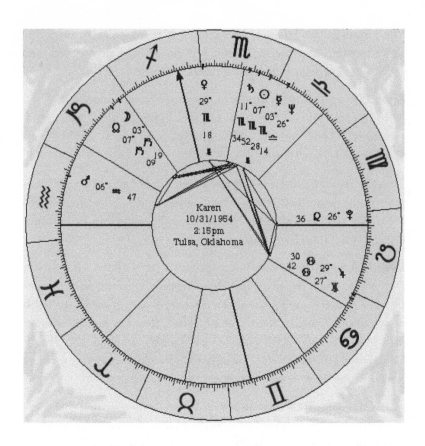

or to be so humanitarian that I allow people too much latitude in their actions toward myself and my goals. I will want to balance that Mars Fire with more Earth so that I can take all the energy of Mars in Aquarius and ground it into positive, practical manifestation for the good of all.

My basic formula before balancing would incorporate an herb or oil of Aquarius for my Ascendant; an herb or oil of Water for Scorpio, my Sun Sign; and an herb or oil of Earth for my Moon Sign, Capricorn. I would take a look at the Planets that naturally rule those Signs—Aquarius/Uranus, Scorpio/Pluto, and Capricorn/Saturn—so I might choose elemi, black copal, and cypress, respectively. I want to bolster Earth in my chart, so I would look at the Earth Signs of Taurus, Virgo, and Capricorn and choose another herb or oil corresponding to the Element Earth. And, because I want to balance that Aquarian Mars in the Twelfth House, I will need to incorporate yet another herb or oil associated with the Element Earth as well. I have the choices of Taurus/Venus, Virgo/Mercury, and Capricorn/Saturn. As Capricorn/Saturn is the earthiest of the Earth signs, I will choose another Saturn herb, patchouli, to add grounded Earth, and I'll pick an herb associated with the Earth Sign Virgo for intelligent discrimination and a clear mind, lemon verbena. This formula would represent and balance my natural Birth Chart.

If I elected to add to my formula the plant energy that is associated with a current goal, I would determine what my goal is and analyze which Sign and/or Planet carries that signature of energy. Let's say that my current goal is to allow others to help me in achieving my goals. Partnerships and working with others is ruled by the Seventh House with its association of Libra. Libra is an Air Sign, and Venus is Libra's Planet. I would choose an herb or oil associated with Air and one associated with Venus. For this formula, I'll go with lavender/Air and rose/Venus.

Thus, my formula is composed of elemi, black copal, cypress, patchouli, lemon verbena, lavender, and rose.

If I were working to resolve a perceived difficulty in my Birth Chart caused by the placement of a particular Planet or its aspect in my chart, I would determine the herb and/or oil that would free the energetic expression of that placement or aspect and include that in my formula according to the Astrological Sign and the Planet's energy that was expressing it.

As you are analyzing a chart, you may see difficult aspects such as squares (two Planets 90 degrees apart) or oppositions (two or more Planets 180 degrees apart). These types of aspects can show you energies that can be working at cross-purposes. For example, in my chart, you can see that Mars is in Aquarius in my Twelfth House of Service, Karma, and Self-Undoing. Mars in Aquarius in this House gives me impetus to use my energies to serve humankind, but I need to be careful not to impair my personal goals while doing so. It is in opposition to my Jupiter in Cancer occupying my Sixth House of Health, Work, and Daily Routine. Jupiter in Cancer in this House inclines me to be successful at work and to enjoy working but also to be a bit naïve as to the real motivations of others, particularly those with whom I work. Mars is a very active Planet working in the Sign of Aquarius—ideals, original thought, and rebelliousness. Jupiter is the Planet of expansion working in Cancer, a Water Sign of emotions.

The opposition of Mars/Aquarius/Twelfth House to Jupiter/Cancer/ Sixth House could cause me to refuse any guidance from others, particularly if the guidance was a warning about the character of another person with whom I work closely. I could have the tendency to lack forethought and to act impulsively and sometimes imprudently, which can cause problems. That Mars in Aquarius with this particular opposition could make me very impatient, wanting everything yesterday and throwing caution to the winds to obtain my goal in my work or routine. Therefore, I would want to ground this energy a bit by injecting an herb to balance Aquarius, making its expression one where I would think clearly before acting. I would want to use another herb to balance Cancer by helping Jupiter in that Sign not become emotionally embroiled. To balance Aquarius, I will choose rosemary; and for balancing Cancer, myrrh.

As you work with any chart, numbers, or Astrological information, always listen to your intuition. If you get a psychic impression that a specific herb, resin, or oil should be included in the formula, listen. Your psychic senses are tuned in to the work you are doing and can give you very helpful directives to make your formula even more effective.

Herbal Materia Magicka

The Magickal herbal practice that I have followed for so many decades is based on the Doctrine of Signatures as developed by Paracelsus and then added to by my own experiments with herbal materials. As time has gone on and my practice has evolved, I have discovered additional Planetary energy applications for some herbs as well as the herbs that correspond with the three other Planets, Neptune, Uranus, and Pluto, which were not addressed by Paracelsus. Every person's experience with the use of herbs and essential oils for Magick is personal and based on their own participation with the blending of the energies. It is all an ongoing work in progress for the modern herbalist/Alchemist just as it was in times past. Your own experimentation is encouraged, and your results will add to future herbal knowledge and lore.

You will find in the following materia magicka, or materials of Magick, that there are some herbs that have a dual correspondence with two Planets. This is due to the inherent nature of the herb, which, as with people, can have several layers of action and result depending on the intention and focus of the herbalist. The following is a collection of energy signatures, lore, and history of the herbs that I utilize the most in my practice. Included with each herb's correspondence to Element and Planet are the parts of the herb that can be used.

Remember to consult a reliable medicinal herbal as you develop your blends to ensure that there will be no contrary physical result from the inclusion of any herb in your formula.

Acacia

Scientific name: *Acacia senegal*

Other name: gum arabic

Element: Air

Planets: Mercury, Sun

Part used: flower

The lovely white flowers of the acacia tree are reminiscent of a cluster of shooting stars. Acacia is traditionally burned to honor ancestors and the afterlife, and its clean scent brings an opening of the psychic senses to Spirit and purification of one's home or temple. The flowers can also be used in Herbal Amulets to draw angelic presence during sleep.

Agrimony

Scientific name: *Agrimonia eupatoria*

Other name: cockleburr

Element: Air

Planet: Jupiter

Part used: leaf

Agrimony is traditionally used in psychic healing, particularly when ill health is the result of a curse. The leaves of this powerful plant are helpful in all protection formulas. Agrimony leaves can also be scattered in front of entrances to the home or office to ward away negativity.

Alfalfa

Scientific name: *Medicago sativa*

Other name: buffalo herb

Element: Earth

Planet: Venus

Part used: leaf

Abundance, plenty, and prosperity are the energies of this plant. Use in Money Amulets or keep a sprig in your wallet, cash drawer, or purse to increase your fortune. An effective Philtre or Condenser can be made with cut alfalfa leaves to promote abundance. An alfalfa Elixir can be ingested by the practitioner or sprinkled over contracts to attract success in an endeavor.

Allspice

Scientific name: *Pimenta officinalis*

Element: Fire

Planet: Uranus

Parts used: berry, essential oil

Allspice berries can be added whole or crushed to Herbal Amulets for increasing money and luck. They are also useful in transforming energy that may be causing obstacles into a more positive flow.

Aloeswood

Scientific name: *Aguilaria agallocha*

Other name: *Lignum aloes*

Element: Water

Planet: Venus

Part used: wood

The ground wood of aloeswood has been traditionally used to add energy and potency to any herbal formula. Used particularly in ceremonial Magick of the Renaissance period, aloeswood is burned as an Incense to promote growth and success in any area of interest.

Angelica root

Scientific name: *Angelica archangelica*

Other names: archangel, master root

Element: Fire

Planet: Sun

Parts used: root, essential oil

One of the most utilized herbs for exorcism and protection, angelica root is associated with the Archangel Michael, vanquisher of the wicked. The energy of the root, when burned, can also be used to provide visions of one's Holy Guardian Angel and one's proper karmic path. Angelica root also has long associations with healing, being one of the herbs burned to cleanse the atmosphere during the various plagues of the Dark Ages.

Arnica

Scientific name: *Arnica montana*

Other names: leopard's-bane, wolfsbane

Element: Fire

Planet: Mars

Parts used: leaf, flower

The flowers of this herb are best used in an Herbal Amulet, as it is poisonous if ingested. Used in the Alps to poison wolves, this plant is traditionally used to protect from shapeshifters and life-sucking spirits.

Asafoetida

Scientific name: *Ferula foetida*

Other names: devil's dung, giant fennel

Element: Fire

Planets: Mars, Saturn

Part used: powdered root

Asafoetida is the dried resin from the giant fennel found in the Middle East. Used extensively in Middle Eastern cooking, it lends the mild taste of leeks to the dish. In Magickal use, when burned, its fetid (*foetida*) odor is excellent in exorcism and banishing. Smell it once and you'll know why.

Balm of Gilead

Scientific name: *Commiphora opobalsamum*

Other names: balsam, poplar buds, Mecca balsam

Element: Water

Planets: Venus, Saturn

Part used: bud

Balm of Gilead is lauded in the Old Testament as an amazing healer, and legend has it that the Queen of Sheba made a gift of the poplar tree to King Solomon, thus bringing it to Judea. The buds exude a sticky, sweet-smelling resin that is used to anoint in blessing. Burning the balm of Gilead bud assists in spirit manifestation in séances.

Barberry

Scientific name: *Berberis vulgaris*

Other names: pipperidge, holy thorn

Element: Air

Planet: Mars

Part used: bark

The root of the barberry is most commonly used in Incenses, Amulets, baths, and any other herbal formula to promote courage, strength, and motivation. The red leaves and thorns from the thin branches can be strewn across the path to one's entrance to bar persons of ill intent.

Basil

Scientific name: *Ocimum basilicum*

Other names: Saint-Joseph's-wort, sweet basil

Element: Fire

Planet: Mars

Parts used: leaf, essential oil

A versatile herb, basil leaves can be used for love, protection, or to attract wealth. Burned in an Incense with rose petals, basil helps to restore peace in a relationship. Strew your floor with the leaves to dispel discord. Use it in the bath or ingest it in a Philtre to restore the vitality of your aura. Added to an Herbal Amulet, it is carried to overcome obstacles to prosperity.

Bayberry

Scientific name: *Myrica cerifera*

Other names: candleberry, wax myrtle

Element: Earth

Planet: Mercury

Parts used: leaf, berry, essential oil

Bayberry is a good addition to any formula focused on abundance. The root, leaves, or berries can be added to Incense or added to a bath mixture to bring wealth. Many people anoint a green candle with bayberry oil and burn the candle with a focused meditation on money. The energy and scent of bayberry also attracts familial love and friendship, promoting harmony in the household.

Bay laurel

Scientific name: *Laurus nobilis*

Other names: bay, laurel, daphne

Element: Fire

Planet: Sun

Parts used: leaf, essential oil

Victory wreath crowns of the noble bay laurel were worn by the winners of athletic contests in Greece. The fresh scent of bay brings protection from negative energy and the strength to combat it. In Delphi, the Pythoness who prophesied to leaders of the ancient world chewed bay laurel leaves to help her in her visions. Burning bay in an Incense or adding a few drops to an oil to develop psychic powers is effective.

Benzoin gum

Scientific name: *Styrax benzoin*

Other names: styrax, gum benjamin

Element: Earth

Planets: Venus, Saturn

Parts used: resin, essential oil

This earthy resin is grounding and stabilizing when added to any formula and is perfect for Home Blessings. A mixture of benzoin, bayberry, and cinnamon is also helpful as an oil or Incense to attract success to a business. Sometimes confused with storax, benzoin has an earthy scent, while storax is sweet.

Bergamot

Scientific name: *Mentha citrata*

Other names: bergamot, orange mint

Element: Air

Planet: Mercury

Parts used: leaf, essential oil

Smelling pleasantly of citrus mixed with a hint of mint, the bergamot, when burned in an Incense or added to an oil, promotes creativity through its gentle stimulation of the thought processes. Bathing in bergamot before engaging in gambling or commerce stimulates luck in the form of opportunities encountered. It also clears the atmosphere of a place or of the human aura when used in any type of formula.

Bilberry

Scientific name: *Vaccinium myrtillus*

Other names: huckleberry, blueberry, whortleberry

Element: Water

Planet: Jupiter

Part used: leaf

The use of bilberry leaf in herbal mixtures draws the energies of peace and tranquility. Bilberries were traditionally gathered at Lammas, and the amount of berries collected was said to foretell the size of the autumn harvests.

Black cohosh

Scientific name: *Cimicifuga racemosa*

Other name: black snakeroot

Element: Earth

Planet: Venus

Part used: root

The root of the black cohosh is used effectively in Philtres, Condensers, and Elixirs for physical healing. Steeped in red wine or added to the bath, black cohosh adds fertility by helping to alleviate impotence.

Black walnut

Scientific name: *Juglans regia*

Other name: English walnut

Element: Earth

Planet: Sun

Part used: leaf

Tall and strong, the black walnut tree's energy is protective, grounding, and stabilizing. In nature, the tree attracts lightning, and in Magickal use, the leaves can attract and absorb directed negative energy and ground it into powerlessness. Powdered dried black walnut leaves can also be used like henna to decorate the body with temporary designs. Applying a Magickal design to the skin like a protective Talisman in times of stress is very effective.

Bladder wrack

Scientific name: *Fucus vesiculosus*

Other names: bladder, kelp, sea wrack

Element: Water

Planet: Moon

Part used: leaf

Bladder wrack enhances psychic ability, attracts abundance, and aids connection to the Element Water to enhance dreams and emotions. Corresponding directly with Water Elementals and the Magickal denizens of the sea, bladder wrack is a treasured offering to Yemaya, Poisedon, and Aphrodite, all Deities connected with water. An Infusion or Philtre containing bladder wrack can be used to wash the floor of an enterprise to attract business and can be consumed to enhance one's intuition.

Blessed thistle

Scientific name: *Centaurea benedicta*

Other names: holy thistle, lady's thistle

Element: Fire

Planet: Mars

Part used: leaf

Blessed thistle has long been used for protection and strength—sprinkle it around a home to divert negative energy, or add it to an Herbal Amulet to protect during travel. An Herbal Potpourri can be constructed with this and other Mars herbs and kept by the front door to protect and strengthen the inhabitants. Sacred to Pan, Herne, and other protectors of woodland creatures, blessed thistle is a perfect Earth offering. It is not advised to add blessed thistle to an Incense, as it can irritate the throat if burned.

Bloodroot

Scientific name: *Sanguinaria canadensis*

Other names: redroot, king root, tetterwort

Element: Fire

Planet: Mars

Part used: root

Added to an Herbal Amulet or carried by itself, bloodroot protects and brings order out of chaos. Used in a Philtre and applied *only externally* to afflicted body parts, bloodroot is excellent for health. Long used to get rid of warts, a bloodroot wash is also very effective to stop the production of tumor cells.

Blue cohosh

Scientific name: *Caulophyllum thalictroides*

Other names: blue ginseng, papooseroot, squawroot

Element: Earth

Planet: Venus

Part used: root

Used for millennia by Native Americans, blue cohosh blesses the home and protects children. Tie an Herbal Amulet containing this herb above the bed of a child to bring sweet dreams. Anoint a baby with a blue cohosh Philtre or Condenser in a blessing to protect and strengthen.

Boneset

Scientific name: *Eupatorium perfoliatum*

Other names: agueweed, Indian sage, white snakeroot

Element: Water

Planet: Saturn

Part used: leaf

Burn boneset in an Incense to balance the energies of a space or to ground and focus your energy. Added to a Condenser, Elixir, or Philtre, boneset promotes health. Mixed with angelica and added to the bath, boneset is excellent for ritual cleansings.

Borage

Scientific name: *Borago officinalis*

Other names: burrage, peace herb

Element: Air

Planet: Jupiter

Parts used: seed, leaf

Borage can be used in Incense, Philtres, baths, and Herbal Amulets to add courage and attract peace. Borage oil applied to the forehead clears thoughts and dispels depression. Sacred to the Celts, it was used to bring knowledge, good judgment, and persuasion.

Brimstone

Other name: sulphur (mineral)

Element: Fire

Planet: Mars

Part used: powdered mineral

While brimstone, or sulphur, is not a plant material, it is useful in such a variety of formulas that it has been included here. When burned, its fumes are very protective, dispelling phantasms and negative entities. Brimstone adds power in any application and has long been used as a hex breaker in the most difficult of circumstances.

Broom tops

Scientific name: *Cytisus scoparius*

Other names: besom, Irish broom

Element: Air

Planet: Mars

Parts used: flower, leaf

Sprinkle the floor of a space with broom tops and let the herb sit for a few hours, absorbing the energy of the space. Next, with the front door open, sweep the floor with an actual broom, sweeping all the broom tops and psychic "dust bunnies" out the front door. Make an aura-cleansing Philtre and add to the bath or sprinkle into the aura of a person to remove blockages and attachments. Add broom tops to an Incense for releasing imbalance and negativity—as the scent floats through the air, see the problems floating away and dissipating.

Buckeye

Scientific name: *Aesculus hippocastanum*

Other name: horse chestnut

Element: Earth

Planet: Mercury

Part used: seed

Carried in an Herbal Amulet, the buckeye is known in folklore as the plant for wishes and hopes. Hold buckeye in your hands, letting your body's warmth heat it, and meditate on the heart to ease heartbreak. Place all the pain in the buckeye, then bury it in the earth.

Buckthorn

Scientific name: *Rhamnus cathartica*

Other name: dogwood

Element: Water

Planet: Saturn

Part used: bark

Used in any herbal preparation, buckthorn brings justice and strengthens legal arguments. For protection, hang buckthorn bark or branches by entrances or burn buckthorn in an Incense.

Burdock

Scientific name: *Arctium lappa*

Other names: batweed, hardock, lappa

Element: Water

Planet: Venus

Parts used: root, leaf

Excellent for healing, burdock can be added to an Incense formula, Herbal Amulet, or included in a Philtre for a health tonic. Burdock also brings courage to act when one is confronted with obstacles, drawing the calm and resolve to do what must be done. In Native American tradition, burdock root is consumed as a fasting Infusion to help clear the mind for spiritual visioning.

Calamus

Scientific name: *Acorus calamus*

Other names: sedge, sweet flag

Elements: Water/Earth

Planet: Moon

Parts used: root, essential oil

One of the four herbs used in the famous formula for Abramelin the Mage, calamus works as an effective herb for healing, luck, abundance, and spiritual visions. Calamus brings control in situations, leading to a positive resolution. Chewing on the root can aid in formulating effective plans and brings wisdom and a larger vision of the situation. Added to Incense, Ritual Oil, or Elixir, calamus binds the energies for manifestation. Creating an Anointing Oil for Qabbalistic work is useful in rites involving the Holy Guardian Angel and the Fountain Breath, a Qabbalistic exercise incorporating focused breathwork (sometimes called the Alchemical Circulation).

Calendula

Scientific name: *Calendula officinalis*

Other names: marigold, summer's bride

Element: Fire

Planet: Sun

Parts used: leaf, flower, essential oil

Just viewing the bright yellow-orange petals of the calendula plant brings optimism and vitality! Burned in an Incense formula or added to a mixture for Ritual Oil, calendula attracts success in every area including legal matters. The petals sprinkled in the bath draw health and vitality into the auric field. Calendula has long been used in protection, its energy dispelling negativity and drawing light to the user. In Mexico, calendula (marigold) flowers decorate the gravesites of loved ones, attracting the passed souls and bringing them joy and comfort.

Camphor

Scientific name: *Cinnamomum camphora*

Element: Water

Planet: Moon

Parts used: gum, essential oil

The scent of burning camphor purifies a space and brings self-discipline, aiding in controlling and transforming bad habits. Long used in the Eastern Hemisphere for temple purification and protection, camphor is excellent for deep meditation and gaining insight. Camphor oil added to the bath clears the thoughts and soothes the soul. A little goes a long way, so if you burn camphor on charcoal, use only a small pinch.

Caraway

Scientific name: *Carum carvi*

Element: Air

Planet: Mercury, Uranus

Parts used: seed, essential oil

The energies of caraway promote memory and intelligence as well as transformative change in mental outlook and attitude. Brewed in a tea Infusion or simply chewed, caraway brings eloquence and persuasion to the speaker. When utilized in any herbal formula, this small seed promotes quick resolution to any Magickal project. Caraway also has been used in weddings, thrown like rice at the married couple to bring fidelity, communication, and luck to the union.

Cardamom

Scientific name: *Elettaria cardamomum*

Element: Air

Planets: Mars, Mercury, Uranus

Parts used: seed, essential oil

An interesting herb with a dual Mercury/Uranus rulership and a correspondence with Mars energies, cardamom connects the linear intelligence of Mercury with the intense, innovative thought processes of Uranus. Its associations with Mars bring warmth, lust, and seduction. Adding the seed or oil to an herbal preparation for a relationship promotes a connection that combines love, attraction, and a union of equals. Cardamom's versatility makes it a good addition to any herbal formula for enhancing a project whose goal is to inspire many people.

Carnation

Scientific name: *Dianthus carophyllus*

Other name: gilliflower

Element: Water

Planet: Sun

Parts used: flower, essential oil

Inhaling the gorgeous scent of the carnation flower will immediately enhance emotions of joy and happiness, so the addition of the oil is perfect for Incenses and oils to dispel depression and disappointment. Carnation flowers attract abundance as well, either as a bouquet or in a formula. Including carnation in a mixture for the sickroom is perfect to aid in the mental aspects of healing.

Cascara sagrada

Scientific name: *Rhamnus purshiana*

Other name: sacred bark

Element: Earth

Planet: Mars

Part used: bark

Cascara sagrada is excellent in rites to release negativity, whether action or thought. As an ingredient in Incense, Herbal Amulet, or Elixir, it vigorously cleanses the energy patterns to return them to a state of neutrality. If you choose to include it in a liquid to be ingested, be warned: it can dramatically loosen the bowels.

Catnip

Scientific name: *Nepeta cataria*

Other names: catmint, catwort

Element: Water

Planet: Venus

Parts used: leaf, essential oil

A mild hallucinatory, catnip, when inhaled in Incense, applied as a Ritual Oil, or drunk in a potion, aids in psychic visions, dreamwork, and intuition. Catnip is also a relaxant and so enhances sexual experience and romantic endeavors. Use in formulas for love, inspiration, and, of course, cat Magick.

Cat's-claw

Scientific name: *Uncaria tomentosa*

Other name: uña de gato

Element: Water

Planet: Saturn

Part used: bark

Used traditionally in Peru for unhexing and protection, cat's-claw bark is particularly useful in shielding animals from harm. Rub a handful on their fur or add a pinch to a locket on the animal's collar. Creating an Infusion from the bark and washing the body with it can release negativity and ill-ness attached to the person.

Cedar

Scientific name: *Cedrus libani*

Element: Fire

Planet: Jupiter

Parts used: bark, leaf, essential oil

Traditionally an herb of the summer solstice, cedar's energy promotes confidence, authority, and plenty. Cedar can be one of the ingredients in any formula to attract prosperity and growth. Objects, animals, or people who are censed with cedar smoke will experience a cleansing and magnetism in their auric fields that draws abundance and health.

Celandine

Scientific name: *Chelidonium majus*

Other names: kenningwort, swallowwort

Element: Water

Planet: Sun

Part used: leaf

Celandine has been used in Incense, bath herbs, and Amulets to deflect entrapment or unfair imprisonment and as an aid in dream- and trancework. For visionary work of this type, celandine's use in the bath or in a dream or meditation pillow is perfect.

Centaury

Scientific name: *Centaurium* spp.

Other name: feverwort

Element: Fire

Planet: Sun

Part used: leaf

One of the Nine Sacred Herbs of the Celts, centaury, when used as a strewing herb, Incense, or in the bath, protects against natural pests (ants, spiders, snakes) and scatters any negative energy directed toward an individual. In addition, the leaf of this plant helps to understand the meaning of dreams.

Chamomile

Scientific name: *Anthemis nobilis*

Other name: manzanilla

Element: Water

Planet: Sun

Parts used: flower, essential oil

Very useful in Herbal Amulets for sleep, chamomile aids in dispelling both insomnia and nightmares. When used as a wash for the hands, chamomile successfully attract money. Sacred to the Egyptian priesthood, the lovely yellow flowers can be added to Incense or strewn in an area to promote purification and vitality. Like centaury, chamomile is also one of the Nine Sacred Herbs of the Celts. (The other seven herbs are mugwort, plantain, watercress, nettle, apple, chervil and fennel.)

Chaparral

Scientific name: *Larrea tridentada*

Other names: greasewood, creosote bush

Element: Earth

Planet: Mercury

Part used: leaf

Chaparral is commonly used by Native Americans in the Southwest for purification and positive change. Burned in an Incense or ingested in an Infusion, chaparral cleanses the soul and draws opportunities for change and to alter bad luck.

Chicory

Scientific name: *Cichorium intybus*

Other names: succory, wild chicory, coffeeweed

Element: Air

Planet: Sun

Part used: root

Brewed as an Infusion, chicory can be consumed or used as a wash to aid in alertness and removing obstacles. When burned in Incense or used in the bath, chicory draws luck and synchronistic events leading to success.

Cinnamon

Scientific name: *Cinnamomum zeylanicum*

Other name: sweetwood

Element: Fire

Planet: Sun, Mars, Mercury

Parts used: bark, essential oil

Cinnamon is one of the herbs used throughout the Far and Middle East for purification and temple cleansing. In addition, cinnamon's energy promotes success, healing, the raising of spiritual intent, and clear psychic vision. It is an excellent addition to almost any Magickal herbal formula, but avoid its use in oils and baths. Many people are very physically sensitive to the potency of this bark and its essential oil. Its application to the skin can cause burns. Very energizing to the human nervous system, cinnamon awakens the mind to clear and quick thought.

Cinquefoil

Scientific name: *Potentilla canadensis*

Other names: five-finger grass, silverweed

Element: Fire

Planets: Jupiter, Mercury

Parts used: leaf, essential oil

The word *cinquefoil* translates to "five leaves" or "five fingers," referring to the number of points on each elongated leaf. Each leaf represents an area of achievement: love, money, dreams, health, and power. Used by Agrippa in Incense of Mercury, cinquefoil has associations with Jupiter as well for the broad number of issues it can address. Combined with mugwort and jasmin in a dream pillow, cinquefoil aids in prophetic dreaming; added to an Incense or oil for love, prosperity, or health, cinquefoil expands the interaction of all herbs in the combination and helps to very clearly focus them. When used in a bath, Philtre, Condenser, or Amulet, cinquefoil purifies and attracts success to any endeavor.

Cleavers

Scientific name: *Gallium aparine*

Other names: clivers, goosegrass, bedstraw

Element: Earth

Planet: Moon

Part used: leaf

As an ingredient in any formula, cleavers works to unblock and remove obstacles or problems. Cleavers is traditionally added to Infusions or Incense for weddings or handfastings to strengthen the commitment and lend the union power.

Clove

Scientific name: *Syzygium aromaticum*

Element: Fire

Planet: Uranus

Parts used: bud, essential oil

Burned in an Incense, clove lends protection, brings joy to the home, attracts riches, and gives inspirational confidence. Add seven cloves to an Herbal Amulet for quick expansion in financial opportunities, or include clove oil in your candle anointing blend to shine light on the truth and stop gossip. Clove added to a child's pillow encourages sweet dreams.

Coltsfoot

Scientific name: *Tussilago farfara*

Other name: coughwort

Element: Water

Planet: Venus

Part used: leaf

Named for its broad, rounded leaves, coltsfoot in an Herbal Amulet, Infusion, or bath increases psychic awareness. Burned in an Incense, colftsfoot smooths the atmosphere and brings peace to the mind.

Comfrey

Scientific name: *Symphytum officinale*

Other names: bruisewort, knitbone

Element: Earth

Planet: Saturn

Parts used: root, leaf

Used extensively in Travel Amulets, comfrey keeps the traveler safe and alert. With its grounding properties, comfrey can be used in any herbal blend to strengthen energy shields and protect the home, business, or automobile from theft. A doubly manifesting herb with its combined correspondences of Earth and Saturn, comfrey can be added to Incenses where the intention is physical appearance of spirit. A small bit of comfrey held under the tongue anchors chaotic thoughts and helps with grounding.

Copal

Scientific name: *Bursera odorata*

Other name: frankincense of the Americas

Element: Fire

Planet: Sun

Part used: resin

Copal's wafting scent is reminiscent of frankincense with a bit of spice added. Traditionally used in Mexico in loveworkings, copal is also an excellent resin to burn for purification and as an offertory to the Gods.

Coriander

Scientific name: *Coriandrum sativum*

Other names: cilantro, Chinese parsley

Element: Fire

Planet: Mars

Parts used: leaf, seed, essential oil

Used the world over for fertility, sexuality, and stamina, coriander can be added to any herbal concoction to enhance the formula's primary focus. Steeped in red wine, the seeds add a subtle spice and enhance virility. Coriander leaf added to food creates a convivial social atmosphere.

Cubeb

Scientific name: *Piper cubeba*

Other name: loveberry

Element: Fire

Planet: Mars

Part used: berry

Associated with sexuality and love in folk Magick, the small, dried berries of the cubeb plant can be added to Herbal Amulets, Incense, or bath herb mixtures to ensure fidelity or help to find a new love. Crush and sprinkle cubeb over food (its taste is close to pepper, though a bit bitterer) and say an incantation to strengthen a romantic union before the food is consumed.

Cumin

Scientific name: *Cumimum cyminum*

Other name: comino

Element: Fire

Planet: Mars

Parts used: seed, essential oil

Used in both the Old World and the New World as an herb to prevent theft, cumin can be added to any herbal formula (when using the oil, add only a drop or two—the smell is very potent). Mixed with salt and sprinkled around a space, cumin breaks up negativity. Like cubeb, cumin seeds are often steeped in red wine to stir the senses and promote fidelity.

Cypress

Scientific name: *Cupressus sempervirens*

Other name: tree of death

Element: Earth

Planets: Saturn, Pluto

Parts used: chip, essential oil

Sacred to Hades, cypress is used to bind and unbind (depending on your focus), to honor the dead, and to ease grief or loss. Cypress chips sprinkled over a gravesite or at the site of a death ease both the pain of those left behind and the soul of the deceased. They can also be used to bind a spirit and encourage it to move on. Cypress chips or oil added to an Incense comforts the heart and uncovers deep subconscious ideas that are contributing to mental/emotional pain in an individual.

Damiana

Scientific name: *Turnera diffusa*

Element: Water

Planets: Mars, Pluto

Part used: leaf

One of the few real herbal aphrodisiacs, damiana enhances drive in both men and women, and as such, it is often used in rites involving sexuality and love. Included in Incense or the bath, damiana also produces slight hallucinations, leading to psychic impressions and visions. Damiana, with its natural sweetness, can be added to wine. It can be smoked in a pipe either as a simple or with other herbal ingredients—it can be slightly harsh, so I would recommend adding a bit of peppermint to smooth out the slight acridness.

Dandelion

Scientific name: *Taraxacum officinale*

Other names: blowball, lion's mane

Element: Air

Planet: Jupiter

Parts used: leaf, root, seed

We all know about making a wish while blowing the dandelion seeds into the wind. The root brewed in a tea brings psychic impressions and dreams. Adding dandelion to an Herbal Amulet for abundance increases financial acumen and opportunity.

Devil's claw

Scientific name: *Harpagophytum procumbens*

Other names: arthritis tea, grapple plant

Element: Water

Planet: Saturn

Part used: root

Used in any herbal mixture, devil's claw confuses and confounds the enemy. Burned on charcoal, this root removes any negativity. Brewed in an Infusion, devil's claw relieves pain and promotes health.

Devil's shoestring

Scientific name: *Symphoricarpos orbiculatus*

Other names: Indian currant, buckbrush

Element: Earth

Planet: Mercury

Part used: root

The low-growing spindly branches form a fortress of protection—add devil's shoestring to any blend to prevent difficulties and to protect an individual, home, or business. In folk Magick, devil's shoestring is used both for gambling and for gaining employment. Create an Herbal Amulet containing this root to take to the casino or on a job interview.

Dill

Scientific name: *Anethum graveolens*

Other names: aneton, dilly

Element: Fire

Planets: Mercury, Venus

Parts used: leaf, seed, essential oil

One of the most popular protection and uncrossing herbs of the Middle Ages, dill can be added to an Incense, oil, or Herbal Amulets to create a shield against negative energy. Added to the bath, dill is said to make one irresistible and to promote fertility. Sprinkled around the bed, it protects the sleeper; and placed in the mouth, it promotes the truth.

Dittany of Crete

Scientific name: *Dictamus origanoides*

Other name: dittany

Element: Water

Planet: Saturn

Part used: leaf

Traditionally burned in Incenses where the manifestation of spirit into corporeal matter is sought, dittany is helpful in séance work. With its close association with physical manifestation of energy or spirit, dittany of Crete can also be used in any herbal mixture where the physical manifestation of the focus is desired—money, love, employment, etc.

Dong quai

Scientific name: *Angelica sinensis*

Other names: Chinese angelica, tang kuei

Element: Earth

Planet: Venus

Part used: root

Known as the female equivalent to ginseng, dong quai acts as a medicinal balancer for estrogen and progesterone. Magickally, dong quai root is sacred to women, giving them strength and protection.

Dragon's blood

Scientific name: *Daemonorops draco*

Other names: sanguis draconis, blood palm

Element: Fire

Planet: Mars

Part used: resin

Truly as red as the blood of dragons, this resin is a powerful herb of protection. Burned by itself on charcoal or added to other Incense ingredients, it quickly banishes any negative energy or entity. Dragon's blood also adds power and potency to any working. Use sparingly in an oil blend or in the bath—it will stain enamel scarlet and leave a stain on the skin. You can create your own pure dragon's blood oil by crushing the resin into a power and mixing in a light oil, such as safflower. Heat gently to melt the resin into the oil while stirring. Do not ingest.

Echinacea

Scientific name: *Echinacea angustifolia*

Other names: coneflower, purple coneflower

Element: Air

Planet: Venus

Parts used: leaf, flower, root

This herb is most often used as an offertory of thanks or petition and can be added to any herbal blend to strengthen the focus of the ritual or meditation.

Elder

Scientific name: *Sambucus canadensis*

Other names: rob elder, ellhorn

Element: Water

Planet: Venus

Parts used: leaf, flower, berry

The lore and use of the elder is huge—contacting Elementals, divination, honoring the dead, protection, and prosperity being only a few of the Magickal uses of this respected plant. Sit near or under the elder and quietly ask a question: in a few minutes, the plant sprite within will give you your answer. Wands or dowsing rods made from the elder branch are traditional tools. Branches or sprigs of elder flowers are sacred offerings to the dead, and elder can be used effectively in Incense, baths, Philtres, Amulets, and more to bless and protect.

Elecampane

Scientific name: *Inula helenium*

Other names: elfwort, velvet dock

Element: Air

Planet: Mercury

Part used: root

The energies of elecampane are helpful in work with the faery realm, either as an offering or an enticement. One of the herbs used by the Druids, elecampane, when burned in a Divination Incense, aids in scrying, whether by crystal ball or on the surface of a clear spring.

Eucalyptus

Scientific name: *Eucalyptus* spp.

Other name: gum tree

Element: Water

Planet: Moon

Parts used: leaf, essential oil

The clear, bright scent of the eucalyptus lends itself perfectly to cleansings of temples, homes, and the human aura. Use in any herbal formula to clean and balance a place or a person. Create an Herbal Amulet or Anointing Oil to strengthen and clear the ill.

Eyebright

Scientific name: *Euphrasia officinalis*

Other name: euphrasia

Element: Air

Planet: Sun

Part used: leaf

Made into a Philtre and used as an eyewash, eyebright has long been associated with both clearing physical eyesight and also enhancing clairvoyance—the ability of Second Sight. In an Incense, bath, or Condenser, eyebright brings forth clarity in a situation as well as the truth of the matter.

Fennel

Scientific name: *Foeniculum vulgare*

Other name: fenkel

Element: Water

Planets: Mercury, Moon

Parts used: seed, leaf, essential oil

Like white sandalwood, fennel enjoys the dual rulership of Mercury and the Moon. It aids in obtaining psychic impressions (Moon) and interpreting those impressions accurately (Mercury). Fennel is also used in protection rites—strew the whole seeds in each room, burn it in an Incense blend, or make an Infusion with the seeds and wash the walls and floor. Burning fennel in Incense or anointing the Third Eye also clears the mind and aids in memory. Fennels seed are tossed at a wedding couple like rice for health and abundance in the relationship.

Fenugreek

Scientific name: *Trigonella foenumgraecum*

Other name: Greek hayseed

Element: Air

Planet: Mercury

Parts used: seed, essential oil

Included in a Philtre or Elixir, fenugreek promotes wisdom and good decisions. As an ingredient in Incense or Ritual Oil (one drop will suffice), fenugreek draws success to any enterprise. Make a Magickal Potpourri money jar by combining fenugreek seeds, bay leaves, and cinnamon in a small jar along with a silver coin. Shake it while you visualize a shower of gold and green drifting down on you.

Feverfew

Scientific name: *Chrysanthemum parthenium*

Other name: febrifuge

Element: Water

Planet: Venus

Part used: leaf

Strew this herb along the walkway or in the entrance of a home or business to prevent accidents. Adding feverfew to an Herbal Amulet for travel helps to keep the journey safe (add some dried or fresh leaf to the suitcase to prevent its loss). Burn feverfew as part of an Incense formula to stop negative influences from ruling decisions that you are making or that are being made about you, such as court cases.

Flax

Scientific name: *Linum usitatissimum*

Other name: linseed

Element: Water

Planet: Moon

Parts used: flower, seed, essential oil

Protector of children and pregnancy, the flax flowers or flaxseeds may be incorporated into Herbal Amulets, Incense, or Elixirs to bless children, increase chances of fertility, or protect an endangered pregnancy. Flax oil applied to a child's forehead or a woman's pregnant belly is protective as well.

Frankincense

Scientific name: *Boswellia carteri*

Other name: olibanum

Element: Fire

Planet: Sun

Parts used: resin, essential oil

This is one herb that you *must* have in your Magickal supplies cabinet. The resin has been burned for thousands of years to sanctify, promote success, protect, connect with the Divine, and consecrate. In an oil blend, frankincense uplifts and opens the user to higher levels of being. A fantastic base for any herbal blend, frankincense is indispensable.

Galangal

Scientific name: *Alpinia officinalis*

Other names: chewing John, low John

Element: Fire

Planet: Mars

Parts used: root, essential oil

Powder the galangal root and strew it about the home for protection, chew a small piece for courage and protection, brew into an Infusion for vitality and sexual energy, or add it to an oil blend for power. The galangal root can be charged with energy by itself and kept on the person to enhance health and energy levels. A relative of ginger, this root brings additional power to any formula.

Garlic

Scientific name: *Allium sativum*

Other names: ajo, stinkweed

Element: Earth

Planet: Mars

Parts used: root, essential oil

Used in every culture for protection and exorcism, garlic is a powerful tool in dispelling negative entities and can be burned in an Incense, hung from the doorway, and strewn throughout a room. Garlic can also be employed in an oil blend for drawing protective symbols on doors and windows to keep illness and spirits out. The essential oil's scent is incredibly strong; a little goes a long way.

Gentian

Scientific name: *Gentiana lutea*

Other name: bitterroot

Element: Fire

Planet: Mars

Part used: root

Arousing desire, gentian root has traditionally been added in Herbal Amulets to draw someone to you or to add sensuality to a relationship. It is also one of the herbs that can be used in a Home Blessing, using the Mars energy with which it corresponds to burn away negativity and bring energy, passion, and health to the home.

Ginger

Scientific name: *Zingiber officinale*

Other name: gingerroot

Element: Fire

Planet: Mars

Parts used: root, essential oil

Perfect as an addition to any herbal mixture, ginger adds force and potency to every working. In a Philtre, Condenser, or Elixir, ginger root acts as an energizing tonic, bringing strength, courage, and health. Ginger can be part of a rite to bring interest back to a romantic union or be a strong addition to a Protection ceremony. Chewing ginger has traditionally been a quick technique for bringing strength to the herbal practitioner as she focuses and releases energy in Magick.

Gingko

Scientific name: *Gingko biloba*

Other name: maidenhair tree

Element: Air

Planet: Mercury

Part used: leaf

Known medicinally as an excellent brain herb, gingko increases the oxygen absorption in the blood cells, increasing clear thought processes and intelligence. Magickally, ginkgo works in a similar fashion, attracting inspiration, new thought, and eloquence to the user.

Ginseng

Scientific name: *Panax quinquefolius*

Other names: wonder-root, eleuthero

Element: Earth

Planet: Mars

Part used: root

Known worldwide as the root that provides strength, stamina, and vigor to men, ginseng is also associated with enhanced sexuality. Using the whole root, you can inscribe the name of your intended romantic partner on one side, your name on the other. Wrap the root in red cloth and visualize the union. Ginseng can also be added to an aphrodisiac Philtre with potent results.

Grains of paradise

Scientific name: *Aframomum melegueta*

Other name: Guinea grains

Element: Fire

Planet: Mars

Part used: seed

Place three seeds under your tongue as you meditate on a desire. Swallow the seeds and expect results in three days, says the lore. A wonderful addition to any herbal mixture to be used in a Home Blessing, grains of paradise attract luck, prosperity, wishes, and a joyful household.

Guarana

Scientific name: *Paullinia cupana*

Element: Air

Planet: Uranus

Part used: seed

Very effective in an Infusion to promote innovative thinking, alertness, and energy, guarana exemplifies the Uranian energies with which it is associated. The ground seeds in an Incense blend promote higher thought processes and a world/Universe consciousness.

Gum Arabic

Scientific name: *Acacia* spp.

Other name: arabic gum

Element: Air

Planets: Mercury, Sun

Part used: resin

Gum arabic is the resin obtained from the acacia tree. When it is burned, its light, clean scent is refreshing and is used for purification of a space as well as an offertory to the Gods. Lore says that the Ark of the Covenant was made from the acacia tree.

Gum mastic

Scientific name: *Pistacia lentiscus*

Other name: mastic

Element: Air/Fire

Planet: Uranus

Part used: resin

A bright and clear yellow, gum mastic is used for rapid change and to attain a high spiritual level. One of the staple resins in many Incenses used in ceremonial Magick, this clean-smelling resin raises the vibrations in a temple and imparts a sense of higher purpose.

Hawthorn

Scientific name: *Crataegus oxyacantha*

Other names: maybush, hagthorn

Element: Air

Planets: Mercury, Uranus

Parts used: berry, leaf, thorn

Used for centuries to protect and bless the home, hawthorn wards off lightning and negativity. Placed in the cradle or in a child's bed, hawthorn stops nightmares and blesses the child with intelligence and health. Known to attract faery folk, hawthorn incorporated into an Incense can be burned or the berries can be sown into the garden to ensure a good harvest. Hawthorn branches carried into the bridal chamber bring fidelity and erotic desire for the partner. In Teutonic lands, Hawthorn was burned in the funeral pyre to lift the soul gently from the body.

Heal-all

Scientific name: *Prunella vulgaris*

Other names: woundwort, allheal

Element: Earth

Planet: Mars

Part used: leaf

Included in an Infusion, heal-all brings health, strength, and vigor. In an Incense or Herbal Amulet, heal-all soothes a broken heart. Strewn in a circle around a place, heal-all sanctifies and creates a sacred circle for ritual or protection.

Henna

Scientific name: *Lawsonia inermis*

Other names: mehndi, al-henna

Element: Fire

Planet: Venus

Parts used: leaf, essential oil

Associated with brides and weddings in India, the intricate patterns left on the skin by using the stain from henna paste are intended to draw the favor of the Gods. When mixing the paste, different essential oils and floral waters can be used that add to the focused energy of the final design. Mixing henna paste with tea tree oil brings purity; rose water attracts sexuality and love; orange oil invites prosperity and happiness. A Talismanic emblem or Magickal square can be drawn on the skin as a part of a ritual. As the henna paste is applied, focus on the intention of the ritual, and as the dried paste is removed, leaving the pattern, release the desire into the Universe.

Hibiscus

Scientific name: *Hibiscus sabdariffa*

Element: Water

Planet: Venus

Parts used: flower, essential oil

Perfect for brewing into an Infusion to connect with the Divine Feminine, Hibiscus is sacred to the Goddess Kali in all her guises. Adding the dramatically red flowers to Incense adds beauty and results in an uplifting spiritual response in the practitioner. This flower can be used to petition for mercy.

High John

Scientific name: *Ipomoea jalapa*

Other names: jalap root, High John the Conqueror

Element: Air

Planet: Mars

Part used: root

High John root is most often taken into court for legal success and can be stored with legal papers prior to a hearing to incite a positive resolution. Adding a small root or bit of root to a carrier oil such as sweet almond and letting the blend cure for two weeks creates a High John oil that can be used to dress candles, Talismans, and other objects for success and overcoming obstacles.

Honeysuckle

Scientific name: *Lonicera caprifolium*

Other name: woodbine

Element: Earth

Planets: Mars, Venus

Parts used: flower, essential oil

The use of honeysuckle in any herbal formula brings increase and energy. The flowers produce a heady, sweet scent that is sometimes used to seduce a lover. Honeysuckle can be used to gently protect—creating an energy space that deflects negativity.

Hops

Scientific name: *Humulus lupulus*

Other name: beer bud

Element: Air

Planet: Moon

Part used: flower

Medicinally, hops work as a sedative, calming and soothing. They work well in dream pillows when a prophetic dream is the goal, and they soothe the ill and ease them into a tranquil sleep.

Horehound

Scientific name: *Marrubium vulgare*

Other name: hoarhound

Element: Air

Planet: Mercury

Part used: leaf

Sacred to the Egyptian God Horus, the leaves of the horehound protect from chaos and aid the thinking processes for clarity and purpose. Before energy healing, the hands are washed in an Infusion of horehound and the body is bathed in an Incense containing horehound to clear the aura.

Horsetail

Scientific name: *Equisetum* spp.

Other names: shave grass, bottlebrush

Element: Earth

Planet: Saturn

Part used: leaf

An excellent herb for clearing the residual energy of sadness and grief, horsetail can be burned or scattered and then swept away, leaving a neutral atmosphere. Rubbed on the skin, horsetail removes emotional attachments. This clearing results in wisdom and understanding in a karmic situation.

Hydrangea

Scientific name: *Hydrangea arborescens*

Other names: seven barks, wild hydrangea

Element: Water

Planet: Moon

Parts used: root, flower

The use of this root disperses negative energy and dispels pain. An Infusion of hydrangea can be ingested, which enhances intuition. Hydrangea flowers planted outside the bedroom aid in lucid dreaming and increased sensuality.

Hyssop

Scientific name: *Hyssopus officinalis*

Other name: yssop

Element: Fire

Planet: Jupiter

Parts used: leaf, essential oil

Used extensively for purification and protection, hyssop can be utilized in all the herbal formulas that focus on clearing a person or a space of negativity. In the Old Testament, sprigs of hyssop were used to paint lamb's blood around the doorways of the Hebrew inhabitants of Egypt, causing the Angel of Death to pass by that home. Bouquets of hyssop were hung in the home during the Middle Ages to deflect the plague as well.

Irish moss

Scientific name: *Chondrus crispus*

Other names: carrageen, pearl moss

Element: Water

Planet: Moon

Part used: leaf

The dried leaf of this moss can be powdered and added to any mixture to attract prosperity and release energy that is causing poverty in the home. In folk Magick, Irish moss powder is placed under the rug in the entryway or front room on the evening of the New Moon to entice prosperity through the door. Pieces of the leaf can be added to Herbal Amulets and charged for attraction of prosperity as well.

Jasmin

Scientific name: *Jasminum offcinale*

Other name: jessamine

Element: Water

Planets: Moon, Venus

Parts used: flower, essential oil

Jasmin enjoys the rulerships of both the Moon, as a night-blooming, white or pale flower, and of Venus for its intoxicating scent. Used often for love and to bring peace and tranquility to the home or emotions, its flowers or oil can be a wonderful addition to all herbal formulas to bring these goals into manifestation. In addition, jasmin oil can be used to anoint the Third Eye when the practitioner is seeking to connect with mystical inspiration for art, music, dance, or poetry. Jasmin can also be utilized for dreamwork and astral projection.

Job's tears

Scientific name: *Coix lacryma*

Other name: tear grass

Element: Air

Planet: Jupiter

Part used: seed

Most often added to an Herbal Amulet for manifesting one's wishes or producing luck, some practitioners use three tears, some seven tears, in the Amulet. With each tear, a statement is made regarding the wish to be granted. In folk Magick traditions, a necklace of Job's tears is strung on red cord for health or on a blue cord for protection of children.

Juniper

Scientific name: *Juniperus communis*

Other names: gin berry, geneva

Element: Fire

Planet: Sun

Parts used: leaf, berry, resin, essential oil

An herb that attracts health, juniper can be used in Herbal Infusions, Incenses, Ritual Oils, baths, and more to bring vitality to an individual. The resin is not generally commercially available but is easy enough to procure by picking some of the juniper sprigs and gathering liquid resin from the bark. Burned to drive out spirits, juniper leaves behind a clean, woodsy scent.

Kava kava

Scientific name: *Piper methysticum*

Other names: ava, awa

Element: Water

Planets: Neptune, Saturn

Part used: root

Drinking a Philtre of kava kava root relaxes the conscious mind and allows psychic visions to occur. Used by the Hunas as a ritual sacrament, kava kava is drunk as an Infusion for communing with the Gods. Sometimes an ill person is instructed to chew on a piece of the root, which is then used by the practitioner in a rite of protection and restoration for the patient.

Knotgrass

Scientific name: *Agropyron repens*

Other names: witchgrass, couch grass, twitch grass

Element: Earth

Planet: Jupiter

Part used: leaf

Growing prolifically, knotgrass brings abundance and repels difficulties. Add to any herbal concoction to attract increase and disperse challenges.

Knotweed

Scientific name: *Polygonum aviculare*

Other names: lady's thumb, nine joints

Element: Earth

Planet: Saturn

Parts used: leaf, vine

Used in folk Magick to confound and entrap enemies, knotweed can be scattered in the perimeter surrounding a home or office to thwart thieves and negative energy. Knotweed is also burned in an Incense or added to an Herbal Amulet for releasing problems. If burning knotweed, visualize difficulties wafting away on the Incense smoke; if using in an Herbal Amulet, fill the Amulet with the energy of the problem and then toss it into a running stream or bury it at a crossroads.

Lady's mantle

Scientific name: *Alchemilla vulgaris*

Other name: stellaria

Element: Water

Planet: Venus

Parts used: leaf, root

Lady's mantle is associated with Goddess energy, including that of the Virgin Mary. Dew collected from the leaves of this herb at sunrise and applied to the face brings beauty. As you may have extrapolated from its Latin genus name, *Alchemilla,* lady's mantle also has been used extensively in Herbal Alchemy over time. Added to any alchemical mixture, lady's mantle adds potency and power to any formula. Drinking an Infusion of lady's mantle imparts emotional focus.

Lavender

Scientific name: *Lavandula officinalis*

Other names: elf leaf, naid

Element: Water

Planet: Mercury

Parts used: flower, essential oil

Lavender is almost an all-purpose herb, and its energies lend focus to herbal mixtures for love, protection, peace, and purification. Dip fresh sprigs of lavender flowers in water and sprinkle them throughout a space to bring protection and purifying energy. Next, dry the flowers to be used later in a Home Blessing Incense or simply display them above the front door to cleanse and bless all who enter. One of the herbs added to love sachets during the Renaissance, lavender brings stability to a romantic union and increases fidelity.

Lemon

Scientific name: *Citrus limon*

Element: Water

Planet: Moon

Parts used: juice, peel, essential oil

Very useful in cleansings and dispelling poltergeist phenomena, lemon helps to break up and absorb etheric energy. For protection during sleep, place a few lemon slices and sea salt in a bowl and keep by the bed. If a room in a house seems "unhealthy," a bowl of sea salt and lemon slices will absorb any negative energy. After three days, dispose of the salt and lemon by either burying it away from the house or tossing them in a running stream. The walls and floors of a home or office can be washed down with a solution of lemon juice and water to rinse away draining vibrations, and lemon juice can be added to a Purification Bath to cleanse the aura.

Lemon balm

Scientific name: *Melissa officinalis*

Other names: melissa, bee balm

Element: Water

Planet: Moon

Parts used: leaf, essential oil

Added to an Incense blend, Ritual Oil, bath, or any other herbal formula, lemon balm attracts love, success, or healing according to the focus of the practitioner. Fresh smelling and tasting, lemon balm lightens the thoughts and the heart.

Lemon verbena

Scientific name: *Lippia citriodora*

Other names: cedron, verbena

Element: Air

Planet: Mercury

Parts used: leaf, essential oil

Long used to end disputes and protect from strife, lemon verbena purifies and opens the Heart Chakra. Useful in a Dream Amulet to protect from nightmares, it brings peace and tranquility. To clear away old patterns and energy, write a keyword on parchment paper describing the pattern and burn it in an Incense containing this herb.

Lemongrass

Scientific name: *Cymbopogon citratus*

Other name: sweet root

Element: Air

Planet: Mercury

Parts used: leaf, essential oil

Lemongrass is a powerful addition to any formula intended to purify, clear energy or thoughts, and discover the truth. Burned, carried, anointed, or ingested, it can be safely used in any herbal mixture. Associated with both Air and Mercury, lemongrass aids with the memory and can be used for study and accessing creativity.

Licorice

Scientific name: *Glycyrrhiza glabra*

Other names: sweetwood, licourace, omolilo

Element: Water

Planet: Mercury

Parts used: leaf, root

Used medicinally for sore throats and hoarseness, licorice root's energy also lends eloquence and humor in speech. Perfect for the actor or teacher, chewing a bit of root brings inspired thoughts and the ability to influence others with words.

Lobelia

Scientific name: *Lobelia inflata*

Other names: asthma weed, Indian tobacco

Element: Water

Planets: Saturn, Neptune

Part used: leaf

Ingested in a Philtre, Elixir, or Condenser, lobelia brings energy of protection, health, and prophetic visions. Burn the leaves and watch for omens in the resulting smoke. Used in storm Magick, both to draw a storm or to deflect one, tradition directs the practitioner to toss the lobelia leaves in the direction in which the storm is brewing.

Lotus

Scientific name: *Nymphaea lotus*

Element: Water

Planets: Moon, Neptune

Parts used: flower, pod, root, essential oil

Prominent in Egyptian religion and Magick, lotus used in Ritual Incense, oil, and Infusions promotes spiritual awakening, peace, and true dreaming. Placed in an Herbal Amulet, lotus attracts the favor of the Gods. The oil of lotus flowers added to a bath aids in psychic development, astral projection, and cleansing of the aura.

Lovage

Scientific name: *Levisticum officinale*

Other names: loveroot, sea parsley

Element: Fire

Planet: Venus

Part used: root

Long added to baths to attract love and romance, lovage also brings peace and love. With a subtle floral scent, the root is an effective addition to Herbal Amulets to attract love, and it can be steeped in wine to be served to a prospective lover.

Magnolia

Scientific name: *Magnolia grandiflora*

Other name: swamp sassafras

Element: Earth

Planet: Jupiter

Parts used: bud, flower, leaf

Placing magnolia flowers near the nuptial bed ensures fidelity, and when added to the bath, they attract honor and recognition. With its rulerships by the Element Earth and the Planet Jupiter, the energies of this dramatic and beautiful tree promote financial increase. After the flower petals have dried and fallen away, the resulting seed cone makes a wonderful aspergil for sprinkling ceremonial waters.

Maidenhair

Scientific name: *Adiantum capillus*

Other names: maidenhair fern, capillaire

Element: Water

Planet: Venus

Part used: leaf

Historically used to attract romance, beauty, and joy, the fronds of the maidenhair fern are stirred through the bath to charge it with erotic energy. Placed under or over the bed, the herb promotes sexual energy.

Mandrake

Scientific name: *Atropa mandragora*

Other names: mandragore, mannikin

Element: Earth

Planets: Mercury, Uranus

Part used: root

(poisonous)

The lore of the mandrake is truly legion. Used for binding, strengthening, protection, and power, this root is quite versatile and has been used for millennia. Pulled fresh from the ground, the mandrake root can be carved into a figure and used in healing and love Magicks to represent a person. The dried root is traditionally placed near the door or in the bedroom to protect the inhabitants. A binding can be performed by wrapping the root with a small piece of parchment on which the name of the person who is causing harm is written and then burying them together. As the parchment decays and dissolves, so does the power of the individual to do harm. Although it is referred to in Genesis as an herb of fertility, this root should *never* be ingested, nor any other part of the plant, as it is very poisonous.

Marjoram

Scientific name: *Origanum vulgare*

Other names: wintersweet, marjolaine, sweet marjoram

Element: Water

Planets: Venus, Mars

Parts used: leaf, essential oil

Perfect as an addition to any herbal love combination, marjoram is sacred to the Goddess Aphrodite. An herb that blends the potent energies of Venus and Mars, marjoram brings strength to the union of marriage. Burned as an offertory, it promotes spiritual bliss and connection to the Divine. As a symbol of familial love, marjoram sprinkled around the perimeter of the home or grown by the front door protects the inhabitants.

Meadowsweet

Scientific name: *Spiraea ulmaria*

Other names: queen of the meadow, joe-pye weed

Element: Water

Planet: Mercury

Parts used: leaf, root

A traditional herb of the summer solstice, meadowsweet brings happiness and increase to the home. Fresh meadowsweet can be cut and placed at the hearth to attract calm, happy energy or burned in the home to disperse negative tension. A sacred plant to the Druids, meadowsweet, fresh or dried, was used as a strewing herb for its pleasant smell and calming energy. Its common name, meadowsweet, comes from the Anglo-Saxon word *medu* (mead), because it was used to flavor this drink made from fermented honey.

Mistletoe

Scientific name: *Viscum album*

Other names: golden bough, holy wood, wood of the cross

Element: Fire

Planets: Sun, Jupiter

Parts used: leaf, berry

(poisonous)

Another plant sacred to the Druid priesthood, mistletoe provides protection when placed near a cradle or hung near the front door. The berries added to an Herbal Amulet attract love and increase the chances of fertility, which is why we have the tradition of kissing under the mistletoe. While the leaves are not poisonous, the berries most certainly are and should never be consumed or added to any herbal combination that might be ingested. Mistletoe will grow on any deciduous tree but that which grows on oak is particularly powerful.

Moss, oak

Scientific name: *Evernia prunastri*

Element: Earth

Planet: Saturn

Parts used: leaf, essential oil

Just inhaling the earthy fragrance of this plant is grounding and peaceful. Used in an Incense or Ritual Oil, this herb attracts stable increase and brings a tranquil focus to any working. Perfect for honoring the sprites in your garden, place some oak moss there to encourage plant growth. Strengthening and enduring, the energies of oak moss lend power and stamina to any herbal formula.

Moss, Spanish

Scientific name: *Tillandsia usneoides*

Element: Earth

Planet: Saturn

Part used: leaf

Traditionally used in folk Magick to stuff gris-gris or poppets (voodoo dolls for healing or other forms of Magick), Spanish moss can also be used to thwart and bind any ill intention. Placed in the wallet or purse, Spanish moss helps to retain prosperity for the carrier.

Motherwort

Scientific name: *Leonurus cardiaca*

Other names: lion's-tail, throwwort

Element: Fire

Planet: Venus

Part used: leaf

Protective of the home and lending extra power and strength to women, motherwort also brings the motivation and the energy to complete tasks and take advantage of opportunities.

Mugwort

Scientific name: *Artemisia vulgaris*

Other names: artemisia, Saint-John's-plant

Element: Water

Planets: Moon, Neptune

Parts used: leaf, essential oil

One of the traditional ingredients in a dream pillow, mugwort promotes psychic energy and lucid dreaming. Used to aid astral travel, it helps the practitioner to leave the body in its etheric form and return to it safely. Added to a Divination Incense, oil, or Philtre, mugwort is a powerful ally in getting and interpreting psychic information. An Infusion of mugwort is perfect for cleansing and charging crystal balls, speculums, pendulums, and other divining tools.

Mullein

Scientific name: *Verbascum thapus*

Other names: Aaron's rod, velvetback

Element: Earth

Planets: Saturn, Mars

Parts used: leaf, flower

Lending the energies of courage, health, protection, and love, mullein can be one of the powerful ingredients in an Herbal Amulet to protect from nightmares and visitations by entities during sleep or kept in the car for safety while traveling. It can be hung over doors to keep any negativity from entering. An Incense composed of mullein and dittany of Crete can be used to give manifestation to the spirits of loved ones at Samhain.

Myrrh

Scientific name: *Commiphora myrrha*

Other name: mirra

Element: Water

Planets: Saturn, Pluto

Parts used: resin, essential oil

Burned with frankincense resin to raise the vibration of temple or home, myrrh protects and brings sanctity and connection to spirit. Used in many ancient Egyptian rites, myrrh was used as an offertory to the Gods and as one of the ingredients in the mummification process. Myrrh resin is sacred to the Goddess Hecate, and burning it during meditations on death and transformation brings deep wisdom.

Myrtle

Scientific name: *Myrtus communis*

Element: Water

Planet: Venus

Parts used: leaf, essential oil

Roman women traditionally wore wreaths of myrtle, an herb long associated with the home and with marriage, to honor the Goddess and to attract a marriage partner. Drinking an Infusion of myrtle leaves or adding them to the bath draws romantic love and youthful beauty.

Nettle

Scientific name: *Urtica dioica*

Other names: stinging nettle, sting weed

Element: Fire

Planet: Mars

Part used: leaf

Utilized extensively for protection and to confound enemies, nettle is a good addition to a Cleansing Bath to remove any negativity from the aura. It also can be placed in an Herbal Amulet to be kept in a sickroom to help the patient recover. The energies of nettle are hot and tend to burn away vibrations that are draining to the vitality of a place or person.

Nutmeg

Scientific name: *Myristica fragrans*

Other name: mace

Element: Air

Planets: Jupiter, Uranus

Parts used: nut, essential oil

The transformative energy of nutmeg attracts positive change, promotes health, and can aid Vision Quests. Included in any herbal formula, nutmeg attracts quick and sometimes quirky changes. An opportunity that you may not have considered before can open up before you. An Infusion that utilizes nutmeg can be consumed or washed over the body to "reset" the electromagnetic nervous system, resulting in a quicker and more creative thought process. In folk Magick, a whole nutmeg can be charged by wrapping it with a dollar bill or simply carried in an Herbal Amulet to draw luck and prosperity.

Orange

Scientific name: *Citrus sinensis*

Element: Air

Planet: Sun

Parts used: peel, juice, essential oil

Bringing confidence, a feeling of well-being, and happiness, the easy-to-obtain orange fruit is truly a wonderful Sun herb. The dried peel can be added to Incense or an Herbal Amulet to bolster strong, positive energy; the juice can be charged with the focus of vitality and health and then consumed; and the essential oil can be added to all herbal concoctions to add the energy and vitality of the Sun.

Orris

Scientific name: *Iris pseudocorus*

Other name: Queen Elizabeth root

Element: Water

Planets: Venus, Moon

Parts used: root, essential oil

This root of the iris flower has long been used in rites of love, beauty, and divination to know the thoughts of the dead. Used extensively in France and Italy in perfumery and love formulas, its oil works well as a fixative in any oil blend to make the scent longer lasting. The iris was also prized by the Egyptians, the image of the flower being carved into some of the temple walls at Karnak. Powdered orris root can be added to herb formulations focusing on romance as well as sprinkled on clothing to attract a partner. The oil adds the Divine feminine energies of the Moon and Venus. Sacred to Iris, the Goddess of the Elysian fields, for whom the plant was named, the root or its derivatives can be used to soothe the souls of those who have passed on.

Passionflower

Scientific name: *Passiflora incarnata*

Other name: passion vine

Element: Water

Planets: Venus, Neptune

Parts used: leaf, flower, vine

Associated with the energies of the Christ, passionflower brings peace, friendship, and familial love. The word *passion* in its name denotes the passion of the Christ, the union of Heaven and Earth in a balanced whole. As an ingredient in Incense, Herbal Amulet, Philtre, or bath, passionflower attracts tranquility and blesses the home.

Patchouli

Scientific name: *Pogostemon cablin*

Other names: pucha-pot, pacouli

Element: Earth

Planets: Mars, Saturn

Parts used: leaf, essential oil

Perfect for promoting lust, patchouli is an ingredient in any herbal formula for romance and sexual intrigue. Its earthy scent also grounds and protects, creating an energy barrier to negativity and ill will. Along with its association with Earth energies and those of Saturn, patchouli attracts the acquisition of property and money for a stable financial foundation.

Pennyroyal

Scientific name: *Mentha pulegium*

Other names: mosquito plant, squaw mint

Element: Air

Planets: Venus, Mars

Parts used: leaf, essential oil

Clearing and strengthening, pennyroyal was used in the Eleusinian mysteries of the Greeks to prepare the initiate for communing clearly with the Divine. Associated with the powers of death and rebirth, which is the focus of initiation, pennyroyal has also been used medicinally to induce miscarriage. It contains a large amount of the chemical pulegone, which causes the uterus to shed its lining, bringing on menstruation. Neither the herb nor the essential oil should be handled by a pregnant woman.

Peppermint

Scientific name: *Mentha piperita*

Other name: lammint

Element: Fire

Planet: Mercury

Parts used: leaf, essential oil

The energies of peppermint renew and refresh. Useful in unblocking stagnant, negative patterns of thought, behavior, and vibration, peppermint clears the old to make way for new vibrations that attract money and health. Used in a dream pillow, peppermint leaves one refreshed and can aid in obtaining useful information in one's dreams.

Pine

Scientific name: *Pinus* spp.

Element: Air

Planet: Jupiter

Parts used: needle, resin, essential oil

The clean scent of pine is uplifting and inspiring. Its needles can be used in an Incense, bath herb combination, or as a strewing herb to purify a space or the human aura. The custom of bringing cut pine branches into the home during the winter holiday season is one that promotes clearing the home of negativity and illness during the winter months.

Plantain

Scientific name: *Plantago major*

Other names: Patrick's dock, snakeweed

Element: Earth

Planet: Jupiter

Parts used: leaf, root

Tying together plantain leaves and hanging them by the door is a traditional method to invite calm, guard against thieves, and soothe the energy residue from an argument. It can be an effective ingredient in herbal formulas focused on healing of the body, mind, or heart.

Poppy

Scientific name: *Papaver somniferum*

Other name: khaskhas

Element: Water

Planets: Moon, Neptune

Parts used: seed, flower, essential oil

Associated with fertility due to its proliferation of seeds, poppy can also be used with good results to encourage prophetic dreams and develop the intuition. As a symbol of sleep and death, poppies were lovely offerings by the Greeks to lost loved ones, and the opium obtained from the poppy plant leads to a hallucinatory experience of the Underworld.

Queen of the meadow

Scientific name: *Spiraea ulmaria*

Other names: meadowsweet, joe-pye weed

Element: Water

Planet: Mercury

Parts used: leaf, root

See *Meadowsweet.*

Raspberry

Scientific name: *Rubus idaeus*

Other name: red raspberry

Element: Water

Planets: Venus, Moon

Parts used: berry, leaf

As with all plants producing an impressive amount of seeds, raspberry is associated with fertility and, used medicinally, helps to stabilize and strengthen the female reproduction system. When grown around the house, this thorny bush serves as a protector, and the branches can be brought inside and hung at the doors, windows, and hearth to keep out intruders, both in physical and spirit form. Steeping the berries in wine and serving them to a lover strengthens the relationship. It is also helpful in protecting pregnant women from miscarriage when used in a bath, Infusion, or Herbal Amulet worn by the expectant mother.

Red clover

Scientific name: *Trifolium pratense*

Other names: shamrock, trefoil

Element: Air

Planet: Mercury

Parts used: leaf, flower

The Celts traditionally burned clover and censed their herds with the smoke to cleanse and purify the animals, ward against sickness, and aid in fertility. Clover has always been associated with luck and the faery folk. Planted near gardens, it attracts the blessings of the plant Devas (spirits) to promote growth and repel pests. Three-leaf clovers are sacred to the Triple Goddess Maiden, Mother, Crone, and protect the wearer. The leaves on a four-leaf clover represent faith, love, hope, and luck. If you find one, make a wish and then place the four-leaf clover between the pages of a closed book. When the wish comes true, return the clover to the faeries by burying it in a natural mound for additional luck.

Rose hips

Scientific name: *Rosa canina*

Element: Earth

Planets: Venus, Jupiter

Part used: hip

Rose hips are the fruit of the wild rose—the seed pod left after the petals have dried and blown away. They can be used effectively in Love Rituals: add them to the bath, drink them in an Infusion with honey, include them in an Herbal Love Amulet, or pierce fresh rose hips with a needle and string them on pink or red silk cord into a necklace. Rose hips contain Jupiter vibration and so can be used to attract wealth: charge the rose hips with energy and add them to an Herbal Amulet that you keep in your cash drawer, purse, or wallet.

Rose

Scientific name: *Rosa* spp.

Element: Water

Planet: Venus

Parts used: flower, leaf, essential oil

In every culture, the rose is linked to love and beauty and was the first plant cultivated purely for its beauty and scent. Sacred to the Goddess Venus, the lore has it that the rose was formed from the tears of the Goddess as She wept over her dying lover, Adonis, the blood mingling with the tears. Different colors of rose signify the essence of the love expressed: red or pink signify romantic love; yellow, familial love; and white, sorrowful love at death. Incenses or oil blends made with rose attract love and affection, and a bath filled with rose petals is perfect prior to seduction.

Rosemary

Scientific name: *Rosemarinus officinalis*

Other name: elf leaf

Element: Air

Planet: Sun

Parts used: leaf, essential oil

The reviving scent of rosemary stimulates the memory and thought processes. Its scent when burned or added to any herbal preparation adds an energy of protection and purification to a space. The oil applied directly to rashes and skin blemishes clears the area, and when inhaled, its aroma aids the memory and brain functions. Sprinkling rosemary leaves over a grave brings comfort to the dead and memories for the ones left behind. Rosemary placed in the bath before bedtime wards away nightmares, and when carried in an Herbal Amulet, it gives confidence and courage.

Rowan

Scientific name: *Pyrus aucuparia*

Other names: mountain ash, Thor's aid

Element: Fire

Planet: Sun

Parts used: berry, leaf, bark

Used for centuries for protection, rowan wards off lightning and creates a barrier to negative energy. A small forked rowan branch is excellent for dowsing, and the berries are used in potions to invoke psychic and creative visions. Plant a rowan tree at the front door or by the front gate to prevent the entrance of enemies or trouble.

Rue

Scientific name: *Ruta graveolens*

Other names: ruta, herb of grace

Element: Air

Planets: Sun, Mars

Parts used: leaf, essential oil

Fortifying and strengthening, rue has long been used for health, purification, protection, and mental focus. One of the herbs used to banish the energies of negative spirits, it can also be used to thwart shapeshifters. Rue is excellent in clearing energy from objects: cover the object with rue and let it sit for three days. During this time, any imbalanced energy is absorbed by the rue and the object is spiritually cleansed. Burn the leftover rue afterward. Rue was used commonly in Europe as a strewing herb to prevent plague, and sprigs of the plant were used to sprinkle the holy water at High Mass. It is said that Leonardo da Vinci regularly ate fresh rue to inspire his creativity and focus. This herb should not be used by pregnant women.

Safflower

Scientific name: *Carthamus tinctorius*

Other names: fire petal, dyer's safflower

Element: Fire

Planets: Sun, Mars

Parts used: flowers, oil

Often effectively substituted for the much more costly saffron, safflower can be used to dye material a lovely red-orange. Its profuse plumage of red, sharp flower petals remind one of thistles, and they can be used in Incenses and Amulets for prosperity. The leaves of safflower end in small, sharp needles, so its utilization in protection formulas is indicated as well. When creating a Solar or Mars oil, using safflower oil as a carrier base adds those energies in abundance.

Sage, Clary

Scientific name: *Salvia officinalis*

Other name: garden sage

Element: Air/Earth

Planet: Jupiter

Parts used: leaf, essential oil

Clary sage has been used extensively in Europe for purification and Home Blessing; in Incenses, Herbal Amulets, and bath herb formulas; burned as a simple; and added to Anointing Oils. Its deep scent is grounding and shielding, and some sage leaf (fresh or dried) is very useful in calming the emotions and clearing the senses. Burning sage or inhaling the scent of the essential oil is very helpful when making difficult decisions, as its energies lend themselves to practical thought patterns and truth.

Sage, white

Scientific name: *Salvia apiana*

Other name: medicine brush

Element: Air/Earth

Planet: Jupiter

Parts used: leaf, essential oil

Like its European cousin, clary sage, white sage is used for blessing and energy cleansing. When its fresh leaves and stems are tied tightly in a wand shape and left to dry, it is often used as a "smudge" to burn and purify the area. If you want to make your own smudge, gather three or four six- to eight-inch stems and place them together. Beginning at the bottom where the majority of the woody stem is present, twist the leaves around each other gently but tightly. With red or white cotton string, wrap the woody end thoroughly and then continue wrapping the string with about an inch between each strand around the remainder of the smudge. Let it dry completely—this will take two weeks. When you wish to cleanse a place of imbalanced or negative energy, light the top and let it flame for about ten seconds. Blow the flame out gently and allow the smudge stick to smolder. It will continue to burn very slowly and will tend to drop ashes, so you will want to hold something under it (like the traditional abalone shell) to collect the smoldering ash. Cleanse the space with the sage smoke, and when you're finished, tamp it out lightly as you would a cigar. You can relight the end when you next wish to cleanse a space or an object.

Saint-John's-wort

Scientific name: *Hypericum perforatum*

Other names: goatweed, tipton weed

Element: Fire

Planet: Sun

Parts used: leaf, flower, oil extract

Perfect for dispersing ghosts and spirits, Saint-John's-wort's ancient name, *fuga daemonum* ("scare demon"), attests to its use in dispelling the negative energies of vampiric spirits. Traditionally gathered around the time of the summer solstice (Saint John's Day is June 24), it can be tossed into the hearth to purify and protect the home. Hung over the door, burned, or strewn, Saint-John's-wort was also used to purify pastoral animal herds to ward off illness. Among its historical uses, this efficacious herb was also given as a tea to calm the mentally ill. Of course, in our modern times, it is used in capsules and as a tea to treat depression and mental illness. To make your own Saint-John's-wort oil extract, place the fresh flowers and leaves in a wide-mouthed jar and cover with extra-virgin olive oil. Close the jar and tighten the lid. Place the jar in a sunny window for six weeks, shaking it a couple of times a day. You will know the oil is being extracted as it turns red. After the extraction period, strain the oil through a cloth or wire colander—actually the foot from some clean panty hose works very well for this!—and decant into a dark blue or amber bottle. Kept in a cool, dry area, this extracted oil will keep for up to two years. This extracted oil can be used in the formulation of any of your alchemical herbal recipes, added to the bath or anointed on a candle.

Sandalwood, red

Scientific name: *Santalum rubrum*

Other names: red santal, red saunders, santalinus

Element: Fire

Planets: Mars, Venus

Part used: wood

Lightly scented, unlike its brother white sandalwood, the energy and color of red sandalwood brings courage, protection, and sexual arousal, hence its affiliation with both Mars and Venus. Burned in an Incense, carried in an Herbal Amulet, or added to the bath, red sandalwood fortifies the strength of one's convictions and gives driving purpose and focus. A writing ink perfect for drawing Talismans and inscribing one's wishes on parchment can be made by bringing water to a boil and then pouring the hot water in a small jar filled with red sandalwood chips. Let the chips rest in the jar and, every few days, lightly masticate them with a small pestle, dispersing the color into the water. After about a month's time you will have your Magickal ink!

Sandalwood, white

Scientific name: *Santalum album*

Other names: white saunders, sandal

Element: Water

Planets: Moon, Mercury

Parts used: wood, essential oil

There may be nothing more uplifting than the scent of white sandal-wood—it inspires spiritual connection and positive energy and is a universal herb for cleansing the temple, home, or human aura. Sandalwood raises any herbal formula to a higher vibration. An herb of calming wisdom, it is perfect for meditation and in rites focused on gaining higher wisdom.

Sassafras

Scientific name: *Sassafras officinale*

Element: Fire

Planet: Jupiter

Parts used: root, leaf, essential oil

The base of the flavoring for root beer, the root of the sassafras tree is grounding and promotes happiness in the home. Its energy attracts prosperity and it can be added to any herbal formula to enhance and enlarge its focused results. According to folklore, the leaves or root bits carried in the wallet or purse ensure that there is always a supply of money there.

Saw palmetto

Scientific name: *Serenoa repens*

Other name: sabal

Element: Fire

Planet: Mars

Part used: berry

Used medicinally as a tonic for the prostate gland in men, saw palmetto is associated with sexuality, lust, and romance. Added to Incense or an Herbal Amulet, the formula can attract a romantic partner. Inscribe the name of the beloved on a whole saw palmetto berry and place it under her pillow to induce romantic dreams of you. Saw palmetto can be added to an aphrodisiac Infusion for a romantic evening—I would suggest mead or a heavy red wine, as saw palmetto has a distinctive taste that is not for everyone.

Skullcap

Scientific name: *Scutellaria galericulata*

Other names: hoodwort, madweed

Element: Water

Planet: Saturn

Part used: leaf

Encouraging enduring love and fidelity, skullcap is a natural for herbal preparations focusing on marriage and unions. Placed in the bridal bed, it brings understanding, commitment, and peace to the relationship. Consumed or sprinkled as a Philtre, Elixir, or Condenser, skullcap works to bring opposites into balance and is thus useful in helping to solve problems in a partnership or marriage.

Slippery elm

Scientific name: *Ulmus fulva*

Other name: moose elm

Element: Air

Planet: Saturn

Part used: bark

Slippery elm is used in folk Magick to protect from gossip. Sprinkle the powdered bark on the front doorstep or in the office to stop slander and lies. A wash can be made by infusing the bark in spring water to release entities or energy "hooks" from the aura.

Snakeroot

Scientific name: *Sanicula marilandica*

Other name: black snakeroot

Element: Fire

Planet: Mercury

Part used: root

Worn or carried, snakeroot is utilized by hoodoo practitioners to attract luck, money, or love. As an ingredient in an Herbal Amulet or added to the bath, the energy of this plant expands opportunities in any of those three areas when charged with intention.

Solomon's seal

Scientific name: *Polygonatum multiflorum*

Other names: lady's seal, sealwort

Element: Earth

Planet: Saturn

Part used: root

Used extensively for protection, healing, and the attainment of wisdom, the root of this plant received its name from the "characters" that appear when the root is cut transversely or when the stems dry and fall from the main rootstock, and which somewhat resemble Hebrew characters. Legend has it that Solomon, "who knew the diversities of plants and the virtues of roots," set his seal upon the roots in testimony of its medicinal and Magickal values. Binding the spirit world to the physical world, Solomon's seal helps to physically manifest the energy and dreams of the practitioner. Small pieces of the root placed on the windowsill, by the door, and by the hearth bind negativity if it tries to enter.

Spearmint

Scientific name: *Mentha spicata*

Other names: garden mint, mint

Element: Water

Planets: Venus, Mercury

Parts used: leaf, essential oil

Refreshing and cleansing, spearmint attracts happiness, peace, and mental alertness. Added to any herbal formula, it brings an uplifting feeling to the atmosphere and to mental attitude. Consumed in a Potion or added to the bath, it draws clean, positive vibrations to a space or person.

Spikenard

Scientific name: *Inula conyza*

Other name: nard

Element: Air

Planets: Mercury, Uranus

Parts used: root, essential oil

Noted in the Song of Solomon—"Spikenard and saffron, calamus and cinnamon, with all the trees of Lebanon; myrrh and aloes with all the chief ointment"—spikenard is associated with wisdom, honor, and learning. It was an ointment of spikenard with which the Magdalene anointed the feet of the Christ, and spikenard was one of the most precious scents in the ancient Semitic world. Spikenard as an ingredient in an Incense or other herbal formula enhances the workings of the mind and allows for the understanding of diverse and complex philosophical works.

Squill

Scientific name: *Urginea scilla*

Other names: sea onion, white squill

Element: Water

Planet: Mars

Part used: root

Growing near the rocky shores of the Celtic Isles, squill has been used for centuries to attract money, provide protection from phantasms, and to turn back the negative energies of a hex. Hanging a squill root or an Herbal Amulet containing squill near the front door reverses misfortune and brings renewal and positive change.

Star Anise

Scientific name: *Illicium verum*

Element: Water

Planets: Moon, Neptune

Parts used: seed, pod, essential oil

The small brown seeds obtained from the star-shaped pod can be brewed into a delicious tea to promote astral projection and psychic ability. You can make a pendulum for dowsing or divination from a whole star anise pod that is perfectly formed with uniform pods. Carefully prick a small hole through the end of one of the pods, pull a twelve-inch strand of silk thread through the hole, and suspend. Add star anise seeds or the whole pod to the bath, Incense, or Herbal Amulets for purification and renewal.

Sweetgrass

Scientific name: *Hierochloe odorata*

Other name: blessing grass

Element: Air

Planet: Sun

Parts used: leaf, essential oil

With a slightly spicy, sweet scent, sweetgrass is used in rites of purification and blessing. Often strands of this long grass are braided together when first harvested and then dried to be burned like the white sage smudge stick. Chant your intention and let it rise on the wafting smoke to receive the blessing of the Earth spirits.

Sunflower

Scientific name: *Helianthus annuus*

Other names: Aztec flower, corona

Element: Fire

Planet: Sun

Parts used: flower, seed, oil extract

Following the path of the Sun, facing East at dawn and West by sunset, the sunflower is true to its name. Sacred to the Aztecs and in Peru, this plant brings life, vitality, and wishes to those who employ its energy. Adding the petals to the bath brings health and happiness, and anointing with sunflower oil sanctifies and draws strength. Folklore has it that charging the seeds with the intention of fertility and consuming them can help with becoming pregnant.

Tansy

Scientific name: *Tanacetum vulgare*

Other name: buttonweed

Element: Water

Planet: Venus

Parts used: flower, leaf, essential oil

Tansy's connection with the Goddess makes it a perfect herb to bless young girls at first menses and to gift to a woman at her Croning. Buried with the deceased, tansy grants a new life and rebirth. In Roman lore, Zues gave Ganymede tansy to grant him immortality, thus it also has an association with longevity. Consumption in an Herbal Infusion is not recommended as the leaves can be toxic.

Thyme

Scientific name: *Thymus vulgaris*

Other name: serpyllum

Element: Air

Planet: Mercury

Parts used: leaf, essential oil

Long utilized in the energy cleansing and clearing of temples in Greece, thyme can be burned or strewn to disperse stagnant vibrations and invite the new. Attractive to the faery folk, thyme can be grown in the garden to entice their plant blessings, and a little thyme under the tongue allows one to see them more clearly. An herb that helps connect with psychic consciousness, thyme in a divination formula aids the mind in understanding and deciphering psychic visions and impressions.

Tonka

Scientific name: *Coumarouna odorata*

Other names: coumara nut, tonqua, love wish bean

Element: Earth

Planets: Venus, Jupiter

Part used: bean

Smelling like spicy vanilla, tonka beans are used in Herbal Amulets and added to the bath to attract love. Three beans placed in a money lockbox or cash drawer encourage prosperity, and small slivers of the bean added to Incense bring courage and the fulfillment of wishes. It is not used in any potion that will be ingested, as it is slightly toxic.

Uva-ursi

Scientific name: *Arctostaphylos uva-ursi*

Other names: bearberry, kinnikinnick

Element: Water

Planets: Moon, Venus

Parts used: berry, leaf

The leaves of this low-growing plant have been added to sacred smoking mixtures by many Native American tribes, as uva-ursi brings dreams and visions of a prophetic nature. The berries can be charged with Magickal intention and eaten to encourage fertility.

Valerian

Scientific name: *Valeriana officinalis*

Other names: allheal, bloody butcher

Element: Water

Planet: Saturn

Parts used: root, essential oil

The original natural basis for the synthetic sedative Valium, valerian promotes dreamless sleep and calmness. In times when it is thought that mischievous spirits are present, the root or oil has been used extensively in rites of protection and purification to calm the situation. This herb can be added to Incense, ceremonial oil blends, herbal sachets, and in various Philtres and Condensers to bring and release negative emotions.

Vervain

Scientific name: *Verbena hastata*

Other names: blue vervain, holy herb

Element: Earth

Planets: Venus, Jupiter

Parts used: leaf, essential oil

Extremely versatile in its usage, vervain's energy traditionally has been used for purification, love, protection, chastity, healing, and as an offertory to the God Jupiter and to the Goddess Venus. It can be an ingredient in any herbal preparation, as it enhances and helps to focus the whole. Sacred to the Druids, vervain was used as an aid to obtain visions and commune with Earth spirits. The Welsh called it *llysiaur hudol,* "enchanting herb." Vervain is an excellent herb for artists; its use before any creative attempt or performances ensures success.

Vetivert

Scientific name: *Vetiveria zizanioides*

Other names: khuskhus, vetiver

Element: Earth

Planet: Saturn

Parts used: root, essential oil

When the root is burned or one is anointed with the oil, vetivert provides grounding, shielding, and protection. Often added to Herbal Amulets for love, it enhances affection and calms quarrels. Also used to discourage theft, the powdered or cut root is scattered outside of the openings to a home or business, and a small sprinkling of vetivert in a cash drawer keeps away thieves. Vetivert also works to keep prosperity flowing toward a business.

White oak

Scientific name: *Quercus alba*

Other names: duir, king oak

Element: Air

Planet: Jupiter

Parts used: seed, bark

Stately and authoritative, the oak has always been a symbol of strength and courage, and it was sacred to the Druids and Romans. Its bark can be burned as an offertory to the Gods, and its fallen small branches, when retrieved and prepared, are perfect for Magick Wands. White oak bark can be an addition to the bath or in an Herbal Infusion to promote strength and resolve. The seed of the oak is the acorn, which is versatile in its use: carve a wish into the acorn and plant the seed; string three or five acorns on red thread and wear them about the neck as you meditate to comprehend your destiny; or draw or carve a different runic or Magickal symbol on a grouping of acorns and use them in divination.

Willow

Scientific name: *Salix alba*

Other names: osier, pussy willow, white willow

Element: Water

Planet: Moon

Parts used: bark, wood, leaf, bud

Wonderful for dowsing and for Magick wands, willow is a plant of intuition, luck, and protection. The bark added to Incense and other herbal formulas brings visions. Use an Infusion made with willow bark to cleanse and charge a crystal ball or scrying mirror, or drink it before settling down in bed to obtain information through dreams. Traditional in Celtic funerary rites, willow is planted near graves to soothe the souls, and it is sacred to Hecate.

Wintergreen

Scientific name: *Gaultheria procumbens*

Other names: patridgeberry, teaberry

Element: Water

Planet: Sun

Parts used: leaf, essential oil

When strewn in the home or business, wintergreen attracts luck and protects. As an ingredient in any formula focused on healing, it brings soothing energy and gentle vitality. An evergreen, this herb is associated with renewal and endurance. The essential oil can be caustic, so add only a few drops to an oil formula.

Witchgrass

Scientific name: *Agropyron repens*

Other names: dog grass, couch grass, twitch grass, knotgrass

Element: Earth

Planet: Jupiter

Part used: Leaf

Added to any herbal concoction, witchgrass brings happiness and luck. Sprinkle the dry herb or an Herbal Infusion of witchgrass about the home to unhex and send any negative energy back to the originator. An Infusion of this herb can also be consumed to dispel depression and bring a more positive outlook. Placed under the pillow of the beloved, witchgrass brings new love and closeness to a relationship.

Witch hazel

Scientific name: *Hamamelis virginiana*

Other names: spotted alder, winterbloom

Element: Fire

Planets: Sun, Saturn

Part used: leaf

Dowsing rods made with witch hazel branches are very effective in divining and water witching, as the thin branches literally bend when they encounter an underground source of water, lost items, or hidden treasures. It can be used in workings to guard against evil influences and to heal broken hearts. This herb provides purification of a space or the aura when burned in an Incense or used in the bath, and a Philtre can be created to wash the body to loosen and release any psychic "hooks" that are embedded in a person or object's energy field.

Wolfsbane

Scientific name: *Arnica montana*

Other names: arnica, leopard's-bane

Element: Fire

Planet: Mars

Parts used: leaf, flower

(poison)

Although another plant, *Aconitum napellus,* is also called wolfsbane, most modern practitioners utilize *Arnica montana,* as it is much less lethal, though it's still toxic. Wolfsbane provides protection from spirits and is one of the hex-breaking herbs. Use this in an Herbal Amulet only; *do not ingest or inhale,* whether in Incense smoke, Infusion, or other combination.

Wood betony

Scientific name: *Betonica offincinalis*

Other names: betony, bishop's-wort

Element: Earth

Planets: Jupiter, Mercury

Part used: leaf

Traditionally used for work with Elementals (the Deva, or spirit essence, of one of the Elements—Earth, Air, Fire, and Water) to entice and communicate with them, wood betony is also an herb that protects from harm and purifies an area. Added to an Herbal Amulet and taken to court, wood betony encourages justice and fairness. Traditionally gathered around the summer solstice, wood betony is tossed onto a bonfire, and then the fire is jumped, cleansing the auric energy.

Woodruff

Scientific name: *Asperula odorata*

Other names: master of the woods, sweet woodruff

Element: Fire

Planet: Mars

Part used: leaf

Added to any herbal formula, woodruff attracts success in all endeavors. Placed in an Herbal Amulet or used as an ingredient in a bath herb preparation, Woodruff protects and blesses. A traditional ingredient in May wine, woodruff brings health to the drinker. Carried alone or in an Amulet, woodruff was used by Teutonic warriors to ensure victory and protection in battle.

Wormwood

Scientific name: *Artemisia absinthium*

Other name: absinthe

Element: Earth

Planets: Mars, Saturn

Parts used: leaf, essential oil

Opening the psychic centers, wormwood allows the user to communicate with the dead, summon spirits, and obtain information in the dream state. Wormwood is also utilized in Incenses, bath herbs, Herbal Amulets, and Elixirs of protection, in which it banishes anger and turns back negative energy. If you add wormwood to an Infusion that you intend to ingest, use only a small amount, as it can cause stomach cramps and diarrhea.

Yarrow

Scientific name: *Achillea millefolium*

Other names: achillea, field hops, milfoil

Element: Air

Planets: Venus, Sun

Parts used: flower, stalk

Yarrow stalks are used in the Chinese system of I Ching, helping to bring clear information and wisdom. It bolsters courage and commitment when used in the bath and is a good ingredient in formulas designed to make love lasting and enduring. Adding a gentle power to any formula, yarrow attracts steadfastness and fortune. Associated with Chiron, the God of healing, yarrow encourages vitality and beauty while attracting Solar vitality to the body.

Yellow dock

Scientific name: *Rumex crispus*

Other names: sour dock, dock

Element: Earth

Planet: Jupiter

Parts used: leaf, root

Traditionally used in herbal formulas for healing the body and soul, yellow dock is also associated with fertility. The seeds are placed in an Herbal Amulet and worn by the prospective mother.

Yerba santa

Scientific name: *Eriodictyon californicum*

Other names: sacred herb, holy herb

Element: Air

Planets: Venus, Sun

Part used: leaf

Yerba santa is used in Magick for spiritual strength and to increase psychic powers. It can be carried in an Herbal Amulet for protection or to ward off sickness or added to an Incense formula to clear the aura. Some people add yerba santa to the bath to gain beauty and joy. When illness is thought to be occurring due to vital energy leaking from the aura, the leaves are used in Healing Incenses to close the energy holes and strengthen the patient.

Yohimbe

Scientific name: *Pausinystalia yohimbe*

Element: Fire

Planet: Mars, Pluto

Part used: root

One of the few real herbal aphrodisiacs, yohimbe is associated with sexuality, lust, and power. Included in a Lust Incense or mulled in wine, it increases the blood flow to the genitals in both men and women and arouses desire. A mild hallucinogen, yohimbe should never be used or consumed by anyone who has heart or blood pressure problems, as it dramatically raises blood pressure.

Planetary Energy and Herb Affinity

You may find in this listing that some of the herbs have a dual Planetary affinity. This is because a particular herb's vibration may have different levels or multiple ways of expressing its energy. For example, white sandalwood is found under the rulerships of both the Moon and Mercury. White sandalwood has an energy that encourages communication between the subconscious mind (Moon) and the conscious mind (Mercury). Myrrh is another herb/resin with dual rulerships: Saturn and Pluto. The scent and vibration of myrrh grounds and binds (Saturn) while bringing into focus spiritual/karmic intention (Pluto).

Sun

Sun herbs promote self-confidence and personal success. They impart a sense of purpose and a strong will. Sun herbs give vitality, health, creativity, dignity, and authority.

angelica	juniper
ash	mistletoe[†]
bay	rosemary
calendula	safflower
celandine	saffron
chamomile*	Saint-John's-wort
copal	sunflower
eyebright	tormentilla
frankincense	walnuts

Please note: The herbs listed here with their Planetary attributes are not necessarily being recommended for internal consumption. Some of them are highly poisonous. Some of them are illegal. Consult your trusted medicinal herbal for directions in terms of internal use.

Moon

Moon herbs are very good in aiding development of the intuition and psychic abilities. As Moon herbs affect the subconscious, they are excellent for breaking old habits and in recalling past lives.

almond	moonwort
anise	mugwort
cabbage	myrrh
camphor	poppy
cucumber	privet
fennel	pumpkin
iris	rose hip
jasmin	violet
lettuce	watercress
lily	white sandalwood
lotus	willow
mallow	wintergreen[†]

Mars

Mars herbs supply vast amounts of energy to projects and health. They give independence and assertiveness and stimulate the passions. Mars herbs protect and deflect negative energies. When mixed with other Planetary herbs, they lend their immense vitality to the other Planets' energies, making the whole stronger.

aloeswood	hawthorn[§]
asafoetida	honeysuckle
basil	horseradish*
black pepper	juniper
briony	mustard*
broom tops	nettle*
cactus	peppercorn*
cayenne*	red sandalwood
cumin	rue[†]
dragon's blood	safflower
galangal	sanicle
garlic	tobacco

gentian   wormwood
ginger

Mercury

Mercury herbs facilitate clear thinking and communication. They aid in business success and in recovery from illness. Mercurial herbs enable the conscious mind to communicate more easily with the subconscious, thus aiding psychicwork with the Tarot or any other divination system that visually incorporates symbols.

bergamot	licorice
caraway	marjoram
cardamon	mastic
cinnamon*	mouse-ear
cloves	mullein†
dill	papyrus
ephedra†	peppermint
fennel	pomegranate
gum arabic	savory
horehound	star anise
hyssop	thyme
lavender	white sandalwood

Jupiter

Jupiter herbs are expansive herbs. They bring growth, both spiritual and material, and are very good in balancing health matters. The herbs of Jupiter expand the mind, allowing for a mental understanding of the Universe.

agrimony	maple
betony	meadowsweet
borage	oak moss
carnation	oak
cedar	pine

---

* Irritating to the skin and or mucous membranes. Also indicates an herb to which many people have an allergy.

† Poisonous: Do not ingest. Use in Herbal Amulets and Magickal Potpourri only, if at all.

‡ Pregnant women should not ingest.

§ People with heart conditions or upper respiratory difficulties should not ingest..

---

cinquefoil
dandelion
figs
fir
hyssop
linden
magnolia

poplar
rosin
sage
sassafras
sumac
wood betony

Venus

Venus herbs bring joy, beauty, artistry, sensitivity, compassion, and appreciation of the Earth and all Her creatures. Venus herbs promote an inner glow and attractiveness that bewitches and delights.

alder
alkanet
apple
beans
blackberries
burdock
catnip
cherry
coltsfoot
columbine
coriander
damiana
elder
feverfew
lemon verbena
lilac
maidenhair
mandrake
marshmallow
myrtle

orris
passionflower
peach
pennyroyal[†]
periwinkle
plantain
plum
plumeria
raspberry
rhubarb
rose
spikenard
strawberry
tansy
thyme
tonka bean[†]
vanilla
vervain
violet
yarrow

Saturn

Saturn herbs give structure, foundation, stability, and an understanding of the physical plane and how it works. They are great teachers of life's "secrets"—self-knowledge and karmic debt. They teach that success comes through perseverance and patience. Saturn herbs are binding and protective herbs.

aconite†	ivy†
asafoetida	mullein†
balm of Gilead	myrrh
beet	nightshade*
bistort	patchouli
boneset	rosemary
comfrey	Saint-John's-wort
cypress	shepherd's purse
dill	skullcap
elm	Solomon's seal
fumitory	spurge
garlic	tamarind
ground moss	valerian
hawthorn§	vetivert
hemlock†	woad
henbane†	wolfsbane†
hyssop	yew

Neptune

Neptune herbs are the herbs of the mystic and are useful in dreamworking, trance, and hypnosis, intensifying the imagination in order to lead to good ideas and concepts far beyond the physical plane. They are useful for those who are developing telepathy and the ability to astral project.

cannabis	orchid†
datura†	peach
kava kava	poppy
lobelia†	skullcap

---

* Irritating to the skin and or mucous membranes. Also indicates an herb to which many people have an allergy.

† Poisonous: Do not ingest. Use in Herbal Amulets and Magickal Potpourri only, if at all.

‡ Pregnant women should not ingest.

§ People with heart conditions or upper respiratory difficulties should not ingest..

lotus   wild lettuce

mugwort   willow

neroli   wisteria

Uranus

Uranus herbs excite, energize, and stimulate. They lend themselves to intellectual inspiration, practical idealism, genius, and the development of telekinesis.

allspice   elemi

betel nut   guarana§

calamus   mace

chicory   mahuang*

cinnamon*   mastic

cloves   nutmeg

coffee

Pluto

Pluto herbs bring about dramatic, sometimes traumatic, change. They promote dramatic growth and insight normally through cataclysmic circumstances. Pluto herbs aid the sexually impotent and help to balance the physical with the spiritual.

barley   patchouli

black cohosh   pomegranate

corn   poppy

damiana   psilocybin†

fly agaric†   rye

galangal   saw palmetto

mushroom   wheat

myrrh   wormwood

oats   yohimbe§

opoponax

---

* Irritating to the skin and or mucous membranes. Also indicates an herb to which many people have an allergy.

† Poisonous: Do not ingest. Use in Herbal Amulets and Magickal Potpourri only, if at all.

‡ Pregnant women should not ingest.

§ People with heart conditions or upper respiratory difficulties should not ingest.

Moon Phase and Planetary Day

The phases of the Moon and the day of the week are important to consider when creating an alchemical blend. You are being very careful to incorporate just the right herbal ingredients to synthesize all the components for an Incense, oil, or other herbal formula to ensure the results you want for successful Magick. You are working with powerful but subtle energies to blend them into a whole; utilizing the traditional tides of Lunar energy and Planetary Day will add to the strength of your formula as well.

Your goal is to connect with the tides of energy most conducive to the successful outcome of your work. Planning to do it at the most opportune Astrological time that adds to and complements the energies you are activating brings you closer to a successful working.

The first thing you want to be sure you understand is the way that the energies of the Moon work. Each *New Moon* begins a new cycle and is excellent for initiating projects and doing ceremony or meditation for increase and growth. The time between the New and Full Moon is known as the *Waxing Moon*, meaning the Moon is growing in size and outward strength, affecting our environment and surroundings. During this time, meditations and spells for increase can be done effectively. The *Full Moon* brings power and energy to the seed you have planted at the New Moon or it fulfills a long-term goal or desire. The time between the Full Moon and the New Moon is known as the *Waning Moon*, meaning the Moon is decreasing in size but gaining in inward strength. It is a time to go inward to receive wisdom and information. It is the time to let go of things, attitudes, or people who no longer contribute to your life or are detrimental to your goals.

When the Moon is waxing (getting larger, from the New to the Full), it is the right time to do expansive, external works. If your formula is designed to affect the outside world—your work, your relationship, the abundance coming to you—you will create your blend during the Waxing Moon. Love, money, fertility, career, and personal success are all aspects of one's external life, which increase as the Moon waxes. Rituals or alchemical herbal concoctions of an internal and/or binding nature should be done when the Moon is waning. Internal works would include developing the intuitive side of yourself, contacting your Higher Self, karmic investigation, and transforming brain patterns or habits. This also includes Magicks for protection, to stop something from happening, control garden pests, cool off passions in another, learn about past lives, and enforce self-control.

You may wish to incorporate the energies of a specific phase of the Moon in your work. New Moons are perfect to initiate new projects and beginnings. Full Moons enhance the concentrated power of your work. The Dark of the Moon (the night just before the New Moon) is excellent for endings, past life–work, and bindings.

You can also incorporate the energy specific to an Astrological Sign of a New or Full Moon. When you check your calendar to see when the New and Full Moons are, also check for the Astrological Sign that the Moon falls in that day. That will tell you what "flavor" of energy the Moon is expressing that day—in other words, what type of energy is the strongest and best suited for your purposes. In general, the following are the types of ritual that work best for each Astrological Sign:

Aries New or Full Moon is good for energy, willpower, and starting new projects.

Taurus New or Full Moon focuses on commitment, material gain, and physical security.

Gemini New or Full Moon brings communication, journeys, new friends, and new ideas.

Cancer New or Full Moon is excellent for spells for motherhood, psychic development, and relationships, and to protect the home.

Leo New or Full Moon is good for animal blessings, creativity, personal authority, and self-esteem.

Virgo New or Full Moon intensifies energy for work, health, intellectual gain, and self-development.

Libra New or Full Moon is useful for workings to promote harmony, partnerships, beauty, and artistic talents.

Scorpio New or Full Moon is effective for occult knowledge, past lives, dreamwork, and sexuality.

Sagittarius New or Full Moon is good for honesty, adventures, prestige, and luck.

Capricorn New or Full Moon attracts energy to realize professional ambitions, stability, organization, and money through your efforts.

Aquarius New or Full Moon brings energy for higher learning, teaching, originality, and to make changes in your life.

Pisces New or Full Moon is effective for spells to develop your intuition, astral projection, romance, and peace.

Put things into motion in such a way that your desires do not manipulate others. Everything can be done in a flowing way that does not force others to your will. Manipulating others ties up your karma with that individual and makes it very hard to make changes later if necessary. And, remember, everything you do returns to you threefold. Some believe this means three times; others believe that the energy is returned to you on the physical, emotional, and spiritual levels.

Magick is the use and release of focused energy: the more positive energy you put out, the more positive energy will be returned; the more negative and manipulative your energy, the more you will receive of the same. Which would you prefer?

You will also need to decide which Planet rules the type of Magick you wish to do, and perform your rite on that day in the proper phase of the Moon.

Rites of the Sun (success, prosperity) are done on Sunday.

Rites of the Moon (psychic development, fertility) are done on Monday.

Rites of Mars (protection, vitality) are done on Tuesday.

Rites of Mercury (career, communication) are done on Wednesday.

Rites of Jupiter (expansion, abundance) are done on Thursday.

Rites of Venus (love, creativity) are done on Friday.

Rites of Saturn (protection, grounding) are done on Saturday.

Rites of Neptune (mystic connections) are done on Friday

Rites of Uranus (genius, change) are done on Wednesday.

Rites of Pluto (transformation) are done on Tuesday or Saturday.

All that being said, there will be times that you will have to create a formula for a ritual that must be performed immediately. A loved one may have had an accident or sudden illness; perhaps your home has been broken into and it must be cleansed and protected. At times of emergency (or even just sudden inspiration), don't limit your efforts by feeling that you must slavishly abide to the Moon tides, Planetary Days, or any other "rule." If you have to do it, you have to do it. You won't have the additional energy that is given by utilizing the Moon tide or Planetary Day, but the focused intention provided by the urgency of the necessary work at hand will be enough.

Elements and Their Corresponding Herbs

You may wish to incorporate one or more of the four Elements in your blends. The Elements correspond to the three states of matter: solids (Earth), liquids (Water) and gas (Air), plus the agent which transforms each of them—heat (Fire). The Elements can be symbolized by many things: the four directions, the four winds, the four seasons, the Archangels, Elemental beings, Astrological Signs, and more.

 Air

Air is the Element of the intellect, mental processes, and communication. It is considered an activating Element. The direction that corresponds to Air is the East, where the day begins. Air is the springtime, new beginnings, and, in the foundations of Magickal thought, Faith. Faith (confidence) in Magickal energies comes from knowledge (intellect) and from understanding the processes of ritual and focused thought, then applying them with sure result.

The tool of Air is the Wand, which is used to direct and channel energy in Magick. When it is used in healing to absorb the energy of the Universe and channel it into the patient, the Wand corresponds to the caduceus of Mercury, a God of Air—you will notice that this same symbol is used by physicians today.

The Astrological Signs associated with Air are Aquarius, Gemini, and Libra. Aquarius is the innovator, the Sign of original thought and ideals. Gemini is the communicator, the comedian, the experimenter. Libra is the balancer and harmonizer, interested in partnerships and relationships.

Air corresponds to the throat, which in turn represents speech, creation, breath, and movement.

The Archangel of Air is Raphael, the Archangel of healing, teaching, and travel. He is visualized on a mountaintop, in robes of yellow and lavender (the colors associated with the Element Air), which blow gently in the wind. In Magick, Angels represent invisible forces, powers ascending and descending between the Source of all things and the world. An Archangel is the angelic entity in its highest and most pure force.

Sylphs are the Elementals attributed to Air and are similar in form to humans, although they are transparent and have lovely, delicate wings. They travel on the wind, and you can hear them talking and laughing as they drift in and out of the trees. Paralda is the name of their ruler. Sylphs are very articulate and logical and prefer the mountaintops where the air is the thinnest. They are related to the nervous system in the human body. Their favorite scents are the mints and light flowery essences such as tulip, and they love the sound of bells and wind chimes.

The herbs, resins, and oils of Air are those with a refreshing scent that enlivens the mind and those of the Planetary energies of Mercury, Uranus, and Jupiter:

agrimony	guarana
allspice	gum mastic
betel	lavender
calamus	licorice
cardamom	magnolia
cinnamon	meadowsweet
ephedra	pine

 Fire

Fire is the Element of Will and Passion and is considered an activating Element. The direction that corresponds to Fire is the South, which we associate with heat. The season is, of course, summer—the time of growth and culmination of that growth. Fire is the drive and motivation used by an individual as he strives toward his goals. In the foundations of Magick, Fire is the Magickal Will. The force of the Magickal Will enables the Magickian to carry through with goals, plans, and dreams. The focused Magickal

Will serves as the force or stimulus for the Magickal energy that is sent forth to act on the physical plane to manifest the goal of any ritual.

The tool of Fire is the Athame, the ritual dagger, which is used to inscribe the Magickal sigils in the ether during ritual, describe the circumference of the Magickal Circle, banish phantasms and defend against them, and heal via the act of removing holes in the aura through cauterization on the astral plane.

The Astrological Signs that correspond to Fire are the Fire Signs of Aries, Leo, and Sagittarius, all Signs of action and vitality. Aries initiates new projects, Leo is the Fire Sign of flamboyance and flair, and Sagittarius is the Sign of freedom and physical activity.

The Archangel of Fire is Michael (pronounced *Mee-kee-al*), the Archangel of authority, victory, initiative, and splendor. Michael is visualized in robes of scarlet and green, bearing before him a flaming sword.

Fire is the activating force giving vitality and energy to the ideas of Air, bringing them into physical reality as we perceive it.

Salamanders are attributed to the Element of Fire. They are not considered a part of the physical flame as such but the essence that enables the flame to burn. Naturally, they are most active in the summer months and geographically prefer the hotter regions. When they live in cold places, Salamanders reside in the hearth. They are full of passion and enthusiasm and for this reason are sometimes considered dangerous, as their unpredictability can be disconcerting. However, they are actually very generous and warmhearted, if treated with the respect due them. Salamanders relate to the heart in the human body as well as to the circulatory system. Their King is called Djinn. Salamanders love the smell of burning wood and spicy odors such as cinnamon and nutmeg. Candles, lanterns, and mirrors are attractive to them.

Fire herbs, essential oils, and resins are those associated with the Sun and Mars and which have an invigorating, spicy scent:

calendula	mustard
celandine	nettles
frankincense	red sandalwood
galangal	safflower
ginger	sunflower

Water

Water is the Element of love, intuition, emotion, fertility, understanding, and imagination. It is considered a receptive Element. Water receives the ideas of Air, the force of Fire, and begins the alchemical process of transmuting them into a form that can be made tangible. The direction that corresponds to Water is the West. Human emotions and feelings belong to the Element Water. The season is autumn, and in the foundations of Magick, Water is imagination. Imagination begins in our dreams and in the language of our subconscious minds. Without it, our rituals would be dry and emotionless. Imagination allows us to see what might be and is therefore creativity, fertility, and inner vision.

The tool of Water is the Chalice, which is used to contain the water of purification when we cleanse a space or an object for ritual. The Chalice holds the ritual wine and the liquid for seeing past, present, and future in the practice of scrying. The Chalice represents wisdom, transformation, and receptivity. In the legends of ancient times, the Grail of Immortality was sought by the valiant for its life-giving and regenerative powers as well as for the knowledge it brings. The Ritual Cauldron is also of the Element of Water, and the stories that surround it—the regenerative Cauldron of Dagda, the Cauldron of wisdom belonging to Ceridwen, and the Cauldron of Baba Yaga—reaffirm the theme of wisdom, life, transformation, and regeneration.

The Astrological Water Signs of Pisces, Cancer, and Scorpio correspond to the Magickal Element of Water. Pisces is the Sign of emotional connection and inner vision; Cancer is associated with family connection and nurturing; and Scorpio is known for occult ability, psychic power, death, and regeneration.

The Archangel of Water is Gabriel, known as the Prince of Change and Alteration. He can be seen on the Judgment card of the Tarot, blowing his horn, which represents fertility and authority. Gabriel is visualized in robes of clear blue and orange, holding a Chalice from which torrents of water spill.

Undines are the Elementals of Water. They are extremely graceful and seductive. Undines are similar to humans in form and the majority of them are female. They will impart psychic knowledge and ability. If you work with them in this area, be sure to give them extravagant and appealing gifts in return, for they have feelings that can be easily bruised. They correspond to the human digestive system, and Necksa is their King. Undines live in oceans, rivers, springs, creeks, and raindrops. Their most beloved scents are cool ones—camphor, cucumber, and citrus fruits such as lime. They delight in beautiful shells, silver jewelry, boxes for their treasures, and flutes.

Herbs, resins, and essential oils of Water are the ones associated with the Moon, Neptune, and Venus and which have a sweet, hypnotic aroma:

cherry	orange blossom
columbine	peach
cucumber	poppy
jasmin flower	raspberry
lily	rose
lobelia	vervain
lotus	white sandalwood
mugwort	

 Earth

Earth is the Element of secrecy, deep wisdom, possessions, creation, perseverance, birth, and death. It is considered to be a receptive Element. Earth receives the idea of Air, the force of Fire, and the transmuted substance of Water and manifests the form into the physical world. The direction that is associated with Earth is the North, the place of endings. Earth corresponds to the bone structure of the human body. The season is winter, and in the foundation of Magick, Earth is Secrecy. Hidden beneath the Earth are many treasures—jewels, minerals, oil—which must be sought out. They cannot be obtained without perseverance and labor. So it is with the Magickal secrets that the Element Earth hides; only through dedication and patience can these secrets be brought to light, yet they must always be protected and guarded.

The tool of the Earth is the Pentacle, which is used both for drawing in and projecting energy. The Pentacle can also used as a shield for psychic self-defense. The Magickal Cords are also of Earth and are used to bind energy.

The Astrological Signs corresponding to Earth are Capricorn, Taurus, and Virgo. Capricorn is the Sign of pragmatism and wealth; Taurus is the Sign associated with sensuality, acquisition, resources, and practicality; and Virgo is the Sign of the healer and the organizer.

The Archangel of Earth is Uriel (pronounced *Ah-ree-el* or *Yuh-ree-el*), also called the Lord of Awe, who presides over protection and strength. He is visualized in robes of olive and russet, bearing a Pentacle.

Gnomes and elves are attributed to Earth and are seen in very small human form. Their King is Gheb (also known as Geb or Gob, as in *goblin*). Earth Elementals are the most mischievous of the Elementals and love a good practical joke. They prefer to live in the forest, crags, heaths, and caverns, although with the human population cutting down on gnomes' habitats, the more sociable ones actually enjoy being around sensitive and sympathetic human beings and will share living quarters. Gnomes and elves love jewels, gold, interesting rocks, moss, and living plants of all kinds. Their favorite scents are resins and woodland smells such as patchouli and vetivert.

The herbs, essential oils, and resins belonging to the Element Earth are the ones associated with Saturn and Pluto and which have a deep earthy smell:

amaranth	patchouli
benzoin	saw palmetto
cypress	Solomon's seal
damiana	rye
wormwood	myrrh
yohimbe	oak moss

Formulas and Recipes

These formulas are complete unto themselves, but you
are encouraged to make them your own by adding or omitting
ingredients and fashioning them in such a way as to create
personal blends derived from your own intuition, knowl-
edge, and inspiration. I have listed the amounts for each herb, essential
oil, and resin in the time-honored unit of parts so that you can make the
amount you deem useful for your workings. A part can be one handful,
one tablespoon, one-quarter cup—whatever volume you prefer. I would
recommend that with any of your essential oils, you consider ten drops to
be equal to one part. After you have blended in your essential oils, let your
creation sit overnight, then smell it to see if you would like to add more
of any oil that you particularly like for a stronger scent according to your
personal taste.

Planetary Formulas

Sun
one part frankincense
one part calendula
one part safflower
one part frankincense oil
one part heliotrope oil

Moon
one part jasmin flowers
one part white sandalwood
one part mugwort
one part violet oil
one part sandalwood oil

Mars
two parts red sandalwood
one part honeysuckle flowers
one part basil
one part ginger oil
one part juniper oil

Mercury
one part lavender flowers
one part gum mastic
one part cinnamon chips
one part cinnamon oil
one part lavender oil

Jupiter
one part cedar chips
one part pine needles
one part meadowsweet
one part cedar oil
one part sage oil

Venus
one part rose petals
one part vervain
one part elder blossoms
one part rose oil
one part ylang-ylang oil

Saturn
one part myrrh resin
one part patchouli
one part oak moss
one part petitgrain oil
one part cypress oil

Neptune
one part white willow
one part orange blossoms

one part poppy blossoms
one part neroli oil
one part ylang-ylang oil

Uranus
one part allspice berries, crushed
one part powdered nutmeg
one part gum mastic
one part clove oil
one part elemi oil

Elemental Formulas

Earth
one part patchouli
one part black copal
one part oak moss oil
one part myrrh oil

Air
one part gum arabic
one part cinnamon
one part lavender oil
one part clove oil

Fire
one part ginger
one part safflower
one part frankincense oil
one part heliotrope oil

Water
one part mugwort
one part orange blossoms
one part lotus oil
one part white sandalwood oil

Formulas for Manifestation of Goals

These Incense formulas are a combination of Planetary energies utilizing herbs, resins, and essential oils well suited for their goal as indicated by the name of the Incense. You are encouraged to alter them to suit your thoughts, intuition, and taste. I have noted the Planet associated with each ingredient to give you a feel for why that particular herb, resin, or oil is being used. If you wish to create a Ritual Oil from any of these formulas, simply use the essential oil rather than the herb, or omit that ingredient entirely if it is not available as an oil or if it is an essential oil that should not be used on the skin.

Abundance
one part frankincense (Sun; success)
one part calendula (Sun; success)
one part oak moss (Jupiter; expansion)
one part orris (Venus; enjoyment)
one part heliotrope oil (Sun; success)
one part cedar oil (Jupiter; expansion)

Aphrodite, Goddess of Love
one part rose petals (Venus; love)
one part jasmin flowers (Moon; emotions)
one part orris powder (Venus; love)
one part rose oil (Venus; love)
one part neroli oil (Neptune; spiritual connection)
one part ylang-ylang oil (Venus; love)

Binding
one part benzoin gum (Saturn; binding)
one part patchouli (Saturn; binding)
one part Solomon's seal (Saturn; protective)
one part rosemary oil (Saturn; protective)
one part frankincense oil (Sun; success)

Change
one part calamus root (Uranus; change)
one part lavender (Mercury; clarity)
one part powdered nutmeg (Uranus; change)

one part cinnamon (Uranus, Mercury; change)

two parts sandalwood oil (Mercury, Moon; communication between
    conscious and subconscious minds)

Courage

one part gingerroot (Mars; courage)

one part dragon's blood resin (Mars; strength)

one part frankincense (Sun; success)

one part myrrh (Saturn, Pluto; grounding and inner work)

one part juniper oil (Jupiter; expansion)

one part cinnamon oil (Mercury; consciousness)

Creativity

one part willow (Neptune; inspiration)

one part safflower (Sun; self-expression)

one part rose petals (Venus; beauty, arts)

one part lotus oil (Neptune; creativity)

one part vanilla oil (Venus; beauty, arts)

Employment

one part gum arabic (Mercury; business)

one part cinnamon chips (Mercury; business)

one part eyebright (Sun; success)

one part pine oil (Jupiter; expansion)

one part bergamot oil (Mercury; eloquence)

one part vetivert oil (Saturn; manifestation)

Fame

one part cedar chips (Jupiter; renown)

one part angelica (Sun; authority)

one part myrtle (Venus; the arts)

one part gum mastic (Uranus; innovation)

one part lavender oil (Mercury; knowledge)

one part carnation oil (Jupiter; expansion)

Fertility

one part fennel seed (Moon; fertility)

one part violet leaves (Moon; fertility)

one part sandalwood (Moon; fertility)

one part rose oil (Venus; connection to the feminine energies)
one part jasmin oil (Moon; fertility)

Grounding

one part myrrh resin (Saturn; grounding)
one part skullcap (Saturn; stability)
one part juniper berries (Sun; confidence)
one part patchouli oil (Saturn; grounding)
one part cypress oil (Saturn; grounding)

Health

one part frankincense (Sun; vitality)
one part basil (Mars; energy)
one part cinnamon (Mercury; nervous system)
one part bay oil (Sun; health)
one part sandalwood oil (Moon; Inner Self)

Inspiration

one part mugwort (Moon, Neptune; Inner Self, inspiration)
one part gum mastic (Uranus; innovation)
one part jasmin oil (Moon; subconscious)
one part neroli oil (Neptune; musk)

Intuition

one part star anise seed (Moon; psychic ability)
one-half part camphor (Moon; intuition)
one part sandalwood (Moon, Mercury; communication between conscious and subconscious minds)
one part lotus oil (Moon, Neptune; mystic)
one part bitter almond oil (Moon; intuition)

Karma

one part myrrh (Pluto; past lives)
one part poppy seeds or poppy flowers (Moon; subconscious)
one part boneset (Saturn; past lives)
one part opoponax oil (Pluto; karma)
one part cypress oil (Saturn; understanding)

Love
one part rose petals (Venus; love)
one part orris powder (Venus; love)
one part red sandalwood (Mars; passion)
one part jasmin oil (Moon; emotions)
one part patchouli oil (Saturn; grounding)

Opportunity
one part meadowsweet (Jupiter; expansion)
one part cloves (Mercury, Uranus; communication, change)
one part frankincense (Sun; success)
one part oak moss oil (Jupiter; expansion)
one part of an oil that represents the Planet ruling the area in which you
    seek opportunity

Past Lives
one part crushed poppy flowers (Moon, Pluto; subconscious, past lives)
one part myrrh resin (Saturn, Pluto; karma, unconscious mind)
one-half part cinnamon (Mercury; memory)
one part jasmin oil (Moon; subconscious)
one part water lily oil (Moon; subconscious)

Peace
one part jasmin flowers (Moon; emotions)
one part myrrh resin (Saturn; grounding)
one part rose petals (Venus; love)
one part lotus oil (Neptune; inspiration)
one part lavender oil (Mercury; communication)

Prosperity
one part calendula (Sun; success)
one part caraway seeds (Mercury; business)
one part pine resin (Jupiter; expansion)
one part bay oil (Sun; victory)
one part cinnamon oil (Mercury; speed)
one part oak moss oil (Jupiter; growth)

Protection
one part frankincense (Sun; vitality)

one part myrrh resin (Saturn; shielding)

one part patchouli (Saturn; grounding)

one part ginger oil (Mars; protection)

one part cypress oil (Saturn; shielding)

Purification

one part copal resin (Sun; cleansing)

one part sandalwood (Moon, Mercury; inner and outer person and
environment)

one part sage (Jupiter; expand spirit)

one part myrrh oil (Moon, Saturn, Pluto; emotions, shielding,
transformation)

True Dream

one part poppy seeds (Moon, Neptune; mystical inspiration)

one part jasmin flowers (Moon; dreamwork)

one part gum arabic (Mercury; memory)

one part neroli oil (Neptune; dreamwork)

one part sandalwood oil (Moon, Mercury; subconscious, memory)

Tables of Correspondences

The following tables are quite useful when planning rituals. Correspondences are materials that share a similar energy/vibration pattern with the Planet with which they are associated. The tables are quick reference guides to the powers, vibrations, and energies of plants, colors, metals, and much more. A Table of Correspondence shows you quickly and easily which materials share corresponding energies so that you can choose your materials and plan your work accordingly. Consulting a Table of Correspondence can enable you to put together and fine-tune everything you want to use in focusing your Magickal energies for a special ritual. You don't have to use them all at one time in one ritual—just choose the ones that will best suit your purposes for your current working.

When designing your ritual, the first step is to pick the Planet (or Planets) that best exemplify the energies you are seeking to use:

Sun: friendship, vitality, luck, money, patronage, peace, confidence, success

Moon: astral travel, safety, childbirth, reconciliation, intuition, creativity, dreamwork

Mars: assertiveness, victory, willpower, sexuality, protection

Mercury: career, communication, conscious mind, learning, theatre, divination, health

Jupiter: ambition, luck, opportunities, abundance, expansion, fame

Venus: beauty, creativity, the arts, love, friendship, pleasure

Saturn: discipline, self-knowledge, the occult, karma, past lives, protection

Neptune: mystical experiences, inspiration

Uranus: quantum mental leaps, the unexpected

Pluto: deep inner issues, fears, instincts

Once you have decided which Planet or combination of Planetary energies will work best for your ritual, the color corresponding to the Planet is the color to use for your candles, altar cloth, or paper, if you're drawing a Talisman. The plants and perfumes are the herbal materials to choose and blend when making your own Incense, Ritual Oil, or Herbal Amulet as you develop your formulas. The metals and gems are materials that you can charge with energy and use in an Amulet (or bury or keep in your pocket or place upon a photograph or contract—your imagination is the limit). The number associated with each Planet represents the Planetary energy, so you could use objects in the same amount as the number associated with a Planet—one candle or stone to represent the Sun; two candles or stones for the Moon, etc. In making a paper Talisman, you would use a three-sided (triangular) paper for Venus, which is associated with the number 3; a four-sided (square) paper for Saturn, which is associated with the number 4; a five-sided (pentagon) paper for Mars, which is associated with the number 5, and so on.

The best day to perform your ritual is determined by the Planet whose main energy you have to tap. Each Planet rules a day of the week:

Sunday	*Monday*	*Tuesday*	*Wednesday*	*Thursday*	*Friday*	*Saturday*
Sun	Moon	Mars	Mercury	Jupiter	Venus	Saturn
	Pluto	Uranus	Neptune	Pluto		

You will notice that because Uranus is the higher octave of Mercury energy, its rites are performed on the same day as Mercury's, Wednesday. Neptune, the higher octave of Venus, has its rites performed on Friday as well; and due to its depth of energy, Pluto shares the energies with both Mars and Saturn. Depending on the type of Plutonian rite in which you are engaging, choose either Tuesday or Saturday for your work. Rituals involving deep-seated instinctual functions such as sexuality or radical transformation of the psyche would be done on Tuesday. Plutonian rites involving resolving karmic debt or ties with whom one has shared a lifetime or lifetimes would be performed on Saturday.

You will also want to plan your ritual by the correct phase of the Moon to capture the best Lunar flow:

Waxing Moon (New Moon to Full Moon, as the Moon is getting bigger) is used to influence events outside of yourself and the environment and people around you, expansion, and growth.

Waning Moon (Full Moon to New Moon, as the Moon is getting smaller) is used for inner work like dreamwork, past life regression, stopping bad habits, and slowing or stopping events.

New Moon is good for new beginnings and blessings.

Full Moon is the Moon in its full-power tide. You'll want to check the Astrological placement of each Full Moon to take the most advantage of its energy at that time.

Table of Planetary Correspondences

On the following pages is a brief listing of Magickal correspondences to the Planetary energies, adapted from author David Conway's work.

Planet	Number	Color	Plant
Sun	1	orange	sunflower
Sun, exalted	8	gold	heliotrope
Moon	2	violet	almond
		silver	sandalwood
Mars	5	scarlet	ginger
		burgundy	red sandalwood
Mercury	7	lavender	lavender
		yellow	cinquefoil
Jupiter	6	blue	oak
		purple	poplar
Venus	3	green	rose
		pink	vervain
Saturn	4	indigo	ash
			cypress
Neptune	11	sea green	kelp
			bladder wrack
Uranus	22	electric blue	coffee
			guarana
Pluto	33	black	mushroom
			rye

Metal/Material	Gem	Perfume
gold	topaz diamond	saffron frankincense
silver	moonstone pearl	jasmin camphor
iron	ruby garnet	black pepper honeysuckle
quicksilver	opal quartz	cinnamon mace
tin	sapphire amethyst	cedar magnolia
copper	jade rose quartz	carnation rose
lead	onyx jet	oak moss cypress
shell	abalone fluorite	neroli amber
titanium	quartz Herkimer	clove nutmeg
pyrite	black opal	myrrh patchouli

Necessary Supplies

To prepare and engage in all the recipes, rituals, and meditations in this book, you will need a wide selection of basic supplies. Over time, you will add to these basic supplies, but the following list will get you started in good style.

Herbal Supplies

Jars and bottles

You can never have enough jars and bottles in which to store all your creations! Wide-mouthed jars are necessary for your Incenses and herbs, for easy storage and removal. A four- or six-ounce jar should be sufficient for most Incense storage, and you will find that recycled baby food jars or small food jars that once contained relish or other condiments are perfect. If you prefer, you can purchase canning jars or wide-mouthed bottles with cork lids at stores that specialize in cookware, like Williams-Sonoma. Stores such as Pier 1 or Cost Plus often have nice jars and bottles at a reasonable price. Keep your herbs and herbal mixtures in a cool, dark, dry place, and they'll last much longer. If you store larger quantities of dried herbs, you may wish to simply keep each of them in a separate brown kraft paper bag, like a paper grocery bag. As long as you keep the bags from getting wet and away from unnecessary heat, they will work just fine for dried herbs and resins.

Vials

You want a laboratory-grade glass vial for your essential oils and essential oil blends. When you purchase an essential oil, it will come in a laboratory-grade vial. It's helpful to have a selection of varying sizes in your vials from one dram size (one-eighth ounce) up to eight ounces. For most oil blends, you will find that one dram, two dram, and one-half ounce are perfect. If you decide to make a massage oil, a four-ounce bottle should be sufficient, and you may prefer to keep that oil in a plastic bottle with a squeeze top for safety. A slippery, oily hand can cause you to drop and break a glass bottle.

Dropper Bottles

You will need at least one one-ounce bottle that has a dropper cap to store alcohol. You use this bottle for dispersing drops of essential oil without contaminating the contents of your essential oil bottles. Using the dropper, you can count exactly how many drops of oil you are adding at any given time. Cleaning out the dropper by drawing some alcohol into the dropper and then shaking out excess alcohol in between applications of the different oils you are using ensures that you don't inadvertently get any essential oils mixed into other essential oil bottles, keeping the scents pure. You just want to be sure that before drawing up a new essential oil into the dropper that you shake all the alcohol out of the dropper. If you drip alcohol into your essential oil, it can make it cloudy.

Labels

Keep a supply of sticky-backed labels on hand so that you can label everything as you make it. You may think that you will remember what a particular bottle or jar contains, but I guarantee you won't! Labels are available at all office supply stores and often at the grocery store as well.

Journal

Speaking of what you won't remember later, invest now in a journal or notebook in which you can record all your recipe blends as you create. You may not believe me now, but the first time you make the most marvelous blend of your life, then want to recreate it from memory, you will wish fervently that you had written it down.

Mortar and Pestle

The mortar is the bowl that contains the herb or resin that you are crushing; the pestle is the rounded implement with which you crush. Glass or ceramic mortars work best as they do not react with any herb, oil, or resin and are easy to clean. Soapstone mortars are iffy as they are porous and can absorb essential oils into their surface. Metal mortar and pestles can react with some herbs and oils and become discolored. A mortar that is at least three inches is the smallest size that is useful; larger is even better. I have known people who have forgone the enjoyment of crushing and blending with a mortar and pestle and actually blend their Incenses in a food processor. I must say I don't relate to this use of an electrical tool, but it works for them. However, if you are ever tempted to crush up your herbs this way, please do not add any resins to your mixture while it is in the food processor. The heat from the moving blades will soften the resin enough to cause it to adhere to the blades and interior of the food processor. This is a big mess to clean up and can even burn up the motor in the food processor if there is enough resin in the mix.

Glass, Enamel, and Ceramic Bowls

You will want to have at least one cereal-size bowl in which to blend Bath Salts. Essential oils can react to metal, so you want your bowl to be made from a nonporous, neutral material.

Herbs

You'll want to have at least one herb or resin for each Planetary energy so that you are prepared to create any Incense, Herbal Amulet, or other implement whenever the need arises. I recommend having the following on hand:

frankincense resin for the Sun (success, personal power)
jasmin flowers for the Moon (psychic ability, subconscious, dreams)
red sandalwood for Mars (energy, courage, protection)
cinnamon for Mercury (memory, mental sharpness)
cedar for Jupiter (abundance, growth)
rose for Venus (love, beauty, art)
patchouli for Saturn (grounding, protection)

white willow for Neptune (inspiration)
nutmeg for Uranus (change, health, visions)
myrrh resin for Pluto (inner knowledge, karma)

Essential Oils

Have one bottle of each of the following oils to be able to create Ritual Oil blends, Bath Salts, and Ritual Incenses:

frankincense oil for the Sun
white sandalwood oil for the Moon
ginger oil for Mars
lavender oil for Mercury
cedar oil for Jupiter
rose oil for Venus
patchouli oil for Saturn
neroli oil for Neptune
allspice oil for Uranus
myrrh oil for Pluto

Trusted Medicinal Herb Book

Many of the blends you create are going to come into contact with your body through ingestion, inhalation, or application to the skin. *Before* you incorporate an herb or oil into your formula, you need to determine what, if any, physical effect that herb or oil might have. Here are some medicinal herb books that I like:

The Scientific Validation of Herbal Medicine by Dr. Daniel Mowrey
The Herb Book by John Lust
The Complete Book of Essential Oils and Aromatherapy by Valerie Ann
  Worwood

Magickal Supplies

Candles

Keep candles on hand in these colors:
white (purification)
black (blocking)

green (prosperity, health)
blue (peace, tranquility)
orange (energy, vitality)
pink (love, beauty)
purple (spiritual evolution, meditation)

You will be purchasing other colors as you develop rituals you want to do, but these colors will cover just about anything you may run up against at the last minute. You will also need a candle snuffer, matches, and at least six candleholders. You will not always need six holders for each ritual, but you'll want to be prepared in case.

Incense Supplies

In a small box, keep your Incense charcoal, matches or lighter, and insulating material (such as sand, kitty litter, or garden soil). You want to keep all moisture away from those items. If your Incense charcoal comes in contact with moisture, it will absorb some of the humidity or liquid and will not light correctly when you are ready to use it. You will want to invest in an Incense burner in which to burn your creations. It's a good idea to have an Incense spoon to dish out a small amount of your Incenses to avoid getting Incense stuck under your fingernails and to dispense the correct amount onto the Incense charcoal. You'll also want a few small containers in which to place your Incense on your altar at each ritual.

Other Ritual Supplies

You will probably end up with more than one altar cloth (you may want to color-coordinate your altar cloths with the type of energy you're invoking at various rituals), but you need at least one black altar cloth around three feet square for general purposes.

Keep on hand sea salt and spring water for cleansing the energy of objects and casting your Circle. You'll need a small container in which to place your salt for use on your altar. Generally speaking, you'll be using your Chalice on your altar to contain your water for cleansing.

You'll need parchment and pen for drawing Talismans and writing spells. Some people like to use feather quills and Magickal inks for this type of work, but you can also use a good quality pen or Sharpies in different colors, too. Rather than using parchment, you may want to visit your art supply store and pick up an array of paper in different colors.

Try to have available the following crystals and stones for general spellwork:

jade or green aventurine for prosperity
hematite or onyx for protection and grounding
carnelian or gold tiger's-eye for healing
amethyst or moonstone for meditation or spiritual work

Go to your local fabric store and check out the remnants section. You can pick up a yard or less of fabric in different colors so that you are ready to create an Herbal Amulet. Just be sure that the material you select is a natural, nonsynthetic one—cotton, silk, or wool. While you are there, get some nonsynthetic cord or ribbon in various colors for tying your Herbal Amulet bags.

Focus and Intention

The most important ingredient in everything you create is your intention. Your herbs, oils, and resins are all tools and definitely contain energy and spirit vibration that do the work, but they must be focused with your intention in the specific direction toward which you are working. A car may sit in your driveway, full of gas, but until you get in and turn the key with your destination in mind, it will not go anywhere. Your Magickal tools of alchemical creation work the same way. You are the main ingredient that causes them to work.

Initially, due to space limitations or budget, you may just store your tools and accoutrements in a cardboard or plastic storage container that you can obtain at your local hardware store. Once you have gotten out all the things you need for a particular working, you can cover this storage box with your altar cloth and use it as your altar as well. Eventually you will need an actual cabinet (it's amazing how much stuff one can collect!) and you may want to check out garage sales or flea markets for a china cabinet to use as permanent storage.

Index

Recommended Books

We are fortunate to have many good herbal books available for our studies. Some of my favorites are:

Culpeper's Complete Herbal: Illustrated and Annotated Edition by Nicholas Culpeper

Cunningham's Encyclopedia of Magical Herbs by Scott Cunningham

The Green Witch: Your Complete Guide to the Natural Magic of Herbs, Flowers, Essential Oils, and More by Arin Murphy-Hiscock

Green Magic: The Sacred Connection to Nature by Ann Moura

The Herbal or General History of Plants: The Complete 1633 Edition as Revised and Enlarged by Thomas Johnson by John Gerard

The Magical And Ritual Use of Herbs by Richard Alan Miller

Master Book of Herbalism by Paul Beyerl

The Weiser Concise Guide to Herbal Magick by Judith Hawkins-Tillirson

ABOUT THE AUTHOR

 Karen Charboneau-Harrison has been involved with Magick, the psychic arts, and occultism since early childhood. Brought up in a household where these philosophies and endeavors were encouraged, she has been using herbal blends medicinally and Magickally for decades. Karen obtained her masters of herbology in 1980 from the Emerson College of Herbology, Montreal.

The proprietress of Moon Magick Alchemical Apothecary since 1978, her blends are used across the nation. She and her husband also own Isis Books & Gifts Healing Oasis in Denver, Colorado (*www.isisbooks.com*), which is the largest and most complete brick-and-mortar store in the United States specializing in world spirituality, Magick, and herbs/essential oils.

Karen is a Scorpio (hidden pathways, alchemy, transformation), with her Moon in Capricorn (practicality, structure, pragmatism) and her Ascendant in Aquarius (innovation, free thought, humanitarian ideals). Throughout her life, she has sought to couple spiritual philosophy and practices with practical techniques to give them form and manifestation in the physical world.

Also in Weiser Classics

The Book of Lies
by Aliester Crowley, with an introduction by Richard
Kaczynski

Futhark: A Handbook of Rune Magic (Revised Edition)
by Edred Thorsson

A Handbook of Yoruba Religious Concepts
by Baba Ifa Karade

*Psychic Self-Defense: The Definitive Manual for Protecting
Yourself Against Paranormal Attack*
by Dion Fortune, with a foreword by Mary K. Greer

*Taking Up the Runes: A Complete Guide to Using Runes
in Spells, Rituals, Divination, and Magic*
by Diana L. Paxson

Yoga Sutras of Patanjali
by Mukunda Stiles, with a foreword by Mark Whitwell

To Our Readers

Weiser Books, an imprint of Red Wheel/Weiser, publishes books across the entire spectrum of occult, esoteric, speculative, and New Age subjects. Our mission is to publish quality books that will make a difference in people's lives without advocating any one particular path or field of study. We value the integrity, originality, and depth of knowledge of our authors.

Our readers are our most important resource, and we appreciate your input, suggestions, and ideas about what you would like to see published.

Visit our website at *www.redwheelweiser.com* to learn about our upcoming books and free downloads, and be sure to go to *www.redwheelweiser.com/newsletter* to sign up for newsletters and exclusive offers.

You can also contact us at *info@rwwbooks.com* or at

Red Wheel/Weiser, LLC
65 Parker Street, Suite 7
Newburyport, MA 01950